S0-CEW-807

THE BARGAIN

"I could take you, you know," Elera whispered, opening her eyes. Her smile was slow. "To my people, that is. And to the place of dragons."

His heart pounded. "For what price?"

When he did not draw back, Elera sat up and traced her fingers over the raging pulse in his throat. She gazed up at him with her answer in her eyes.

"I will not," he whispered.

Elera inclined her head. "A kiss, then. If you cannot resist a simple kiss, Karl, your place is not with the Mattaen."

She was holding something back, of that he was certain.

"No hands," he said finally, cursing himself for wanting the taste of her as much as he wanted the knowledge she offered.

Elera nodded. "No hands. Mine, scholar, not yours. Yours may roam as they please."

BREATH
OF
FIRE

TAMMY KANE

LOVE SPELL   NEW YORK CITY

*To my husband, for quietly ordering takeout whenever
I burn dinner or simply forget to make it...and for
sending me lilies anyway.*

To everyone who believed in me,

Thank you.

LOVE SPELL®

July 2009

Published by

Dorchester Publishing Co., Inc.
200 Madison Avenue
New York, NY 10016

Copyright © 2009 by Tammy Cobby

All rights reserved. No part of this book may be reproduced
or transmitted in any form or by any electronic or mechanical
means, including photocopying, recording or by any information
storage and retrieval system, without the written permission of the
publisher, except where permitted by law.

ISBN 10: 0-505-52816-9
ISBN 13: 978-0-505-52816-2
E-ISBN: 978-1-4285-0691-6

The name "Love Spell" and its logo are trademarks of Dorchester
Publishing Co., Inc.

Printed in the United States of America.

10 9 8 7 6 5 4 3 2 1

If you purchased this book without a cover you should be aware
that this book is stolen property. It was reported as "unsold and
destroyed" to the publisher and neither the author nor the publisher
has received any payment for this "stripped book."

Visit us on the web at www.dorchesterpub.com.

BREATH
OF
FIRE

ONE

"You must not do this."

The men ignored his sharp command. With a sigh concealed by the hood of his black robe, Karl of the Initiates stepped forward and stopped just shy of the angry wall of villagers standing against him.

His gaze shifted to the object of his concern ... a young woman, no more than twenty, being led into the rocky plains below the village. She wore a simple gown of pure white, with thin straps that bared her arms and back. The hands gripping her wrists and pulling her along were not altogether gentle. The barren land beyond the enlightened realm bred little more than barbarism in its people—even paganism, if the rumors surrounding his monastery were true.

The girl stumbled then, and was quickly caught up by the guards at her flank. The mass of men and women watching from the village cheered.

He studied the line of men before him. Their voices joined the calls of their brethren, but their eyes were wide with fear. A man trained to join the highest order of Mattaen monks would have no problem overcoming their superstitions. Not if he was worth the ceremonial blade strapped to his thigh. "I assure you, your fears are based on the myths of a people long past—"

"You think to fool us with high talk," interrupted an elder, garnering strength from his peers' nods of encouragement. "But your kind knows little of this stretch of land."

"There is little high talk in me, wise one, for you are right. I know nothing of these lands."

He threw back his hood to reveal bright green eyes. Flame red hair spilled from the neck of his robe to hang well below his shoulders in a mass of coiled, braided, and free-flowing tresses.

"But I tell you now," he continued quietly, "that the sacrifice of this girl defies the sanctity of life, and of choice."

Karl arched a reddish brow at their blank stares, though his expression remained carefully neutral. He tried a different approach. "Do you not have murder in these lands?"

"This is not murder, Initiate." The eyes of the elder shifted uncertainly to the girl being marched to a platform against the cliff wall. "It is sacrifice, and the girl is willing."

Their willing sacrifice chose that particular moment to balk. Breaking free of her captors with a cry, she ran only two steps before being caught and slung over a hulking shoulder.

The elder grumbled beneath Karl's sidelong stare, "Willing or not, we cannot lose an entire village to spare one girl's life ... and she'd be dead anyway."

He fell silent. Now manacled against the cliff, the girl began sobbing. A tortured groan accompanied her cries from behind a hut near the path where they stood. Running a hand over his hair to disguise his search, Karl found a man of similar age to the girl below. As soon as she started pleading for help, the young man covered his ears and dropped to his knees.

"The girl is no virgin," Karl said quickly. "Do you not require a virgin sacrifice to appease the wrath of a *dragon*?"

His growl caused a few villagers to take an involuntary step back, but they quickly resumed their positions. The code of his guild, which allowed a Mattaen to defend himself but never to attack another, was well-known even here.

Karl inhaled slowly and reminded himself that these people had little access to education, or higher learning of any kind, for that matter. He had to repeat the breathing technique twice before his calm returned, but when it did, the disapproving lines around his lips eased.

"She must be a virgin," someone whispered, casting a doubtful look at the girl. "Who would have dared touch her?"

"I mean no disrespect to the girl or her family," Karl pressed, "but a single moment of weakness on her part will condemn your village if you choose to continue on this course. I ask only that you give some thought to—"

"We must find another virgin!" someone shouted. A volley of agreements followed with enough volume that the men in the plains looked back in concern.

"Enough!" commanded the elder, his gaze pinning Karl with the closest he had seen to true intelligence outside the realm. "Have you forgotten that the one suggesting this blasphemy is the very stranger who argues against the existence of such beasts? The girl is a virgin. I have it on her father's word. We will have our sacrifice."

Karl returned the pointed look. "Tell me, wise one, if you can: What do these dragons of yours look like?"

"They have slavering mouths filled with teeth as big as a man's hand!" a voice from the crowd shouted before the elder could respond.

"Nay, as big as a man's arm!"

"And terrible red eyes that can kill you with a single look! Or take your mind ..."

The descriptions continued, growing more ingenious as the game progressed, until even the elder wilted beneath their ludicrous tales.

"Have you ever even seen a dragon?" Karl asked gently. "Has anyone?"

The wind picked up, gusting through the village. Karl's hair whipped in it, his long robe clung to his frame, and still no one answered his simple question. He was about to continue when the elder held up a gnarled hand for silence.

"I heard one once. A terrible sound that shook the ground with every bellow … and hiss." The elder's eyes glazed in revulsion. "I was a child, and my mother's sister was the sacrifice. I never saw it take her, but she was gone nonetheless. It was not a sound I would ever forget, monk of the realm."

Excitement sparked in Karl's eyes, but for only a moment. He knew it was ridiculous to entertain even the notion that dragons were real, though rumors of their existence spread from the outskirts of the realm like the mythical fire the beasts were said to breathe.

Karl shook his head. The old man seemed certain of his tale, but children had a tendency to confuse fantasy with reality. It was one of the first lessons he had learned from the Guild.

The villagers were swayed by their elder's conviction, so Karl changed tactics. "Leave the girl to be devoured by the dragon that comes for her. Spill not one drop of her blood yourselves."

If they were as fanatic as they seemed, he would have to interfere before she died from exposure or other predators when the dragon never arrived. However, their concession would buy time. And as any worthy Initiate knew, time was the key to successful negotiations.

The elder glanced at him in disdain. "Of course we will not spill her blood. We are savages by the standards of your guild, but we are not murderers." He tapped his cane on the ground. "The girl will die by the will of the beast that comes to claim her."

"Very well, I will not interfere."

"But you do not believe anything will come?"

"We shall see," Karl said simply, pulling his hood over his head and leaping onto the stone passage descending into the steppes. Cliffs encircled the area, some with peaks reaching into the clouds. Others had long ago crumbled to the same level as the steppes, which were riddled with narrow chasms that led into the misty depths below.

Such was the landscape of the barrens beyond the realm.

Karl crouched on the edge of the rough-hewn stairs with his hands tucked into his sleeves. Not once did he take his eyes off the girl—not when she started begging for release, not even when the guards passed him on their return. Tempering his anger for her pointless suffering, he kept a silent watch.

As the hours passed, the sun dipped behind the mountains and cast the steppes in crimson shadow. The girl had long since fallen silent in defeat. Or perhaps exhaustion, Karl amended, noting the steady rhythm of her breathing. The wind from across the frozen peaks lashed cruelly against her bared skin.

Shifting his eyes toward the men standing vigil, Karl lifted a hand to beckon the elder near. "In very little time you will not have to spill a drop of her blood to kill her. When no dragon comes, you will be held accountable for the murder of an innocent."

"You are wrong, man who would be monk."

"And the teachings of a millennium? Are they wrong, as well?" Karl asked dryly.

He could tell these people that no physical sign of a creature the size of a dragon had ever been found, much less recorded. The barrens did not contain enough of a food supply to support the appetite of any such predator. He could even pinpoint the origins of their dragons in the fantastic writings of centuries past...the fantastic and *fictional* writings. But looking at the zealous belief on the elder's face, he knew it would be for naught.

"Release the girl. I will take her place." When the watchers on the wall scoffed, Karl lifted a brow. "Or am I mistaken in my assumption that it is virginity your dragon craves, and not the sex of the sacrifice?"

Most of the men gaped, but the elder narrowed his eyes. "Why would you do this?"

"Because there is nothing coming, old man," Karl said, losing patience as the girl renewed her weeping. "And I will not watch that child suffer a moment longer for the ignorance of your people."

For a moment, the elder stared at him in silence. Then, with a nod of acceptance, he raised his hand to the five closest men and beckoned them to follow. "You will regret your generosity, Initiate."

"I regret my faith in your compassion," Karl spat, warning the guards away with a cold stare and leading the descent himself, "or I would have offered sooner."

By the time they reached the girl, the orange horizon barely kept the approaching night at bay. And even though she wept with gratitude for the stranger's sacrifice, the girl still clung hard enough to the man who released her bonds.

Karl stepped onto the stone platform and raised his hands to the manacles. His long sleeves fell about his shoulders, revealing the rippling muscles born of a lifetime devoted to discipline and training. The fools slapping cold steel around his wrists didn't even suspect he could have them off at a moment's notice.

But since it was ignorance and not the people themselves that Karl wished to fight, he chose to ignore the pinch of the cuffs. Already, his hands were going numb.

A sudden rumble in the distance sent the brave villagers running for the safety of their huts.

"It is but an earthquake," he grumbled. They were common in these lands, and the ground had been rumbling for days.

"Or perhaps an eruption of the fire mountains across the

barrens?" the elder mocked, coming around the side of the slab. He frowned. "Will the Mattaen come after us for this?"

"Since there is no dragon, there will be no harm. And if there is a beast," Karl continued over the other man's objection, "then what choice did you have, really?"

The elder hesitated, glancing to the skies. "What is your name?"

"Why?"

His weary eyes met Karl's stare. "Because I would mark a grave for you on the morrow."

The corner of Karl's lips curved, but by then the elder was already racing across the steppes. He was quite fast for a man of his years. Karl supposed he would have to settle for the mark of *Initiate* on his grave site. Or perhaps *Fool of the Realm*, if there was a grave to be marked at all.

He chuckled, and was still laughing quietly when a shadow fell across his platform. Karl frowned in confusion. The ground shook, jarring the cliff at his back. He swallowed nervously ... and turned to watch the shadow taking slow shape around him.

The shadow moved, each motion shaking the ground and setting loose stones dancing. He craned his neck to try to see what lurked behind him, but the boulder blocked his view. Heat radiated from the rock at his back.

The shadow on the ground took on the unmistakable outline of wings.

"Impossible," he breathed.

He twisted against his manacles, lifting his body halfway up the boulder by bracing his sandaled feet against the stone. Neck and forearms rippling, he strained until he could see over the rocky ridge. His breath froze in his lungs.

Bright red eyes glared back at him. Snarling lips pulled back to bare a set of slime-slicked teeth.... *Far more teeth than seems logical*, he thought.

He watched, stunned, as those membranous wings stretched to a span easily twice the length of the creature's sleek gray body. Its scaled shoulders hunched, its massive head lowered, and the low hiss emanating from its mouth made his flesh crawl.

Creeping ever closer, the beast lowered its belly in anticipation. The position elevated the spiked ridges of its spine, creating a bony fin that traveled from the base of its neck to the end of its blade-tipped tail.

Karl held the dragon's stare, deft fingers already manipulating the steel on his wrists ... though where he could run remained a mystery. It seemed he wouldn't get even the chance to try, for just then the creature lunged.

Karl opened the eyes he'd squeezed shut in reflex. The dragon had stopped on the brink of the slab. "My friend," he said calmly, hearing the clink from the first manacle, and then the second. "You do not exist."

Pulling his body swiftly up, Karl dove beneath the creature's head.

Good reflexes, Elera thought as she watched the man from behind a boulder on the opposite side of the steppes. Her dark brows rose appreciatively when he rolled again, avoiding a claw that swiped a hairbreadth from his torso.

She waited. When the man leaped over the dragon's hide, twisting in midair to avoid the backlash from his tail, her eyes widened with wonder. Not for his skill—the man was of the Mattaen order, after all—but in appreciation of the exquisite view, which laid to rest any questions she might have had regarding what, exactly, a monk wore beneath his robe.

She grinned, then glanced at the red hair concealing his features. He was no monk yet, but an Initiate only. The Mattaen shaved their entire bodies.

While she stood admiring him, the dragon finally trapped

the man beneath his claws. Still the Initiate made no move toward the ceremonial blade she had seen on his thigh. She'd heard that the blade must never draw blood. Not that it could against the thick scales of a dragon, but that he would adhere to the decree even now ...

Enough staring. Elera was here to slay a dragon, so slay a dragon she must. With another lopsided grin, she leaped atop the boulder with her longbow and arrows in hand.

"Hope you're ready, dark one," she whispered, and, with just a slight hesitation, released the arrow.

The dragon bellowed across the steppes. Taking advantage of the beast's distraction, the man wiggled free and ran, all the while searching the cliffs for the source of his deliverance. When his eyes landed upon her, she tipped her head and let another arrow fly.

The beast targeted her now, spreading his wings to their full width and gliding from the ground. Elera spun and raced across the steppes.

The dragon overtook her in moments. Ducking beneath his wing, she rolled to evade grasping claws. Once he overshot her, she paused just long enough to ensure that the man was watching ... then deliberately shook her head as if dazed. When the dragon spun in the sky and dove back with a roar, she bolted to the very edge of the cliff.

She was in little danger from the dragon, but the man was closing the distance between them faster than she'd anticipated. He was near enough now that she could see the color of his eyes, as unusual and striking as his fiery hair.

Elera looked skyward and set another arrow in her bow. She glanced back in the moment before its release, and saw fear in the eyes of the man pursuing her.

Fear for her?

She smiled at him. Once she was certain that he watched her, she winked, then released the arrow. The dragon shrieked as his massive body contracted in the air. His wings folded as he plunged from the sky ... straight toward her.

"Faster," she whispered urgently, keeping her eyes on the man, who was nearly within reach. And it did seem as though the speed of the beast's fall increased, until he crashed into the earth with an explosion of rocky debris. Momentum drove him forward, forging a path to where Elera stood ready.

Ignoring the Initiate's warning shout, she dove over the creature's shoulder, rolling across scales that felt like fire under her skin. She nearly tumbled off his back, and would have broken more than a few bones if his long tail hadn't arced suddenly in the wind.

Elera managed to hook her bow around a bony ridge, slowing her fall as the dragon's body skidded to a gradual stop. Dropping to the ground, she casually retreated from its unmoving form. She heard the loud slap of sandals just before rough hands turned her around.

She had time for just one thought—*Tall*—before the edge of the cliff crumbled under the substantial weight of the dragon.

Shoving the man back, Elera stepped away from the cracks webbing beneath their feet. Only after the ground finally settled did she answer the question in his eyes.

"My name is Elera, daughter of the dragonslayer Shane." Running her eyes over his muscular form, she added throatily, "And you, Initiate of the Mattaen, are my virgin prize."

Two

Karl cleared his throat as the woman sauntered to the edge of the cliff and looked down. While she stared into the chasm, he stood quietly until blood no longer pounded in his ears. This took much longer than seemed proper, thanks to the effect her purring voice had on his uncooperative body. He would never taste a woman, but that didn't mean he was immune to the curves on this one. Or the strength in her shoulders, which were left bare by the black hair coiled at the nape of her neck.

Karl glanced away until the stirrings left him, then drew near to ask, "You are a *dragonslayer*?"

Elera shrugged without looking back. "Don't you learn about dragons from your Mattaen mentors?"

"No," he said simply. "Step back, Elera of the dragonslayers. It is unsafe."

"I am waiting," she said softly, though she did as he asked when more stone crumbled away from the edge.

The ground shook from an impact far below the mist hovering between this cliff and the next. Karl peered over the edge in fascination. He scanned the terrain leading down, measuring the distances between footholds, locating loose stones that could send a man plunging to his death. His blood raced at the thought of examining a creature never before recorded....

He looked up. The woman was getting away.

"Where do you go?" Karl called, sprinting to her side when she did not pause in her march toward the mountainside village.

"To collect payment for my services."

Disappointment deepened the lines around his mouth, though he said nothing to dispute her claim. "I would very much like to speak with you when your business is concluded."

Elera laughed. "You talk calmly for one who came so near death just moments ago."

"No more than you." He glanced ruefully down. "And less so, I think, since you are laughing a great deal, and mainly at my expense."

"You cheat yourself, Initiate," Elera said as she turned to wink at him. "It is *all* at your expense."

He smiled at her audacity until he noticed how dark it had become. Night had completely shrouded the steppes in the time they'd lingered on the cliff, and there were other predators about. Perhaps not as large, but teeth and claws were not exclusive to the dragon she had just felled.

Karl frowned uncertainly as a rustling sound drew his attention back to the path. By unspoken agreement, the pair quickened their pace until they reached the stone stairs. Villagers lined them with torches in hand.

Unease knotted his shoulders. "It does not seem you are very welcome."

"Most likely they cannot meet my price," she said simply.

Karl nodded. "Then I will provide what they cannot."

Her lips curved in a secretive smile, but the approach of the elder prevented him from pressing for an explanation.

The man's gaze fell upon Elera. He seemed surprised as he studied the dragonslayer, but quickly masked the emotion with a glare. Shaking his walking staff, he spat upon the ground at her feet. "You expect payment when none here called for you?"

Elera's eyes narrowed. "I was called, old man."

His staff lowered slowly to the beaten earth. "None would have dared. We cannot pay...." He swallowed his words as his eyes darted nervously across his people. "We provided a sacrifice."

Elera slashed her hand to command silence, and jerked her head to the Initiate standing at her side. "The lover of the one you would have sacrificed called me, and I care not if he had the blessing of your village. Payment or penalty. Make your choice."

Color flooded Karl's face as he realized she assumed that the young man was his lover. "Elera, I am not the sacrifice, or at least I was not meant to be. There was a girl.... I do not have such tendencies ... and I—"

"Of course you have no lover, Initiate, or at least not of the male variety." She winked up at him. "I did notice your interest earlier."

"I am of the Mattaen," he said stiffly, folding his hands beneath his robe to conceal his fists.

Elera cast him a level look before returning her eyes to the elder. "The lover of the *girl* you would have sacrificed called for me." She knelt, pulled a wrinkled parchment out of her boot, and handed it over.

"Nathan," the elder whispered, hands shaking. "Nathan!"

At once, the young man pushed through the crowds, falling to his knees at the elder's feet. "Forgive me, but I could not let her die. I will pay the price, I swear." His eyes turned warily to Elera. "What is the price?"

"Fool!" shouted the elder. "You negotiate a contract and do not ask the fee? She can take your life as payment then, for it is not the doings of this village that brings about your dishonor."

Elera raised a brow. "My price is not so high, old man. I ask only for what is my due, as have all who came before me."

When confusion flickered across the faces of the crowd, Karl turned to look at her. "You might state it aloud, Elera of the dragonslayers, to expedite matters."

She sighed. "Shelter and sustenance for the night ..."

Surprise for the simplicity of the request widened Karl's eyes.

"... and fifty silver *tarlae*."

Ah, he thought with an inward smile. Herein lay the reason for their anger. That sum would take this village more than a decade to earn.

"If you provide the accommodations, elder, I will pay the fee." Karl glanced down at Elera. "Surely that is acceptable. It was my hide you saved, after all."

"It is a generous offer, but I wasn't finished." Her eyes trailed down the length of him before rising slowly back to his face. "I will also take the intended sacrifice to my bed this night."

The first thing he noticed when he could think once more was the challenge in her eyes, the humor on her lips ... and the stark determination of her stance.

He dipped his head in contemplation. He could not honor this agreement, but an open refusal might exacerbate the situation. "If I had not replaced the girl?"

"Then I might have forgone this payment altogether. But a male sacrifice is too rare for me to relinquish my prize now— especially one so appealing to my tastes."

"I cannot. Nor do I recognize your rites, or even your race."

"This village recognizes both, and as it was they who called me, my price will be met. Or my penalty."

Karl glared at the young man cowering on the ground. "I will pay the penalty then, if it is a life. I will not break my vows."

"You haven't yet taken your vows." Elera paused. "Loyalty to your creed is a commendable trait, Initiate. But your offer is mine to accept or deny, and I most assuredly do not accept. Tell him the penalty, elder." She shifted her stare to the night sky with a sigh. "I am weary of talk."

"But you can't." Only now did the elder sound as old as his years. "You wouldn't."

Elera said nothing.

"The penalty"—he looked shakily at Karl—"is forfeiture of every man, woman, and child of this village. She'll kill us all."

"I'll do no such thing," Elera said sharply, before returning her gaze skyward. "The dragon I lure back to this place will do that in my stead."

Karl hissed, appalled by the threat and the casual manner in which she issued it. "The dragon is dead. I watched your arrow fly true."

"And, of course, the beast is the only of its kind," Elera drawled. The dragonslayer kept her eyes averted as she was bombarded with threats and pleas, as if she cared nothing for the turmoil she had caused. As if the outcome of this debate was inevitable, and of course it was. A Mattaen could not allow an entire village to be destroyed, and Karl could not fight unless she followed through with her threat.

He was struggling with that rule, his body humming with the urge to commit violence, but he reined in his anger with a few long breaths and some whispered words of ritual that eased his clenched fists.

"I cannot," he said again.

"That is unfortunate."

"You misunderstand." He wrapped his hand around her arm, halting her return to the plains. "I am unable. My training prevents it."

He watched as Elera's mouth twitched suspiciously. "I see," she murmured.

The men of the village stared at Karl in horror, and the

elder was no exception. He opened his mouth to speak, squeaked, then tried again. "We can give you another man, dragonslayer—"

"I have reconsidered. I will take the bed, the meal, and this Initiate's fifty silver *tarlae*, after all." Elera paused. "And I will settle for the *company* of his person in my room for this night, where we may substitute an intellectual merging for a physical one. You did mention the desire to speak with me, did you not?"

Karl stared warily down at her. "You will not try to change this agreement during the course of the night?"

"I most certainly will," she teased, but then her expression turned grave. "I cannot force you to my bed. Nor would I, as some in my race do."

Karl sighed, resigned to a less than pleasurable lesson where most of his energy would be spent controlling the part he claimed could not perform. His eyes held hers. "I do not understand how it is that none have ever seen your kind."

"Enough have seen my kind that a boy on the outskirts knew how to call me."

Conceding the point, Karl nodded. "I accept your terms, daughter of Shane. We will pass the night in study."

"I-I will," the elder stuttered, glancing between the two, "I will prepare a meal."

"Feast," Elera corrected absently.

"A feast. Yes, of course." A weary groan escaped his lips. "And a room."

"Do that," she said. Karl looked down in confusion as she pulled her arm from his grasp. Had he been holding it all this time?

"What is your name?" she asked.

He hesitated, unwilling to give her even a small advantage. "Karl."

"Just Karl?" she asked. "No clan, no—"

"Karl of the Mattaen Initiates," he said firmly.

"We will see." She drank greedily of a water flask just now being offered and did not try to stop him when he walked away to collect his thoughts.

"The slayer awaits you, Initiate."

Karl nodded thanks, though it was obvious the elder had been watching for him to return from the cliffs where he'd been prowling. Equally obvious were the four posted guards on lookout... and their failure to have noticed his approach.

The humor faded from his lips the moment he stepped into the hut. A fire glowed from the center of the room, comfortably heating the air. Two lamps cast shadows over the walls. In front of the bed stood a steaming tub of water. And in it, Elera bathed.

"Close the door, Karl," she said, peeking over her shoulder. "You're letting the heat out."

She shifted back into the water, lifting her arms to finish lathering the mass of dark hair piled atop her head. Ignoring the soft arc of her neck, the barest glimpse of her breast, Karl let the door fall closed and took a firm step within.

"Eat if you're hungry." She motioned to the table laden with fruits and bread. He sat, but made no move to eat. "I will finish in a moment. I arranged for another bath to be brought for you."

"That's not necessary."

"Don't be foolish, Karl," she drawled. "You are every bit as filthy as I was. I promise not to jump in with you if you're still afraid."

She ducked beneath the water to rinse her hair, and so missed his less than flattering response. He was standing directly in front of the bath when she emerged. When his gaze skimmed the surface of the water, her breath quickened.

He leaned forward. "I am not fool enough to deny that many men would kill to be in my position this night. But though I might acknowledge and even appreciate your allure, Elera ... *it is not for me*."

She stood slowly and smirked when his breath caught in his throat. "If you say so."

"I do." He took a quick step back when she got out of the tub and reached for him. "Elera ..." he growled.

"Yes, Karl?" With a grin, she lifted a towel from the hook behind him and pulled it to her.

"You toy with me."

"Does it bother you?"

He swallowed. "It does."

"Good," Elera whispered, finishing with the towel and donning the poncho left for her use. Ignoring the ties that were meant to close it at the sides, she took a seat at the table with one knee lifted to her chest ... leaving the curve of her thigh, the dip of her waist, and even the subtle swell of her breast exposed.

Karl sighed and took the seat across from her, watching as she contemplated some of the berries. Her eyes widened when she popped one in her mouth.

"This is amazing," she whispered. "Will you not try some?"

Karl frowned. "You've never tasted a raspberry?"

Elera eyed another of the red berries and shook her head. When he did nothing more than watch her, she asked, "Do you have no other questions for me, then?"

"I would wait until you are rested."

"I am," she assured him, moving to the fire to comb her fingers through her hair. Loose, the wet strands reached her waist, and it seemed no easy task unknotting the tangles. "Go ahead, Karl. I can see the impatience in your shoulders."

While she was partially bent over, the poncho doing nothing to cover her breasts, Karl took a long drink from a water flask on the table. "Where do your people live?"

"Beyond the barrens."

"I have been beyond the barrens, Elera. I saw no signs of life, much less evidence of an entire people."

"Were you looking for signs of life?" She plopped onto the animal skin on the floor and stared up at him. "We are there, I promise you."

After a moment's pause, he asked, "And why do you hide yourselves from the realm?"

"What makes you think we hide?"

"Are all your answers to be questions, then?"

Elera smiled. "When do you take your vows?"

"On the day of my thirtieth year," Karl answered, then frowned when he realized she still had not answered his question.

"And when is that?"

"The day after tomorrow." Every Initiate took vows on the last day of the month in which he reached thirty years of age. The day of Karl's acceptance into the brotherhood would coincide with his day of birth. His voice vibrated with energy. "I will have been an Initiate seventeen years on that day."

Elera's grin faded. "Who were your people to let you be taken so young?"

"That is too personal a question," Karl said quietly, inclining his head when she rose and placed her hand over his. "And no one took me, Elera. It was my choice."

"I didn't mean to offend you."

He squeezed her hand gently before slipping away from her touch. "I chose the Mattaen to gain knowledge, and I stayed to improve my body and mind. But I join, not only to gain access to the sacred scriptures ... though that is surely a boon"—he winked at her—"but to quench the yearning in my blood. I have studied worlds of knowledge and still found nothing to whet my interest except the desire to learn more."

Karl paced back to the fire.

"My people have traded the power of knowledge for the power of blood," Elera offered sadly, standing at his side when he moved to allow it. "They fight, they kill, and yes, they rape if the need takes them. It is ambition for some and lust for others, but there is no thought to the future. I fear we are at the brink of extinction."

"I am sorry for you."

"You are sincere," she said, and he could see her surprise. She nodded. "I have learned some of what it takes to join your order. You develop the skills of a warrior, and then you are forbidden from using them for any purpose but the defense of others."

"Our minds are trained as well, Elera." Karl glanced down and realized he was twirling a lock of her dark hair around his finger. He let it fall and took a small step away, but it still drew his eyes … a mystery of black, and when the fire hit it, a richness to rival his own. "If a Mattaen cannot use his knowledge to avoid violence, he isn't worth the blade strapped to his thigh."

"Yes, I saw the weapon. When you did that …" She mimicked his flip through the air with her hand and grinned when his cheeks bronzed. "Personally, I find the forgoing of mating to be the most difficult of the trials you face."

Karl lifted a shoulder. "It gets easier with practice," he said, then listened to Elera's humming as she reclaimed her seat on the floor.

"Elera?"

She looked up at him.

"I have lived my life for the Mattaen…." He paused when the villagers carried another tub of water through the doors. They set it by the fire, collected Elera's tub, and left without a word. Karl caught her gaze and continued. "Joining them is all I have ever wanted."

"Then bathe, Karl of the Initiates." Elera waved her hand. "And I will tell you everything I can of dragons and their history."

THREE

Karl stayed rooted to the spot, lips curved. "I do not trust you."

"An intelligent choice," she said, ruining her solemnity with a wink. "But I promise not to take liberties while you bathe."

"But you will watch?" As soon as the words were out of his mouth, he flushed angrily. He would not grovel to this woman, even if she did look at him with hungry ... nay, ravenous eyes. He set his jaw and quickly drew the robe over his head.

But where her blatant desire had merely unsettled him before, it absolutely paralyzed him now. Her lips parted on a sudden breath. Her dark eyes drifted briefly to his before slowly skimming every inch of his naked body. The pulse in her neck quickened, and for reasons he could not fully comprehend, Karl's own blood began to race as he watched her.

With a curse that was forbidden on the lips of an Initiate, he stepped out of his sandals and plunged his body beneath the water. He had only a moment to enjoy the effects of the soothing heat on his overtaxed muscles before Elera knelt at his back.

"You're injured," she whispered. Her hands hovered above his skin, but did not touch the raw flesh at the base of his shoulder. "It needs tending."

Her words were nearly a plea. Karl caught himself just before he nodded acquiescence. "It is nothing, I assure you. And you promised, Elera."

"It bleeds still," she pressed, then fisted her hands and backed away. "I will send for someone else, then."

Whispering something in a language he didn't understand, she moved to the door to give instructions to the villagers standing outside. By the time she turned back, he had soaped the wound and started unraveling the braids and coils in his hair. She moved to sit before the fire.

"So ... do you want to hear about dragon history, dragon physiology, or dragon behavior?"

"All."

She grinned, but tilted her head in acquiescence. "They are female, with the exception of a single bull. Gray in color, with subtle differences in shades ranging from charcoal to slate. Very instinctive, very bright, though not possessed of the intelligence ascribed to them in tales. You have these writings in the Mattaen archives?"

Karl nodded, then dunked his head beneath the water to rinse the soap from his hair.

"There are no dragonriders, then?" he asked after he finished, frowning in annoyance when a soft knock drew her to the door. He waited impatiently, eager to learn more.

She shut the door and carried the gauze and salve she had requested to his side, only to leave them within his reach and return to the fire. Stretching her arm into the flames while contemplating how best to answer him, she let heat redden her skin, then watched the burn fade when she withdrew her hand.

"What of the breath of fire?" Karl asked.

"How can you know of ..." Elera sputtered, spinning around with wide eyes. She paused for a moment, then realized he meant the fabled breath of the dragon. "I have never seen a dragon with this ability to breathe fire. Their bodies run hot, but not from any fire within. They simply absorb the rays of the sun."

"How close to the sun do they live?"

"Not beyond the boundaries of this world," she countered, amused by his curiosity. "They are skybound, living in a land that extends as high as the atmosphere allows life."

"And I suppose this place is also beyond the barrens?" Karl asked.

Elera started, then saw that he had asked the question merely to gauge her reaction. The man was far too astute. She had to wonder how much he intended to glean from her in such a way. Everything, considering the way he watched her. She had to be wary.

"It is only logical that a people who know dragons, who hunt them, would live near enough to study them," Karl prodded.

"Yes," she said simply, staring into the fire.

"Have you ever been to this place?"

"It would require wings, Initiate." She fell silent for a moment. "Stop hedging and get out of the tub before you take ill from the cold."

"You have not told me everything you know," Karl said stiffly. "And I enjoy the cold."

Elera remained quiet. When she heard an exasperated growl, she figured her ploy had worked and felt only slightly startled when he sat by her side with her towel wrapped low on his hips. In his hands were the salve and bandages, which he held out to her.

"Do not overestimate your abilities," Karl murmured, running long fingers through his hair until the snags loosened. He shifted to give her access to his shoulder.

The wound was not as deep as she'd first thought, mostly raw with abrasions from the times he'd fallen on it that day. It did not require stitching, and so she set those tools aside. Even though the salve must have burned, he made no reaction other than to tighten his forearm.

As Elera rubbed the medicine into the entire area, she spoke again. "The dragons have been in existence longer than we have, I think." She leaned in to inspect her work and let her hair fall over his shoulder.

Karl's hand balled into a fist. "Do you possess physical evidence of this?"

"Like skeletal remains, you mean?" She shook her head. "I do not think any exist. I think …"

Unraveling the gauze, she taped it into place, smoothing its edges with slow strokes. Her poncho slipped, causing the curve of her breast to brush against his back.

His other hand twitched. "You think …?"

Smiling, she whispered, "I think they do not die at all except in battle."

His brow furrowed in thought … until she pressed her lips to his shoulder blade. By the time Karl turned to warn her off, she was moving to the table with the remains of the healing supplies.

"And that would mean," Elera continued, turning to face him, "that our dragon today was the oldest living creature on the face of this planet, struck down by a mere girl's bow." Holding his eyes, she loosened the ties at her neck and let the poncho slither to her ankles.

She watched as his gaze slipped down her body, studying her golden skin, her narrow waist, the dark curls at the juncture of her thighs.

"I have been tempted before, dragonslayer. I will not forget myself, no matter your tricks."

Elera chuckled. How many hours of meditation would he spend trying to erase this encounter from his mind?

"I imagine you have been tempted by all sorts, Initiate. The forbidden always have a sweeter taste." She was also forbidden to him, and her words were warning and invitation alike.

Karl growled again.

"I like this sound you make," she murmured. "I long to feel it against my throat—"

"Stop this game, Elera!" He shot off the floor and glared down at her. "I will not be led from my—"

Karl's words ended abruptly as he noticed she was no longer looking at his face, but quite a bit lower. Her eyes lingered there hungrily before lifting slowly back to his, but she kept her tone light. "You lied, Initiate. There is nothing *unable* about you."

He shifted to hide his obvious arousal, and she saw him tense when she stepped near and lifted her hand to the hair hanging down his back.

"I have never seen hair the color of fire before," Elera whispered. The drying locks fell through her fingers like a wave of satin. "It seems wrong to waste such beauty."

He reached out to her... then remembered, and quickly moved away.

She closed her eyes. "Tell me, my scholar, do you know *anything* about the rites of mating?"

"I have studied."

"Studied?"

"Various techniques and positions... areas of greatest stimulation."

Elera's eyes popped open. Forgetting the spell she was weaving, she darted forward, grasped his cheeks, and pressed her lips smartly to his. There was no passion in the kiss, simply affection, and she was gone before he could push her away.

Karl frowned. "You will not benefit from these learnings, I assure you."

"As you wish," she said, trying to contain her laughter. "The Mattaen are sadists to give you such knowledge and deny you the experience!"

"In truth, I admit to having thought the same at the time." His mouth curved in a wry grin. "But the purpose was to teach the reasons for mating. One cannot fight something without first understanding the motivations behind it."

Her brow furrowed. "I would have thought understanding brought about embracing."

"Perhaps because you think overmuch of such things," Karl teased, though color rose in his cheeks when he saw her slow smile. She yawned then, moving near the fire to stretch out. "You should sleep," he said. "I will leave you."

"We agreed on the entire night," she said. And while he might not have recognized the regret in his voice, she certainly did. "It is far from over."

She was silent so long, Karl was certain she had fallen asleep. Moving quietly closer, he knelt at her side and indulged in a more detailed study of her features.

She was an uncommon beauty. Her nose was straight, her jaw angled and stubborn. Her lips were full, but not pouting, as if she hid a wealth of secrets within their enigmatic curve. He should not be fascinated by the delicious puzzle she posed, but how could he resist?

"I could take you, you know," Elera whispered, opening her eyes. Her smile was slow. "To my people, that is. And to the place of dragons."

His heart pounded. "For what price?"

And was he excited by the woman or by her offer?

When he did not draw back, Elera sat up and traced her fingers over the raging pulse in his throat. She gazed up at him with her answer in her eyes.

"I will not," he whispered.

Elera inclined her head. "A kiss, then. If you cannot resist a simple kiss, Karl, your place is not with the Mattaen."

"How long to reach this place?" he asked, ignoring her challenge.

Elera shrugged. "It depends on the perils of the path. There are the barrens, of course. The shrouding mist that must be breached, the heavy storms of ocean winds and rain." Lifting a finger, she traced the small scar on his bottom lip. "An unseasoned traveler might take months to find the marks of passage."

"Elera . . ." Karl warned, biting back a groan when her hand slipped around the back of his neck.

"Two days for me," she said, scraping her nails over his sensitized skin.

Too long to get there and back. Karl grimaced. "I join the temple in two. I cannot miss it." He would not be given a second opportunity to take his vows.

"I will wait for you."

"You would . . . Why would you do this?"

"If you indulge me in a kiss, Karl, I would wait as long as it takes."

She was holding something back; of that he was certain. Why was it that her eyes seemed to hold such sorrow?

"No hands," he said finally, cursing himself for wanting the taste of her as much as he wanted the knowledge she offered.

Elera nodded. "No hands. Mine, scholar, not yours. Yours may roam as they please."

She waited quietly as he struggled to align his will with his desire. Karl knew what she was doing, knew that she wanted this kiss far too much, knew he should consider her motives. Instead, he said simply, "Take it."

FOUR

Karl clenched his hands at his sides, bracing himself against the sensual assault as Elera came to her knees and slowly closed the gap between them. Their bodies did not touch, but the heat of her skin was just as potent. He had to dip his head to bring their lips within range. He watched her wait, passion darkening the smoky gray of her eyes, until he closed his own and lowered that final inch.

The first touch of her lips was soft enough that he might have imagined it. But he could not have mistaken her teasing sips over his scar.

"Open for me," she whispered.

He parted his lips for her, and she ran her tongue along their inner seam.... She drew back slightly to murmur encouragement, coaxing him to part further.

He did so, hesitantly.

At once, she deepened their kiss. She slid her tongue along his, lightly at first, withdrawing to nibble his lips again, and then returning within to thrust deep.

Karl jerked back as he processed the new sensation. She scraped her teeth along the column of his throat instead, nipping sharply at its base. Elera laved the tender spot, then moved back up to nip at his tightly clenched jaw.

He had to regain control of the situation before it got any worse. "You promised—"

"It is still just a kiss, Karl." Elera followed the path of her teeth with her tongue until she reached the tender skin above his collarbone. And then she truly used her teeth on him, clamping down and moaning as he tangled his hands in her hair.

"This is not the kiss I agreed to," he rasped as she licked the taste of him from her lips.

"It is my kiss." Elera turned her head and nuzzled his hand. "And you did not specify the nature, scholar. It will be as I wish it."

She closed her lips over his thumb, suckling it within her mouth, circling her tongue around its tip. She nipped the base before allowing his thumb to slide from between her lips, and the contrasting sensations made his shaft grow thick beneath his towel.

All the while her eyes remained locked on his, capturing his gaze, immobilizing his body ... freezing his objections over this line she claimed not to be crossing.

"Forgive me," Elera murmured, "for I have no choice."

Behind them, the fire crackled furiously. Karl turned to look ... and saw that it had *changed*. No longer orange, it faded away to nearly nothing, then rose higher than before, with blue flames that cast the room in shades of twilight.

The same colors flared in Elera's eyes. Their smoke gray reflected the light of the fire and swirled with blue flame.

Karl shuddered, his sex swelling with an almost painful surge. "Stop. What are you ...?" His body thrummed; his blood burned. She was bewitching him! "Elera, do not, I beg you!"

Too late, he thought as she blew softly over his lips.

Her warm breath caressed his skin, stimulating every nerve, every sense, every repressed and aching desire. Karl closed his eyes and moaned her name....

Elera watched him, relishing the stark beauty in his face as he surrendered to the moment of the sexual rite. It was the breath of fire, sacred to her people, sacred to her ... and if he had none of the strength or intelligence he claimed, he would never know why it should also be sacred to him.

Karl was still dazed, breathing erratically, unable to absorb the full physical assault on his senses when she ordered in a husky voice, "Remove the towel."

He obeyed at once, his mind susceptible to her command when his senses were so overwhelmed. He sat at her side. Her eyes dilated in desire, straying only briefly to the blade he had not removed from his thigh even to bathe. She could not risk her temporary control by ordering him to set aside something that might have an even stronger influence over him.

"Lie back," she whispered, keeping her lips against the center of his chest as he reclined. She straddled one of his thighs and placed her hands on the floor on either side of his head.

She could take him as he lay helpless. The deed would be done before he could stop her. Many of the men in her race who cared nothing for a woman's resistance used the thrall in that manner.

But she wanted better for Karl's first experience, and so she would wait. It was only moments before his eyes cleared. When they narrowed sharply upon hers, she knew the thrall had left his mind. His splendid body would burn for some time, control or no.

"What did you do?" he rasped after he glanced down at his naked body.

He would remember tossing the towel aside, she knew. But he would not understand why he had done it. Lowering her head, Elera licked the hollow of his throat. "I have broken no word to you."

His eyes narrowed further. "Then our bargain is met?"

"Are you certain you still wish it to be?"

She slithered down his leg and scraped the skin of his abdo-

men with her teeth. His body jerked. A few phrases he must
have picked up before his life as an Initiate fell from his lips.

Elera chuckled.

"What have you done to me?" He groaned again, rearing
up when she blew her breath along the length of his shaft.
"Stop; I cannot! You…"

She closed her lips over him, and his voice faltered. Sweat
dotted his brow, slicked his skin. She started to move, circling
his tip, drawing him in.…

His hands were wrapped in her hair, his hips lifting as he
sought more from her than teasing tastes and whispered
touches. In one swift movement, he grabbed her arms, dragging her up his muscled body to press her against his arousal.

Karl gasped as her body rubbed against him. Nothing, no
scroll or lecture, could have prepared him for this. His body
was on fire with every urge he'd ever repressed. Instinctively,
his hips arched again, rubbing against the soft skin of her inner
thighs.

"Karl … knowledge without experience *is* weakness," he
heard her whisper against his temple. He sipped at the base of
her neck, licking its slender column, grazing her jaw. He
watched her as she moaned and then fisted her hands to keep
her word. Cursing himself, he lifted her higher, drawing her
peaked nipple into his mouth and suckling. When she cried
his name, he felt a fierce sort of pride.

The sound fueled his awakening ardor. He stroked her
back, reaching lower to knead the firm mounds of her bottom, and lower still to skim his fingertips between her wet
folds. By the time her scent hit his nostrils, Karl was bucking
against her slim body, his sex so hard it was almost painful. Elera slipped free to slide enticingly across the seeking tip of his
arousal.

She paused when he froze, then met his rage and passion with arrogant calm. "Our bargain is met. You may leave if you still wish it."

He trembled beneath her, sweat slicking his skin as he tried in vain to fight her spell. When finally he shuddered, they both knew she had won.

Karl closed his eyes, despising himself for his weakness even as he whispered, "I will hate you for this."

"I know ..." she said softly. He felt her rock back onto him, heard her moan as she worked herself onto his thick crest. He moved, driving deep ... then deeper still until she began to tremble. "I'm sorry. Give me a moment...."

He growled, flexing his hips. She would not deny him. Not now.

"Karl!" Elera cried.

Cutting short his forceful thrust, he opened his eyes, then narrowed them upon her tight features. "You are no virgin, witch."

"I'm neither, I hope." The corners of her lips curved. "But you are no small man. I need only a moment to adjust, if you ..."

They both gasped when she eased farther down, taking more of him. Reaching for his hands, Elera lifted them to her breasts, ran his knuckles across their peaks.

He could feel her tight sheath ease a little more, but he could wait no longer. He ran a hand down her satiny skin. When he reached the curls where they were joined, Elera held her breath in anticipation ... and cried out at the first flick of his finger against her nub.

He touched her gently as he recalled his learnings, moaning as she flexed around his shaft. "Elera," he whispered, circling the nub with purpose now. "Elera, it must be ..."

She pressed down hard, sheathing him fully. Yet even

through his ecstasy, he remembered to keep touching her. For every downward thrust, he flicked her center.... For every slow rise, his fingers circled rapidly.

Frantic cries fell from her lips, matching his as she quickened her pace, stroking him with her inner muscles until his hips thrust endlessly beneath her. The pressure between them built, thickened. "Wait ... I cannot hold ... I cannot ..."

Seizing the nub that was swollen from his touch, Karl rotated it firmly between two fingers. Elera screamed, her head thrown back, and the sensation of her inner muscles clamping around him shredded the remains of his restraint.

He rolled her beneath him, driving deep and fast, with no thought to the strength of his hands as he held her there.

"Elera ...!"

Karl's eyes went wide and blank. He wrapped his arms fully around her, buried his face in her neck, desperate now for the same dark pleasure that had taken her. Pumping further ... and further still ... until his body jerked without warning, quaking in pleasure with every pulse pouring into her.

Raw and untried, his cries echoed through the village and far into the steppes below.

Afterward, she curled against him. And despite his anger, despite his failing, Karl did not have it in him to turn her away. Perhaps it was the intimacy, albeit forced, or the tears rolling down her cheeks long after she fell asleep. But he pulled his robe over them both, curled an arm around her waist, and slept.

Dawn trickled through the cracks in the hut and roused Karl from his dreams. Cold air was slipping beneath the robe tossed carelessly over his shoulders. He stretched lazily, unused to the languid sense of ease that had overtaken him.

His hand met empty space and Karl stilled. Had he comforted Elera in her sleep, just so she could leave him in his? His eyes cracked open, shifting to where the scent of Elera still lingered, but he saw no sign of the woman herself.

And as he sat up, every good feeling vanished with the reminder of what had been done the night before.

His life's work had been for naught.

His search for knowledge ended.

Karl rose slowly to his feet. Unconcerned by his lack of clothing, he walked to the window and stared out. No one moved about the village, and little surprise that. The moon and the sun still clashed, and even the dawn that had awoken him barely glimmered against the gray sky.

He clamped a hand over the dread churning in his stomach. He would not join the Mattaen tomorrow. It was the greatest dishonor, and he had embraced it with eager lips and pathetically little thought to resistance.

Not so, his mind whispered. *She did something to you.*

Remembering that moment, Karl bit back a moan. What had she done? Her breath had flowed over him, into him, flaming a path that burned hotter and hotter until his very will had been consumed.

The dragonslayer had tricked him, knowing full well she would have him with that bargain. Karl sighed. He had been arrogant to think he could barter that part of himself to begin with ... arrogant and hungry for greater knowledge. He wasn't sure even now if he had betrayed the Mattaen for the woman, or for the secrets she had promised.

Karl scanned what he could of the village and steppes. Finding nothing, he turned back and searched the room for signs of her. But it wasn't Elera's absence that told him she had fled. Or even that her clothing no longer lay beside the bed ... although he considered that fairly conclusive.

It was the blade no longer strapped to his thigh. The black blade meant to draw not a single drop of blood through his entire journey as Initiate.

She'd known. All along she'd known the blade of an Initiate took only the life of its master, if he failed in his quest and chose not to live with the shame. No other weapon could take its place, for no other held the ceremonial power to grant him final honor in death.

She had taken it to keep him from choosing that path.

And she was gone. Without ever intending to keep her end of the bargain, she had taken everything ... and left him lost.

His knuckles whitened at his sides. Temper, rarely shown and only hinted at in the color of his hair, flared now. Jerking his robe over his head, Karl reached for the pocket holding his coin ... and snarled.

She would take his life's work, disregard the pact they had made, but she would not take the fifty silver *tarlae* she had demanded? They would see about that.

The village had just begun to stir when Karl stomped to the stone stairs leading into the steppes. Emerging folk took one look at him and slunk hastily back into their huts. Even the men on watch on the stairs shrank against the walls as he passed.

He barely noticed them in his pursuit of the woman. Not that tracking her path proved to be a strenuous activity, and Karl took time to appreciate the irony of someone so small leaving so many clear imprints of her boots in the gravel.

Then he reached the edge of the cliff where her trail broke abruptly off. And he thought that perhaps she could afford to be careless after all. Few, if any, could descend this cliff.

Scowling still, Karl tied his robe about his legs and leaped over the ledge. His fingers sought and grasped minuscule nooks, slipping only once on loose rock. But he was too angry to fear falling to his death, and scraped his arms raw to find better purchase.

Blood filled his mouth as he slammed into the flat of the cliff, honing his focus with its metallic taste. But the deeper he descended, the thicker and more putrid that mist became as it drifted up to meet him. By the time he was a few dozen feet down, Karl had to rely on touch to continue his path. And when he finally felt solid ground beneath his sandals, his fingers were covered in cuts.

Tentatively transferring his weight from his hands to his feet, he balanced precariously atop the new surface. Still he could see nothing. No signs of a path or any danger that might lie in wait along it. He could barely see his hand waving before his face.

There was sound, however. Karl tilted his head to listen. Water, he realized, and fairly close. Holding one hand out as a guide, he crept along the rock until the roar of falling water blocked out all other noise. He moved forward as the spray started clearing patches of the mist, showing him glimpses of level ground ahead.

Karl took a deep breath ... and stepped directly into a chasm hidden at the edge of the rock.

He didn't fall far, and caught himself on the opposite edge of the chasm with bloody fingertips. He pulled himself up and over the rock. He looked down and discovered that he hadn't found the bottom of the cliff after all. He'd just reached some sort of plateau.

Had Elera continued to descend? Considering his options, he rose to his feet on the plateau and stole just a moment to catch his breath before running again. The level ground quickly gave way to a swampy embankment resulting from the humidity and mist, and it was here that he again picked up Elera's trail. The longer he sprinted through fronds of moss, evading various creatures and leaping over bogs of mud, the fresher her tracks became.

Finally he slowed his pace. There she was, walking lightly along with his blade slung across her shoulder. Karl's eyes narrowed. She looked back once, head tilted curiously, but continued on her way with a careless shrug. Some time later she started whistling, and Karl had to bite his tongue to keep from snarling her name. He climbed a ridge rising alongside the path she traveled and shadowed her. But at last she stopped, climbing the base of a rotted tree stump nearly twenty feet around.

Karl dropped from his perch and landed on the ground directly in front of it. Already he anticipated seeing her eyes widen in alarm, that berry-kissed mouth part in surprise or even fear.

His pride smarted when she did none of these things. Instead she smiled and held out a satchel of berries when he climbed onto the stump to glower down at her.

"Karl." Elera winked, popping a raspberry into her mouth. "I had wondered when you would arri—"

Her voice cut off when he raised her up until they were nose-to-nose. "I came only to claim what is mine," he snarled.

For a moment, he saw something flare in her eyes, something too quickly shielded for him to guess at its meaning. His body began reacting to those curves pressed against it, and that was enough to renew the anger that was just beginning to subside.

He shook her once, and dumped her back to her feet to reach for his blade. The tips of his fingers brushed its hilt....

Elera jumped into his stance, twisting full circle and booting him hard in the chest. The unexpected attack sent him sprawling off the edge of the stump. He grabbed her foot and pulled her down after him.

Taking the brunt of the landing, Karl rolled before she could react. He pinned her beneath him, then used one hand to imprison both of hers above her head. The other stripped the black blade from its clasp upon her shoulder.

"It's cowardly to use that," Elera accused, lifting her chin and standing her ground when he pulled them to their feet.

"It's cowardly to leave without having to face what you did," he snapped back. "And you forgot something."

Starting as he thrust something into her hands, Elera glanced down at the pouch overflowing with silver *tarlae*.

Her lips parted. "Karl—"

"Say nothing, witch! Your price is met, so you will leave that town in peace." Stepping away when her eyes flashed hurt, Karl lowered his voice. "And you've no right to that look."

Elera nodded and paced to the lip of a ravine nearly concealed by vines and foliage. "Where will you go now?"

He needed only an hour alone to complete the ritual, so there seemed little point in answering her question.

"I see," she whispered, turning back. "I never lied to you, you know. And I gave you everything a man of your knowledge should need to find his way. It's your failing if you choose to ignore it."

"Never lied," he repeated dully … then grabbed her arms and shook her with all the fury of his betrayal. At her cry, he stepped back, rubbed his hands over the marks they had made. Softer now, he whispered, "Why did you betray me?"

She didn't answer. Even if she had tried, her words would have been lost to the thunderous noise coming from the ravine. Karl pulled her farther from its edge, stumbling over the stones bouncing with each expanding thud.

His fingers tightened on her arm. "What's this?"

"You're hurting me, Karl," Elera said calmly.

He immediately released her and glanced over the ravine, seeing nothing but greenery. "Elera, I believe we should—"

"Karl? You don't *really* think I made it down that mountainside on my own?"

Suspicion dawned as he dropped his eyes to measure the much smaller span of her reach. He recalled the half dozen times he'd nearly fallen when no hold lay safely within his grasp.

Karl's gaze lifted slowly back to hers, just as a massive gray paw slammed into the earth at his feet.

FIVE

He tossed Elera over his shoulder and ran ... until a massive membranous wing slammed into the ground directly in front of him. In a single fluid motion, he twisted and jumped clear of the wing without ever losing his grip on Elera's waist. A blast of air warned him to brace himself as the animal leaped over them.

It landed in their path with fangs bared and spiny fin extended. The beast hissed, its tail poised in the air ... and even a lifetime of training could not help Karl dodge the lightning-quick lash. Searing pain followed as a rib cracked beneath the blow. If the creature had struck him with the bladed tip of its tail instead of its blunt length, Karl would certainly have been skewered.

"Forgetting your own suspicions already?" she whispered from around his shoulder. "I think he's starting to take it personally, you standing between the two of us."

Karl froze, as much in response to her words as to the hiss emanating from the dragon's slavering mouth. But that was all the distraction Elera needed to ease the black blade from his fingers and skip out from behind his back.

A sharp claw sliced into the ground a hairbreadth from his foot, blocking his attempt to grab her. He swallowed, moving backward very slowly as the beast bared its teeth mere inches from his face.

The dragon's head tilted suddenly as a small hand touched its snout. Elera moved closer to the dragon and pressed her forehead to its lips, smoothing its snout with both hands.

Wanting to scream and whisper her name at once, Karl gaped when the beast lowered its head, allowing Elera easier access to the lighter gray scales along its forehead. The look in those ruby eyes did not become any less menacing when the dragon glanced at him, but its hiss had been replaced with a softer sound, almost a purr.

He sneered as she comforted the beast. "Elera the *dragon-slayer*."

Although the creature's spine rustled in warning, it remained flat beneath her hands. "I never claimed to be that, Karl. Not once."

"You never claimed to be many things," he said, staring as she gripped a scaly ridge and climbed to the crest of the dragon's neck. "It was a … a ruse? Was the whole thing just a trick?" Fury made him ruthless. "Your people are scavengers," he hissed, "feasting on the fears of the ignorant to steal the very food from their mouths. Leaving them to rot in poverty because you—" He broke off when he saw her trembling. The dragon shook with her, though a few expert strokes and whispered words in a language unknown to the realm helped it settle.

"You faked the killing of this beast, took payment you had no right to demand. You took everything I am … was," he amended, choking on the words. "And for what?"

"I did what I had to, Karl. I—"

"*Whore!*" he shouted, ignoring the hiss of the beast she rode. "*Whore* to your lies and your pleasure, *whore* to—"

The pouch of silver struck him in the chest, and he snarled as it glanced off his cracked rib. He could see the fury in Elera's eyes now, fury reflected in the spine and extended wings of her dragon. The beast lifted its tail, ready to strike.

The lash never came, but Elera's words sliced into his pride. "I told you I would attempt to change our agreement, and so

I did. I warned you not to trust me, but you did. We bargained ... a bargain you had no right to make according to your creed, as well you know. And you dare stand there and blame me for your loss?"

Karl took a slow breath, trying and failing to calm his anger. "I blame you for breaking your end!"

His roar earned him a lash of that vicious tail, though he managed to duck just before being struck. It was a warning only, for he'd seen it coming and knew the beast could move much faster.

Elera raised a dark brow. "I promised to take you to the land of my people and to the dwelling of dragons. I never said they were two separate places. Or that I would hold your hand through the journey, or even walk at your side." Lifting his blade, she met his eyes over its gleaming edge.

"I have given you everything you need to find this place and me. When you do, if you still want to use this blade, I'll give it back. Until then ..."

The dragon reared on powerful hind legs, its wings unfolding to rip the surrounding fronds and vines as if they were of no greater substance than the mist. They beat once, twice ... and with a final swing of its tail—this time forcing Karl to drop to the earth to avoid its lash—the dragon dove over the side of the ravine.

Karl rolled to his feet, sprinted to the ledge, and stared grimly into the vacant drop.

They were gone.

Elera sat astride the bull's neck with her boots planted against the scales under his crest as they flew. Below them, partially obscured by the clouds, lay Verteva.

The land itself had evolved from a long-dormant fire mountain, now mostly crumbled into the ocean. What remained was an island in the sky, many miles around, and supported by a matrix of solid granite and rock. It thickened in a gradual ascent from the ocean.

The fertile tip of her land had begun to erode into the water below. Each year, more of the mountain's natural infrastructure fractured, eroding the borders of their skybound home. It would be decades before it became a real problem, Elera admitted, studying the honeycombed sections where the dragons loved to romp. But decades spanned barely a single breath in a millennium.

Sensitive to the slightest pressure from his rider, the bull flared his wings and began a slow descent. Clawed feet cut through the clouds, skimming over the scarlet and midnight colors decorating the various Houses. Banners flapped in the wake of their passing, while gray dragons unfurled their wings and submissively ducked their heads.

Elera grinned, leaning down to caress a sensitive area beneath the bull's crest. All the dragons below were female. His personal harem, and less than half his size … though she'd seen him flop meekly to his side when indulging a favored few.

At least, it seemed like that to her, though none could say for certain. She hadn't lied when she'd told Karl that dragons did not possess the intelligence granted them in fables. They were animals to the last, and whatever wisdom or tolerance they exhibited came from their immortality and their relationship with their riders. Affection connected rider and dragon, and the greater that affection, the more susceptible the dragon became to its rider's mood.

Elera looked over the crowd that had gathered, waiting for her to land. The bull growled. She stroked the ridge of his spine, then surrendered control and let him guide them down. He landed lightly and folded his massive wings at his sides.

"Thank you, my friend," Elera whispered in the ancient

tongue as she slid off his lowered neck. "Go. There are many who missed you."

His great body coiled for flight. But before he left the ground, his tail swung around, whistling past the head of a warrior stomping toward her. The man's dodge was pure reflex, and he glared at her in reproof.

She shrugged. "He knows I have little liking for you."

The warrior raised his fist, commanding his men back. Black hair fell nearly to his waist, its color accentuated by the deep crimson of his tunic. He wore a dagger on each thigh and an ax slung across his back. This rider was the greatest warrior of her people—feared, respected, and single-mindedly ambitious.

He stopped a foot away from her, running his eyes over her body as if to claim her. "Liking or not, you dare much to leave the fold with neither permission nor protection."

"The bull is all the protection I need," she answered, hefting her bag from one shoulder to the other. "I'm tired, Ronin. Let me pass."

His charcoal eyes narrowed in suspicion. He stepped closer, lowering his head to breathe her scent. His nostrils flared, and she watched his face purple before he swiveled his gaze slowly to hers. "Who has touched you?"

She lifted her chin, saying nothing.

"I have asked you to come to me when the need takes you," he said stiffly.

"You have told me to come to you when the need takes me," Elera corrected, brushing by once he allowed it. "But it is more than simple pleasure that you seek. And I have said no too many times to repeat myself now."

"Stop."

She sighed, but stopped and turned as he commanded.

"If I thought you went to another for reasons other than physical, I would be ... displeased."

"Because you care so much?" Elera mocked him.

Ronin closed the distance, and she could see him trying to understand how one girl could defy him when his own men would be quaking before his wrath. "I will be sovereign here. And I do not share what is mine."

She knew he included her in that list. But this was an old argument, and Elera stared as if bored. With a curse, and then a quick step back in response to the rumbling bull, Ronin vaulted atop his charcoal female and took to the sky.

Three of his warriors stayed in his stead. They stepped respectfully aside, allowing Elera passage into the ivory manor built along the side of a nearby cliff. Most of their deference, she admitted, came from her unique status as the sole female rider. Dragons did not forge same-sex bonds with riders, and the woman who rode the bull was naturally held in great esteem.

Her grandfather waited within the arched doorway at the top of the stairs. He took her arm and pulled her gently into his embrace. "I missed you, my son's daughter."

Moving back, Warwick studied the shadows under his granddaughter's eyes, and glared at the men easing up the stairs. In a volume that belied his age, he called to them, "I do not recall giving you leave to enter here."

"Did you have trouble with my disappearance?" Elera asked, retreating inside with him when the warriors returned to the bottom of the stairs.

"Nothing I could not handle." When she looked at him in concern, Warwick scoffed. "I am the father of a dragonslayer, living in a world of those who practically worship the creatures. You, my dear, are the very opposite of trouble." He paused to wink and add, "In comparison to your father, of course."

Chuckling mostly for his sake, Elera followed him to a

rooftop terrace, where a meal sat ready. She longed for a bath and her bed.

"I know," Warwick said, smiling at the girl he'd raised as his daughter. "But I am an old man with the patience of a tot. You'll indulge me with the story of your adventure."

His impatient look sent the servants scurrying from the terrace. Only then did he sit at the table, lean back, and fold his hands. When his feet started tapping the floor restlessly, Elera sighed. For a man well into the fourth quarter of his century, he neither looked nor acted the part. His silver hair hung long and straight, and his gnarled knuckles could still straighten and grip the hilt of his battle-ax.

It was the hard grooves cutting into his cheeks, lining his eyes and brow, that gave evidence to his long years.

"It's done," she said.

Her grandfather's sigh echoed hers, relief and regret at once. "And will he come?"

"Oh, he'll come," she said firmly, lifting a brow and grinning. "If only for my neck."

"If only for…" The furrows in his brow grew deeper. "What manner of man did you take?"

Elera studied her hands, readying herself for his disapproval.

"Elera…"

"An Initiate," she said.

"A *Mattaen* Initiate?" He narrowed his eyes when she flipped her hands to study her palms. After she nodded, he stared in disbelief. "How did you manage—"

"I spotted him roaming the barrens," she explained quickly, "shadowed him until I was certain of his path, then allowed the bull to prowl around the land near the village where the man would cross … as our men do when they want to claim a sacrifice. By the time he reached their borders, the people had readied a girl, and a slayer had been called. I meant to play the slayer with the girl ... and then try to claim him out of the crowd as part of my payment afterward...."

Warwick lifted a brow in expectation.

"But I saw him arguing with the elder. I decided to wait and see if he argued out of compassion for the girl or disdain for the ritual. I thought perhaps he might try to free the girl ... but I did not expect him to trade himself for her as the sacrifice, though it was certainly easier to claim him as my prize because of it."

"Mmm," Warwick murmured, staring blandly. "Your father's blood does run hot in you."

Elera's eyes blazed. "I don't consider that an insult."

"Nor do I," Warwick said, softening. "But Elera—"

"He has a true chance against Ronin, if it comes to that."

"It will," he warned when she stood to pace the terrace. She heard the bull rumbling in the distance, responding to her agitation.

"But more than a warrior," she whispered, returning to kneel at his feet, "we need a ruler who can think to the future ... who can show compassion to a people not his own. If there is a chance we can survive in the world below when this land crumbles to the sea, we need someone who can find it. None here could rise to this task."

"There is one." Warwick crossed his arms. "But she takes chances far too great for an old man to condone."

Elera's eyes shone with mischief, and she winked before turning to where the bull flew amidst a flock of smaller forms. He was playing, and she struggled to keep her mood light for his sake. The bond between them was precious, but it made her a pawn to her people. And a prize to Ronin.

Men ruled in Verteva, which was no different in this regard from any other society she had seen. But the customs here revolved around the dragons her people had held sacred for millennia. It might seem natural that the rider of the most powerful dragon would rise to rule. But the rider of the most powerful dragon was a woman. Therefore, it was not the rider of the bull who rose to sovereign status, but the bonded mate of the rider herself.

For years, Ronin had ruled the people of this land with the might of his ax and fist, but without Elera's bond any ambitious rider could challenge him. If she bonded with another, his rule would be over.

Out of respect for the bull, he hadn't attempted to force their mating. But until now she'd made little protest against his leadership except to refuse him her bed. If he discovered what she had done in the world below, their peace would come to an end. Not even the bull would be able to protect her from Ronin then.

She shuddered, but masked her revulsion with a prideful toss of her head when she felt the eyes of the bull turn her way.

"I should have forced you to find a mate as soon as you came of age," Warwick continued, scoffing when she scowled at him. He had been weak with love for the child of his fallen son, and so had let her have her way. "I watched Ronin rise to power. I knew he would come for you, and though any man would have been better than him, I wanted more for you than a mating based on necessity. And now, despite my wishes, this is all you will have."

Elera's shoulders twitched in reaction to his statement, and her grandfather leaned forward to examine her expression, trying, no doubt, to discern the nature of her experience with the Initiate. "If this man is less than what you say, Ronin will kill him before he has a chance to accept your bond."

Elera shifted her eyes and sadly stared into his. "Then we are lost."

* * *

Night fell fast, leaving the manor completely dark except for the stars shining directly above. Warwick had left her alone, and she sat on the terrace outside her room, knees drawn up and a shawl tossed over her shoulders to ward off the evening chill.

She heard him coming long before he swung first one leg and then the other over the railing.

"Ronin." Pulling the shawl tighter, Elera narrowed her eyes. The bull did not take kindly to trespass on these grounds. "You'll be lucky if he lets you back down."

From a nearby hilltop, where he lay burrowed between two females, the bull rumbled.

Ronin leaned against the wall. "I am regretting the leniency I've shown you these last years."

Careful not to show fear for either his trespass or their solitude, Elera watched him close the distance to her table. He crouched before her and gripped the arms of her seat, not quite forming a cage, though it served to remind her that he could.

"Elera . . ."

She started in surprise. Rarely did he use her name.

"Why?" he asked simply. Elera knew he could smell her fear. It wasn't his intention to frighten her, but she didn't think he was opposed to it either. "It must be someone, so why not me?"

"Would you like to hear all of my reasons, or just a few?" Elera asked flippantly. She gasped when he tipped her chair back, keeping one hand on her arm to stop her from falling.

He used it now to pull her close. "You mock me, and I simply ask a question." His dark eyes lowered to the flesh barely covered by her slip, now that her shawl had slipped to her feet. "The time will come when I do not ask so much as take."

"You would rule this place with no thought to anything but your own ambition."

"Not so," he murmured, bending closer. "I would give you anything you want."

"To get what you want," she said, jerking her arm back, only to be pinned against the wall. When his hands dragged at the straps of her slip, she snarled, "You can force my body, but not my bond."

Ronin's hands hovered over her skin, clenched once, and then slowly lowered to his sides when a brief glance showed the bull already taking to the air. "I burn for you, Elera, and I—"

"You burn for the rider of the bull, with little care for the rider herself."

"And I," he pressed, lowering his mouth and forcing her to feel his breath, "am weary of waiting for what is my due. If you don't come to me by the first crescent of the next waxing moon, I will forgo the bond and force you to take me."

Elera lifted her chin. "Your rule would forever be in question."

"By whom?" Ronin whispered, backing away from her as he straightened. "There is no one to stop me, Elera ... and you will know it by the end."

He ducked and rolled, just managing to keep his head atop his shoulders as the tip of the bull's tail whipped over the railing. The momentum of his flight slammed the bull into the manor, where he gripped the wall with claws that chiseled through the ivory.

Elera scooted behind the shelter of his wing, straightening her shift as she ran. From the corner of her eye, she saw Ronin leap over the railing and swerve in midair to avoid the slash of the bull's wing.

"You will know cruelty in my bed if you force my hand," he shouted, landing smoothly atop the female rising to meet his fall. "Best for us both that you come willingly, and soon."

The bull drew his wing reluctantly back, unwilling to risk

striking his female to reach her rider. Nor would he leave Elera's side when he could sense her distress.

She glared into his garnet eyes. "You don't completely disapprove of him or you would have been here sooner."

Lowering his head, the bull butted her until she ran her hand along his scales. The familiar act worked to calm her as nothing else could. Only after he nudged her gently before shooting back off to his hill did Elera succumb to her fear and sink to the terrace stone.

Even Karl couldn't find this place before the next waxing moon. And the breath of fire—the rite of bonding she had given him—was for life. Even if he never came to claim her.

Even had Elera wished it, there was nothing left in her for Ronin now.

SIX

The day that Karl should have joined the Mattaen arrived too quickly. He spent it sitting on the wall surrounding the temple, listening as the faithful took their vows. More than one baffled look got tossed his way as the day progressed and he did not enter. No one had considered that he might have succumbed to temptation, and it was no surprise when light steps skipped up the wall and a familiar face appeared at his side.

"What has happened?"

For a long while, Karl stared silently ahead. Finally, he sighed. "I am failed, brother."

"Tell me."

So he did, with neither inflection nor sentiment in his tone. Karl left nothing out ... not the dragon, nor the woman and their night together. When his tale was through, the man at his side simply shook his head.

"As dragons do not exist, and dragonriders even less, I say come. Enter the temple and be at peace."

"And you have the power to issue such a decree?" Karl grinned, and finally turned to look at the Initiate by his side. Though they shared no common blood, the two had walked as brothers for more than a decade. "Go take your vows, Simon. It's what I came to see."

Indecision showed in Simon's face. "I might forgo them to walk with you instead."

"I cannot allow that," Karl said softly, clasping his hand over the other man's shoulder. He smiled again. "One of us must know the secrets in those tombs."

"True," Simon said gravely, although his eyes sparked as he tilted his head. "Do you remember the day we learned of the vents in the barrens? And of the insects that could manipulate passage through them without ever being caught in their bursts of steam?"

Karl nodded, fond of that particular memory. "I followed a firemoth through to test the validity of the legend."

"We were nineteen," Simon said. "And I thought you were crazy, first to need proof of a Mattaen teaching, and second to risk your life on it." He fell silent for a while, watching the line of Initiates dwindle as each was accepted into the temple. "You always needed proof, brother. You were never convinced without it."

"You think I should find her."

"I think you will find her, if only for your honor." Simon sighed then, ready to leap from the wall and take his place. "There are six fewer to take vows this month than there were last. I will mourn only you."

"You'll be much too ecstatic over all the secrets I will never get to know to even remember my name," Karl quipped, but he nodded his head in recognition of the concession.

Still, Simon hesitated. "Will you truly leave me in ignorance, my brother?"

"Ask, then, and be gone," Karl growled. "I do not wish to think ill of you this day."

Simon grinned. "What was it like?"

Only three Initiates were left in the procession, and still Simon waited, his patience as enduring as the steadiness in his calloused hands.

"Almost worth it," Karl admitted finally, with more sadness than he'd intended to reveal. But there was little he could hide from this man.

"Effort is the difference between *almost* and *absolutely*, my brother." With those cryptic words, Simon leaped from the wall and raced across the grounds.

Karl watched him go, clenching his jaw as vows were taken, robes discarded, and hair shorn. Shaving the body symbolized shedding identity ... and all ties with their former lives. He fingered one of the red braids hanging over his shoulder ... the traditional hairstyle of his father's people. He would have given it up to become one with the brotherhood.

He let it fall with a resigned sigh. During his brother's turn, he mouthed the words that should have been his.

Simon turned once, just before taking his first anxious steps inside the temple.

Walk well.

"Well or not," Karl said, reading the silent message and then slipping over the opposite edge of the wall, "I walk."

The Mattaen temple sat in the center of the realm. One could meet a Mattaen monk and join their Initiates only if one had the fortitude to ignore the wonders and comforts in the surrounding city.

Karl walked amidst those wonders now, weaving past merchants as they bartered wares and services in the brick-lined streets. Children raced along, playing in the sunlight under the guidance of multiple tutors.

As the day progressed, women smiled invitingly down at him from their carriages when they noticed his robe, while tradesmen nodded respectfully as he passed their shops.

The time had come to change his clothing. He was no longer an Initiate, and he should not be receiving the attention due their status. He had just switched course to the nearest clothing vendor when two young boys grabbed his hands and started pulling him in opposite directions.

Karl observed from beneath his hood as the pair continued

to fight over where his attention was needed the most. Even after they decided to cooperate and pull him to the left, he stood stock-still. The boys stared up at him in confusion. The oldest was the first to sigh, slapping the younger on the back of his head. "You have to ask him first, nit."

"No, you ask," the younger hissed, gasping when Karl twisted his arm, reversing the boys' grip so he now held their wrists.

Lifting both boys to a single crate on the side of the street, Karl threw back his hood and met their eyes. "Ask me what?"

"We have a bet, sir," the youngest said, gnawing his lip until Karl motioned for him to continue. "With our sister, see."

"And what exactly is this bet?"

"She thinks she can join the Initiates and be a Mattaen, and we want you to tell her she's wrong."

"Why do you say she's wrong?"

The boys gaped. "Because she's a bleeding girl, that's why."

Karl's hand shot out, caught the stone hurtling toward the younger brother's head, and frowned sternly over his shoulder at the girl with the sling. There were tears streaking down her face as she stared mulishly up at him. Her delicate silk dress was thoroughly stained with grass and dirt.

"Please, sir, tell her."

"And what do you get if you win your wager?" Karl asked the boys, tossing the stone back to the girl.

"I don't have to wear a dress through the schoolyard," the oldest announced proudly. "And Jayden doesn't have to weave his hair."

"I see," Karl said, ignoring their expressions as they noticed the braids in his hair. "And if your sister wins the wager?"

"She doesn't have to wear the bleeding dress either."

The smirk on the girl's lips was hard to miss. She recognized the one-sidedness of this particular wager. It was hard enough to keep from smirking himself while wondering how she'd wheedled it.

"You are both right, and both wrong," he said finally. "Worth determines an Initiate, not gender. However, no woman is permitted entrance into the temple. So on the last day of the month in which she reaches her thirtieth year, any female Initiate is once again a citizen of the realm."

Though all three siblings were deflated by their wager's impotence, the girl seemed to be considering his words. Her eyes lifted curiously to Karl's. "Why bother?"

He lifted the boys down from the crate and crouched before her. "If you can't answer that, little one, then it isn't the path for you."

Digging into her pocket, she pulled out enough silver *tarlae* to make her brothers goggle. "Is this enough to join?"

"Ten times that, perhaps." Karl tucked it quickly back into her pocket, adding two to her stash. "If you ever earn it all and reach the temple, ask for the monk named Simon. Tell him that Karl thought you were worthy."

Soft amber eyes studied him carefully. "I will."

Karl stood with a nod and started walking away. He chuckled when he heard her tell her brothers that since they had all won the wager, they should all honor its terms.

He was still grinning when he handed over a large sum of silver in exchange for leather breeches, a tan tunic, a poncho, and a pair of black boots. He folded his robe neatly, tying it with rope and tucking it carefully into his new pack along with the poncho.

Karl felt fairly satisfied until he realized that his new clothes were annoyingly constricting. He twisted and stretched until the material no longer threatened to strangle him ... even though the neck of his tunic barely brushed against his collarbone. But there was nothing to be done for it ... or for the alien feel of his boots over feet too familiar with sandals. So after nodding grudging thanks to the merchant, Karl walked through the darkened streets.

Somehow the realm became even more vibrant at night. Music and laughter filled the air, accompanied by the sounds of good-natured brawling. Sweet scents of hallucinogenic smoke drifted from a nearby tavern. Karl stepped onto a pedestrian bridge and pressed forward, leaving the bustle of the city beneath him.

Surrounding him now were the rising towers of the city, many of which scraped the very sky Elera had promised to show him. From his current height, he could even see the way candles flickered against their open windows and blended in with the stars themselves. Without ever taking his eyes off the view, Karl continued his travels for most of the night. He didn't need to watch his footing. This was a path he'd walked more times than even *his* mind could count. Far too often had he been drawn to the great barrier wall to watch the sun rise and bathe the untamed regions in flame.

He stood and watched, this time facing the realm, while shadows from the towers receded before the sun. He ducked his head inside the hood of his new poncho. The barrens lay to the east, and to the east he would go. He leaped lightly from the wall, rolling into the landing with scarcely a wince for his cracked rib ... and walked.

He walked straight into a hailstorm. Angry welts had risen on his back and arms by the time he reached the first of the outlying villages. He stormed into the nearest hut, wincing as its occupants began shrieking and throwing things.

"Wait," he protested, raising his hands. "I seek shelter only. I have payment!"

Throwing his hood back, Karl managed to cross the single

room and back the guilty couple into the wall without ever laying a hand upon them.

Their missiles fell harmlessly to the floor.

"Is this how you treat all ...?" He sighed before saying, *Initiates*, and ran a hand over the rain dripping off his brow. "I mean no harm and seek only shelter from the storm."

The silver he pulled from his pouch produced an instant and more amiable response from the couple. Karl was surprised that the man did not offer his wife for the night.

And so he did, following a meal and a drink. After refusing—politely, he'd thought—Karl found himself nearly tossed out of the hut by that very woman for his insult. It was more the silver in his pocket than her husband's sharp reprimand that finally settled her as Karl took to his bed and lay back to rest.

Sleep would not come to him. Not when his hosts' bickering filled the breaks in the storm, and not with the question of how he was to find a place not marked within any route, map, or mind of the realm.

Hadn't Elera said she'd given him the tools he needed to find his way?

Karl quashed that line of thought as quickly as it sprang to mind. Tossing back the blanket, he stalked to the shuttered window and stared through its cracks. Wind and rain cooled his face, soothing some of his ire. He turned to look at the couple.

"Have you changed your mind, then?" asked the man, glancing invitingly toward his wife's ample bosom.

Hesitant to answer and start yet another row, Karl helped himself to a drink. Outwardly, his face was a mask of complacency, but his constantly active mind was busy analyzing every word Elera had spoken concerning the place of dragons. Whatever clues she'd professed to have given him remained elusive.

With a sigh, he looked back at the couple ... and tilted his head with a sudden thought. "If I were to seek a dragonslayer to save a sacrifice, how would I do this?"

They gaped at him.

"Never mind," Karl said immediately, seeing from their expressions that this village was not deep enough into the barrens for them to have adopted superstitions. It was the closest to the realm, after all, and almost always passed through by any citizen seeking adventure beyond.

He was completely unprepared for the woman's shriek, and flinched hard enough to spill his drink over his arm. She continued to screech, hitting her husband on his head and shoulders, until finally the man shouted for silence. She did not obey, but he seemed to make sense of her rants, for his arms shot up in acquiescence just before he ran from the hut.

Karl cleared his throat, uncomfortable with the look in the woman's eyes as she measured him from head to toe. Her gaze lingered on his hair. He turned away, ready to leave and find her husband, when the man shot back through the door. Another man raced too close behind, and both went sprawling to their knees. With a few sharp words, the wife berated the pair for their clumsiness.

Raising a brow upon hearing so many forbidden curses being used so lightly, Karl sized up this newest visitor ... and was surprised to be measured equally in return.

"Are you the fire-hair?" the newcomer asked gruffly.

Karl inclined his head, neither assent nor denial, as he waited to see what the man would tell him.

"He asked the question," said the husband. "The one she said he would ask. And anyway his hair is red, and that was what she meant by fire-hair."

And suddenly he knew who they were talking about. Slamming his fist against his thigh, Karl breathed, "Elera."

Nodding at the mention of her name, the newcomer pulled a parchment from his robe. "She said to give you this when you came."

"And how did she know I would come?" Or that he would ask such a question at all? When the trio stared, Karl snatched the parchment away.... It was heavier than he'd expected.

"Now you have to go," the husband said, pushing Karl from the hut with the aid of the others. "You must leave at once, before great disaster comes to us. She said ..."

She had somehow managed to rekindle Karl's fury, even though *she* was likely across the barrens on the back of the beast by now.

"You have not answered," he snapped, resting the flat of his palm on the door to hold it open. "How would I find a dragonslayer if I had need of one?"

"Is it a game?" the woman asked, looking at her husband.

"A trick, more likely," the newcomer answered, refocusing his energy on closing the door that wouldn't budge.

"Can you not answer the question?" Karl asked calmly, despite the wind and rain pelting his back and whipping his hair. At least the hail had stopped.

"How?" asked the husband. "Can't find something that doesn't exist, now, can you?"

"Right," Karl muttered, letting the door slam inches from his face. He *was* too close to the realm for such beliefs.

He reached the borders of the mountains of mist before he sought shelter beneath an outcropping of rock. He removed from his pack the package Elera had left him and opened it.

She'd left him a blade—not black, but silver tinted with blue. That was not the only insult. Drawn on the underside of the parchment, and accompanied by symbols in a language he could not hope to decipher, was a red-inked map showing the way to a land that extended into the sky.

Closing his eyes, he took the rest his body demanded. His dreams, when he had them, were of Elera's sweet neck between his hands. All things considered—the bed of rock, the muddy slope, the frigid air and sopping clothes—Karl slept very well, with a smile on his lips.

It took him nearly a week to reach the boundaries of the barrens, and another three days to arrive at the cracked grounds of the fire-mountains. The land was dark and bare, stripped by storms whipping through from afar. The air could sear a man's lungs if he breathed a bit too deep.

Karl ignored the sting in his eyes and chest as he marched along. He'd made this crossing twice in his life: the first on his own, the second with Simon. Yet despite his assurances to Elera, Karl hadn't been this deep within the barrens for nearly a decade, and it seemed he had come to a fork in the path. Undecided, he stood motionless and pulled out the map. He'd given up trying to decipher its language, and had taken to relying on its faded illustrations instead. Finding nothing new to assist with his choice now, he stuffed it away. Elera's clues had not been particularly helpful thus far. While he stood considering his options, steam began evaporating from the scorched ground. The vapor rose and thickened.

With a quiet curse, Karl attempted to see through this shroud of mist. If he could just get his bearings, he might find some sort of . . .

Shrouding mist?

Had Elera mentioned that? Karl thought back to their night together. Feeling almost sick, he withdrew the map again. Nothing on it described this phenomenon. There were only symbols he didn't understand, words he couldn't decipher.

But jagged black streaks ran along the tattered borders of

the parchment. Karl flicked his eyes to the east, where lightning sketched the sky in hot, brilliant lines.

And through the shroud of the rising mist, the lines were black. Karl's blood thickened, and his boots thudded over the ground. The moon, illuminated only briefly behind the clouds, glimmered full.

SEVEN

Deep in the catacombs of the temple, Simon squinted at his stack of sacred scrolls. Candlelight gleamed off the novice Mattaen's newly shaved scalp. He'd been sitting here for days, cross-legged and forgoing food and drink in his obsession with knowledge.

Scientific formulas danced up at him. Mathematical equations explained the stars. Even the heretical writings of fallen civilizations passed between his fingers.

Taking a breath to calm his mind, Simon set these newest scrolls aside and reminded himself that his readings had a purpose. He couldn't be certain that his brother had understood what he had seen. A pagan sacrifice, a mysterious creature, a sexual encounter … Perhaps Karl had seen what he needed to see, in order to justify straying from his chosen path.

Simon shook his head. Either way, if there were dragons or any mention of a race of people who slew them, then the scrolls acknowledging their existence should be buried in these tombs.

If they contained something to grant his brother peace on the path Karl now walked alone, he would find it.

"What is it you search for?" Inclining his head to apologize for his intrusion, the monk glanced with amusement at the jumbled papers on the floor. "You leave a trail in your wake, brother."

Simon sighed, then grinned ruefully. "Dragons."

He waited for an indulgent look and was surprised to see anger flash in the other man's eyes.

"What is the reason for this?" the elder asked.

Simon was no fool. If he was reading malice in the other monk's stance, it could mean only that the monk *wished* for him to see it. "Rumors, brother," he answered carefully. "From the barrens, where I spent most of my wanderings as an Initiate."

"With he who did not take his vows?"

Simon nodded.

"Sometimes"—the monk entered the room and knelt at Simon's side—"a rumor is just a rumor. You could search these tombs ten lifetimes over and still find no evidence."

"Then I will get back to it."

Simon unbound the next scroll and settled back to peruse its contents. Not long after, he was once again lost to secrets, though he did notice when the elder left him. Bread and broth were at his feet two days later, since his absence had now gone noticed by many.

On his sixth night in study, Simon finally came across the scrolls he sought. Or at least he believed so, since each bore a seal in the design of a dragon.

"Not even one lifetime, then," he whispered, trembling from lack of sleep and sustenance. Steadying his hands, he chose a scroll and carefully tore open its seal. The words within were smudged from age, but he was able to piece together a few excerpts.

> By terror and fire and force, dragons entered the world. They were worshiped as deities, offered human sacrifices to save mankind from their awesome wrath.
>
> But there were those who hungered to harness such power for themselves, men who thought dragons should be tamed and ruled. And in the struggle for supremacy that followed, the world was laid to waste in a war that neither race had won.
>
> Dragons disappeared into myth and fable, and humanity

started anew, ruling the world in blood and steel as mankind once again succumbed to war . . . this time with one another. A billion deaths followed, a trillion nights of flickering survival, until finally arose the realm.

And at its heart, the Mattaen.

Simon had paled with every word he read. Could this be an accounting of the origins of time, origins that recorded the rise and fall of the ancient world . . . *that acknowledged the existence of dragons?*

His hands trembled as he reached for the next parchment.

We were wrong to think dragons were sentient. Their actions are so close to human that we were fooled. We should have seen the truth in our understanding of these acts. For it is human to rape a sacrifice, tearing her from home and family. It is human to make war, and human to expect deification.

And it is the human on the back of the beast who makes the beast.

Simon frowned then. The rest of the words were written in a language not taught by the realm. He set the scroll aside and opened another.

The innocents of the world are pillaged by riders whose women can no longer bear the issue of their loins. Two dragons have been slain—a horror to those who ride . . . a balm to those who have suffered loss.

In the midst of conflict, a truce has been wrought. The line of the protected realm is marked by a wall, which separates the realm from the outskirts. It is from these barren lands alone that the riders may pillage for the virgins they crave.

So long as they honor this agreement, no blood of a dragon will ever again be spilled. And while we mourn for the loss of these ignorant innocents, we must protect what we can.

The world is not yet ready for a second war between slayer and rider.

"The scroll in your hand is more than six hundred years old, and it did not fall to you by chance." The same monk who had visited him earlier held out his arm and assisted Simon to his feet. "But even by us it was once forgotten, along with all knowledge of these creatures. Until forty years ago."

"When...?" Simon prodded.

"When a young Mattaen by the name of Shane accidentally stumbled across them."

"I don't understand."

"Shane restarted the forgotten Order of Slayers, trained for years, then took an army of seven beyond the realm with the intention of finding this lost place of legends. None were seen again." The monk reached out and steadied Simon as he swayed on his feet. "One year to the day of their disappearance, eight black blades mysteriously appeared atop the wall of the realm. And that, my brother, was twenty-four years ago."

The elder reached down to retrieve the scroll Simon had dropped in his shock.

"'The world is not yet ready for a second war between slayer and rider.'" His eyes were grim. "We do not know if he succeeded, or what he might have told them about us if he did. Tell me, brother. Would you believe these scrolls and help prepare for a war that could wipe our order from existence? Or would you betray your oath to warn the brother you mourn?"

Too late, Simon remembered to school his features.

"On the heels of your brother's failing and disappearance,

you become obsessed with these creatures." The elder monk inclined his head. "We inquired of the other Initiates when you started studying. No one can recall your ever showing any curiosity about them prior to this."

Simon frowned in disgust.... Any novice could have reasoned out his motives, and his undisciplined reaction had only confirmed them.

"No one can possess this information except for us. Your brother failed.... Wherever the path takes him, it must take him alone." His eyes lost all semblance of emotion. "I would have your answer."

"The wrong one will see me dead this day." Although his words had not been phrased as a question, the elder nodded in answer. Picking up another scroll, Simon slid down the wall and rested it upon his knees. He whispered, "I am Mattaen."

"Then rest, Simon of the Mattaen," the elder murmured, taking back the scroll. "For none but a slayer may have this knowledge. Your training begins on the morrow."

Karl woke with the taste of Elera in his mouth. Though he knew it was but a lingering effect of his dreams, he could do nothing to ease the hot spikes of need that accompanied it.

There was *something* he could do. But he refused to give Elera this final shred of his control ... even if his dreams were filled with images of her spread beneath him, of her nipple growing hard in his mouth as he drew on it, of the thick surge of his member when she slowly licked the tip....

Karl grimaced as sweat slid down his back. His sex throbbed within the confines of his infernal pants. If he didn't temper his thoughts, his body would find release without any physical assistance from him!

He sat up and considered his journey thus far. It had taken him almost two weeks to complete what he'd planned as a four-day crossing through the fire-mountains. His frustration had peaked the night before, when he'd finally reached the end of them and found only further barrens. He had simply been too weary to face more of the wasteland, and so he'd set up camp and gone to sleep.

However exhausted he might be, it did not seem to affect his ability to *rise* in the morning. Grumbling under his breath as his body continued to throb, Karl concentrated on regaining what had once been an impeccable control ... and heard footsteps approaching directly behind him.

There was nothing wrong with his reflexes. Grabbing the boot aimed at his face, Karl flipped his attacker to the ground, and quickly twisted the man's arm behind his back.

"Just a bit of fun," the stranger croaked beneath the knee pressed against the nape of his neck. He gasped when the pressure on his wrist increased. "No harm, friend ..."

Easing off just a bit, Karl leaned low and asked, "Your purpose here?"

"My ..." The stranger's grunt was close enough to laughter that Karl twisted his arm. The man sobered quickly. "I'm here for her, of course."

Karl released his hold, stepping a full three paces away while the stranger struggled into a crouch. "Her who?"

When one golden brow lifted in amusement, Karl lunged forward ... and saw familiar gray eyes staring back at him.

"You're one of them," he said.

"And you're moving much too slow. I've been waiting four days for you to get this far." The stranger said nothing for a moment, wilting a little beneath Karl's patient study. But finally he nodded, rose warily to his feet, and spat on the steaming ground. "Name's Tem. And I'm here to hasten your pace."

The man crooked a finger, then walked partway around the ridge before noticing he was alone. He quickly backtracked.

From where he stood waiting, Karl lifted a curious brow. "Why does it matter, the pace of my arrival, or even that I arrive at all?"

Tem looked surprised. "Didn't tell you much, did she?"

"We will see," he said simply, kneeling to retrieve his pack and poncho. He didn't follow the man as much as he followed the heat rising along the horizon.

Karl's placid expression vanished when they came around the final ridge. Once again, he stood face-to-face with a dragon. The beast was not as large as the one Elera had ridden, but no less formidable with its bloodred eyes and black-tipped claws. Its massive wings flapped in the breeze.

Without a break in his stride, the rider leaped onto the back of his pale gray beast. Hooking his boots beneath its wings, he stared arrogantly down at Karl.

Karl swallowed. "You mean to quicken my pace on the back of this animal?"

"I'd assure you of her gentle disposition"—Tem grinned—"but I refrain from untruths as much as possible."

"Might want to teach Elera that virtue," Karl drawled, still focused on the scaled and rippling torso of the female before him. She lacked the ridged spine that the bull had used to form its deadly fin. But he still had to leap back when she reared suddenly and raked the air with her claws.

"Careful, friend." Tem was quiet, soothing his dragon in nearly the same manner as Elera had the bull, but his eyes flashed with anger. "I will forget you said those words so I do not lose my head later, when you regret my having overheard them."

Deciding to save that puzzle for another time, Karl carefully inclined his head. That quickly, the rider grinned affably once more … though his dragon continued to snarl.

He stared. "I believe I will take my chances with the walk."

Most men would have given way under so much laughter coming at their expense. Karl simply shrugged and started off.

"Wait …" Tem called, setting his dragon at an easy pace beside Karl. "I do not mean to imply that you are a coward."

This time it was Karl who laughed.

Tem shook his head and tried again. "I ask you to reconsider, seeker."

"Give me a worthy reason to do so …" He paused. "Seeker?" He hissed when Tem stuttered and averted his eyes. "Thinking up an untruth, rider?"

Tem sighed. "Thinking of a way to avoid one, actually. I can't seem to do it, so I will say nothing at all."

Karl stopped. "Tell me why I should hurry my pace, then."

"In three days, Elera is … There is a rider who … She will be forced to …" He growled between his teeth. "I can think of no way to answer without breaking an oath to her."

"Elera is in danger?" Karl suggested dryly, rolling his eyes when Tem broke into a wide smile and started nodding frantically. "Why does this concern me?"

The rider's smile faded, and Karl did not have to understand his language to get the gist of his oaths. When he finally finished, Tem said, "I didn't actually believe her when she told me you would say this. I can't pretend to understand what makes you so hostile—"

"I wasn't sulking over why I *should* care, rider," Karl snapped, turning to stare at the horizon with a frown. Quietly, he added, "But pondering why I do. Very well," he said finally, taking a step toward the wary rider and his beast. "Take me to her."

In all the languages he had studied, there was not a single word to describe that ride—the ground rushing by beneath them, the raw power of the beast shifting between his thighs. As the wind whipped through the coils of his hair, Karl closed his eyes to revel in pure, unadulterated sensation.

He gripped with his thighs when their pace slowed and just barely managed to keep his seat when the dragon landed. He sat for all of three seconds, until one flared wing swung back and knocked him off.

"How is it a girl managed to tame such a beast without breaking every bone in her body?" Karl grumbled, shaking sand from his hair and face.

"She broke a few." With a laugh, Tem hopped down and pulled him to his feet. "But that was just a love tap, seeker. My beauty enjoyed the ride as much as you, though I'd be inclined to bloody your face if you thought to call *her* a beast."

Crooning into her overlapping fangs, he let her nuzzle his throat in return.

Karl pivoted away with a grunt … then gaped in surprise at the sight of the ocean just a few paces away. A low fog hung over the waves lapping at the shoreline, and the soft breeze carried the taste and scent of salt. Karl was stunned at the distance the dragon had carried them.

"Beyond the ocean," he whispered, too softly for the other man to hear. Not that Tem paid him any attention, strutting into the foamy water while pointing out the cliffs rising from the fog nearby.

"There are countless passages to get to the cliff you need, but only one that doesn't end in water. So you'll be taking—"

"The lowest ridge and wettest path, directly through the center of the fifth ridge," Karl hesitated, studying the horizon before finishing, "due south."

Tem stared in horror at the piece of parchment Karl had removed from his pack.

"Problem?" Karl asked shortly. He consulted the map and then folded it away as he led the way toward the cliffs.

"I …" Tem cleared his throat before shaking his head. "It's not forbidden, I suppose. But definitely frowned upon."

"The map is frowned upon, but not the visitors themselves," he repeated. "Do you have many visitors from among the outskirts?"

"A visit implies an end, so my answer is none ... at least, not in my lifetime." He frowned. "You should have been told something of our ways. She should have ..." Tem trailed off as the curiosity in his eyes was replaced with suspicion. "Tell me, seeker ... what manner of man reaches your age without ever having taken a woman?"

So even this was known.

Celibacy in the order was no secret, but he no longer wore the robes of an Initiate. Had Elera discussed him ... and their intimacy ... with this man?

Embarrassment and anger flooded his cheeks as he clenched his jaw. "You can think of none?"

The rider stumbled to his knees in the surf, gulping a mouthful of the salt water that blasted him in the face. By the time he'd flipped the sodden hair out of his eyes and drawn his blade, his expression was stony. "I can, but if you were of that creed, I would regret my help this day."

Though his hand crawled to the blue-tinted dagger strapped to his thigh, it was neither shame nor fear that prompted Karl to incline his head in a nonthreatening manner. Rather, it was his adherence to the creed he had abandoned. "Then you regret nothing, friend."

And if the rider could not reason that he was referring to his *former* allegiance with the Mattaen....

Karl shrugged. He was now fighting the waves of the rising ocean. With one eye on Tem, who had yet to lower his weapon, Karl dove, reaching a ridge in the first cliff before the need for air dragged him back to the surface.

He made no move to climb out of the water. In fact, he made no move whatsoever, out of healthy respect for the dark claws scratching rock less than a foot from his own hands.

Slowly, Karl raised his eyes to the dragon and her rider.

"I do not know whether to wish you luck, seeker ... or ill," Tem said quietly.

Apparently the man could reason, after all.

"But you rode with neither fear nor pride," Tem continued, "which earns you a warning, if you would hear it."

Karl nodded.

"Three days will find you at our land if you do not falter. I cannot be your friend there, though I was this day. Remember that." He leaned down. "This is my warning: Unless you arrive by the end of the third night, don't come at all. Elera will be dead, and any who seek to avenge her will follow swiftly after."

Karl pulled himself onto the sharp rock, then ducked as the dragon sprang into the sky. He shouted up at her rider, "Take me to her directly, then!"

"You do not wish her harm," Tem called back, circling overhead, "and that might earn my friendship. But already the help you've been given will be answered for in blood. None but she, I think, would mourn the loss of yours."

Leaping over loose stone, gripping mossy rocks to vault atop a ridge, Karl raced after the dragon until she flew behind the clouds. Even after he dropped to his knees in exhaustion, adrenaline pumped through his veins.

It was fear. Instinctive, gut-clenching ... and all for Elera. He stood and ran ... sliding down crevices and embankments when the rock grew slick from the ocean mist. He found what he hoped was a shortcut—until the tunnel took him below sea level and added time to his journey. The gift of Elera's blade came in handy there, saving him from a variety of cave creatures seeking an easy meal, and Karl traveled through the high ridges after that.

Three days. The words hounded him, chasing him through the day until night fell and dawn arose again. But after an all-out run carried him to the end of that final day, with still no sign of the end of the cliff, Karl slammed his fist into the rock and bellowed his frustration to the crescent moon rising above.

How could he help Elera if he could not find her?

Under the light from that tiny arc, something shimmered in the distance. Easing his panic with a few controlled breaths, he squinted through the heavy ocean fog.

Karl ran, the burn of lungs and muscles forgotten, until finally he stood on the precipice of the cliff, staring for the first time at a matrix of branching columns of rock. They spiraled out of the ocean, thinning and thickening in spots as they rose past the fog and into the cover of the clouds.

Renewed purpose gleamed in his eyes as he measured the gap between the edge of the cliff and the skybound ladder. A glance down revealed jagged rocks jutting out of the ocean, but he could see no other way to cross. Karl made a few quick calculations in his head, tightened the pack around his back . . .

And dove.

EIGHT

The first crescent moon was always a cause for celebration in the skylands of Verteva. Feasts were prepared, women were adorned, and riders took to the sky. It seemed to mean something to the dragons, that shimmering scythe of light. They would charge toward it, wings outspread, claws extended ... diving down just before the air become too thin to breathe. From below it looked as if the dragons dove through the arc itself.

Tonight they seemed particularly festive. While people looked on from the ground, the riders, clad in ceremonial red and gold, played in the sky and put on a show for their audience.

Elera rested with the bull, watching their antics from his favorite hill near her manor. Once the display ended, there would be feasting, sport, and contests among the riders.

After the competitions would come the dancing and drinking.

And Ronin.

He hadn't approached her since the night she had returned from below, hadn't even spared her a glance in all the occasions that their paths had inadvertently crossed. But she could feel his anger growing with every night he slept alone, and knew he had not forgotten his threat.

Elera glared at the six riders lurking nearby. Ronin had undoubtedly ordered them to guard her in case she thought to flee tonight. She sighed when they stared stonily back at her, then turned her attention back to the sky.

Laughter bubbled in her throat when Tem's dragon swerved and nearly ousted another rider from his seat. Not that there could be any actual mishaps in ritual pattern—the instincts of riders and dragons forbade it. But the few men who shared Tem's humor would play little pranks to amuse the onlookers.

Too few, she thought, thinking of her childhood friend. Possessed of a good nature, fierce loyalty, and, at the moment, a powerful anger toward her, he was her greatest love besides her grandfather. If he'd ever shown the faintest desire to lead, she might have chosen him when they were younger instead of searching the realm for a mate.

But leading their people wasn't for him. Though he would have accepted the role had she asked him to, Elera could not have betrayed either of them in that way. Even if he *hadn't* spoken a word to her since returning from the barrens ... except to snap that it was done. She should have known he would realize the origins of the man she had sent him to help.

The bull moved restlessly beneath her hand. "Anxious to get up there and chase them from the sky, are you?" Elera whispered. The bull always seemed to enjoy seeing his females scatter and flee before his might. *Typical male*.

Sliding her legs over the sides of his neck, tightening her thighs to steady her seat, Elera rubbed the ridge of the bull's crest. "The quicker the end of our flight, the sooner the end of this night. And I am not looking forward to—"

The bull took to the sky so fast her heart leaped into her throat. When they'd flown so high that the crescent moon seemed almost within reach of her fingertips, he twisted in the air and roared. Every female in the sky spun in a frenzy of fleeing forms.

Elera laughed, fear and politics forgotten in the passion of the moment. Throwing back her head, she urged him on the chase.

★   ★   ★

Still heady from the power of their ride, Elera took her seat at the head of the riders' table amidst a sea of welcoming smiles. She stiffened as Ronin claimed the seat next to hers and turned toward her. "I trust the night has brought you favor," he said.

Ignoring him, Elera took a large gulp of fire-brew.

"I've no real wish to harm you," he told her, clearly unconcerned with prying ears. Not many men would dare to stand against him, and even fewer would succeed if they tried.

She watched as his gaze lingered on the skin exposed by her crimson gown. The sparkling silk hung open in the back, drooping just below the swell of her hips before gliding lazily to her ankles. When she leaned back against her chair, his attention shifted to the ankle-to-hip slits that allowed her to straddle the bull.

Ronin leaned over and inhaled her fragrance. "Status or no, I would have you beneath me this night."

"Not willingly," she said. "And not without a fight."

"All the sweeter," he whispered, standing and lifting his chalice to the sky. "To the feast, the riders, and the blood!"

Feet stomped the earth, and fists pounded the tables as the riders responded to his cry. Ronin waited until the crowd quieted, and grinned widely as he drew his ax. "To the victors go the spoils!"

He vaulted over the table to take his position in the center of the battle circle. Then, raising his ax, letting it gleam in the fires behind him, he beckoned forth the first of many challengers.

"Where is your grandfather?" Tem asked quietly, taking the seat Ronin had vacated.

Smiling a little, Elera turned her eyes to his. "Talking to me again, are you?" She sighed when he shrugged. "He won't be at a feast where the end is …"

"Your end?" Tem finished softly, touching her hand after she dipped her head. "I would not want to quarrel on this night."

"Nor I," she whispered, wrapping her fingers around his.

"Elera—"

"No," she said, more sharply than she'd intended. Ronin's men stared at them until she glared so pointedly that they fidgeted and returned their attention to the ongoing battle in the ring. "There is nothing to be done, and nothing you will do when it is over."

She could not break the bond she had given Karl. If that meant fighting Ronin to the death when he tried to take her, then she would fight ... and lose. But no one else would die because of the path she had chosen to follow. She could not allow Tem to place himself in harm's way for her sake. He was not a king, but her people needed him, needed the humor and spirit of men like him if they were ever to flourish.

"You ask much of me," he whispered stiffly now, pulling his hand back despite his words not two moments earlier. "Too much, I think."

Elera watched him stalk away, then turned back to the merriment.

As he swung his leg over the final hump of land, Karl heard the bull's primal roar, felt it vibrate through the rock and dirt beneath his fingers. He looked up to see the dragon streaking across the starlit sky, and knew that Elera sat at its crest.

By the time he had journeyed within hearing distance of what seemed to be a celebration, night had covered the fields and cliffs in almost total darkness. The stars remained, much closer than he was used to and especially bright. But that tiny slip of a moon offered little light.

It took a great deal of his training to maintain even breathing. The high altitude made him feel as if he had one less lung and a third more mass. Discipline kept the spots from dancing behind his eyes, but only pure adrenaline and his fear for Elera kept him moving across the land at a rapid pace.

So attuned was he to the needs of his body that he nearly missed the shadow skimming overhead. But he ducked at the last moment, rolling flat against the earth while the wind of a passing wing brushed over his skin. He twisted to avoid the clawed foot slamming into the ground beside him.

"You have a personal vendetta against me, beast?" Karl grumbled, leaping a good distance back from its whipping tail. "If this is your version of a love tap, I'll pass."

To his surprise, the dragon furled its wings, flopped to its stomach, and rested its massive head atop its claws. Its red eyes dimmed to orange.

Karl stood motionless, even after the creature shifted its eyes toward the festivities. A low grumble rose from its throat. But moments later, the beast snorted ... and, in what seemed like a blur of motion, unfurled its wing to tuck a diving female against its massive body.

Two other dragons fell from the sky, although the first must have been a favorite, since none of the others enjoyed the shelter of the bull's wing. But they did sprawl close enough to touch its tail and paw.

Karl could not contain his grin when the bull lifted its head to stare straight at him. If it were capable, he was certain the beast would have smirked at him. But after a while, as it nuzzled the favored female, its orange eyes drooped and closed.

Immortal.

The word ran through Karl's mind until his heart was thudding from more than just his efforts to breathe. Had Elera lied to entice him here? Or could these creatures truly have seen the dawn of time and everything since? Unsure of the answer, or even that he wanted it, Karl resumed his walk amid the growing field of dragons.

Something butted his back without warning. He whirled, stomach clenched, but the dragon standing there simply lowered its head to his hand.

"Tem's beast," he whispered, and rubbed the female's scales as she made a purring sound in her throat. "Don't tell him I called you that, now."

A rumble from the bull had her spinning, and Karl ducked to avoid the lash of the female's tail. With a new appreciation for his reflexes, he stared warily at the blades and spikes lining the tail's tip, then watched as the dragon found a place among the others at the bull's side.

Karl pushed forward, growing cautious as he passed a few manors. They were dark and quiet compared to the noise coming from the gathering grounds beyond.

Those grounds nestled between high cliffs, Karl realized, as he searched for the best path between them. He quickly chose the route least visible to the warriors standing guard atop the ridges. Using shadow as his cloak, he slipped through the narrow passage completely undetected.

He stopped before entering the grounds, ducked quickly beneath an overhang of rock ... and stared at the woman who had stolen his heritage.

By the order, she was breathtaking! The silken gown, the bared skin, the silver bracelets circling her upper arms ... all that hair tumbling down her back and shining in the light of the fire. In times of old she would have been a goddess, he thought feverishly. Tonight, she was seductive, elusive ... a stimulating mix of promise and raw passion.

She stood in the arms of a dark-haired man, swaying slowly to the beat of a primitive tune.

When the man slid his hand up her back, wrapping his fingers in her hair as he aligned her mouth with his, Karl growled. But before he could lunge from his spot, the warrior released her to leap atop a boulder.

Frowning when the man shouted for silence, Karl settled back.... He wanted to hear what put such stark fear on the face of Elera of the dragonriders.

When Ronin released Elera, Tem stepped toward her. She warned him back with a quick shake of her head. His interference would only provoke Ronin's temper. As rider of the bull, she was required to honor the victor of each contest with a dance. She'd spent most of these last few hours on her feet, with a great bellyful of drink from all the toasts made to their prowess.

Ronin had bided his time until the first of the men began dragging their women into shadows. When the music slowed to a steady throb, he'd come to claim his dance.

She bit her lip, thinking with sadness of the man who *hadn't* come. The fire-brew she had drunk to dull her fear was only partially responsible for her unsteady legs when Ronin addressed the crowd.

"The crescent moon begins its fall!" Obvious as his remark might seem, the crowd responded with a roar. "For more than two decades we have been without sovereign, without legitimate rule, and without the pure strength such could bring. But before the sunrise on the morrow, I, Ronin of the House of Samson, would change that for you."

His dark eyes turned to Elera.

"What say you, Elera ... daughter of a dragonslayer, longchild of the warrior Warwick, rider of the bull? Will you give me your breath in bonding and bring stability to our world?"

"If I thought it might do so"—Elera tilted her head and pretended to think—"not even then."

The crowd stepped back when Ronin jumped down from the stone. He would not take kindly to her refusal ... especially when it was delivered as an insult. But he merely took Elera's arm and steered her away from the people.

His voice was quiet. "You would force my hand?"

"You will do as you wish," she said just as quietly, jerking out of his grasp. "As you always have. But you are not the man to lead our people from ruin. And I will not secure a rule I know is wrong."

"Then you have sealed your fate instead," he snarled, twining her hair around his hand before dragging her body to his.

The tension in his muscles told Elera that he expected her to fight. He just didn't expect her to fight mean. When he moved to toss her over his shoulder, the knee she brought up between his legs dropped him to the dirt. Wasting no opportunity, she braced her weight and rammed her foot into his mouth.

She landed on her back in the next moment, both feet kicked out from under her. Ronin rolled, then straddled her.

"I will have your bond, Elera, or you will have this...." She watched him raise his fist high and braced her body for the blow....

It never came.

Instead a man's arm hooked around his elbow, halting his strike. Before surprise could even show in his eyes, Ronin had been flipped off Elera and sent rolling a dozen feet away.

"You would do well to stay your ground," Karl warned. His words were quiet, but she could see the urge for violence in his eyes. He offered his hand to Elera. "Are you well?"

His attention shifted immediately back to the warriors circling around him, then to the guards above who aimed their bows at his heart, and he missed her nod. When she grasped his hand, he pulled her to his side with a quick tug.

She turned her head into his shoulder, desperate with relief. "I wasn't sure—"

"That I would come?" Karl chuckled darkly, glancing down at her in reproof....

"That you would make it in time," she whispered, biting her lip when Ronin advanced, ax in hand.

"You dare much, stranger, to trespass in these lands. And far too much to interfere with what is mine." His eyes narrowed, and his free hand beckoned. "To my side, Elera. Now!"

"I commit no trespass, as I was *invited*," Karl said clearly, tossing Elera another dark look. His fingers tightened on hers, just in case she felt inclined to obey the other man's decree. "And I think she cannot give you this breath that you demand."

Ronin stumbled midadvance, and now Elera bore the brunt of two sets of furious male eyes. The rider could have been angry for any number of reasons, but Karl was angry for just one. She reminded herself that his intelligence had factored greatly into her choice of him.

"I think she cannot," he continued, looking only at her, "because she has already given it to me."

NINE

A cool night breeze blew through the feast. The men stood, shocked and uncertain, looking to Ronin for guidance. Someone stoked the fire, sending embers fluttering about the ground.

"Impossible," he whispered, letting his ax fall to his side. He turned to Elera. "This is why you left? To betray ... to set a stranger above a rider, above even me?"

"I did what was needed." Her words were clear, and Karl could tell that they were as much for his benefit as for that of Ronin and the riders. "And it was my choice, my right to choose a mate from below, as it is for you all."

Karl heard a noise and looked up. Bows and arrows quivered, held poised in the hands of the men above them.

"He would have to have been a—"

"Virgin, yes." Elera lifted her chin and ignored his hiss. "He was."

"It is not the same," Ronin rebuked, now that color had returned to his cheeks, "and well you know it."

She scoffed. "There is no law that says different."

"Elera ..." Karl warned, trying to gain her attention as the warriors began to advance toward them.

"My breath is given," she continued, paying him no heed. "It cannot be undone whether you wish it or—"

Karl covered her mouth with his hand, sensing her shock at his audacity. But her shock was nothing compared to his when one of the nearest men drew his sword, hesitated ... then dropped to his knee with his head bowed.

Unfortunately, the man's humble position was responsible for his failure to see Ronin's ax swing around. Struck on the head with the flat of its blade, he slumped to the earth.

"Keep your feet!" Ronin roared to the few people who'd started to kneel. "Her claim is not accepted, and this stranger is no one to you." Turning to Karl, he added softly, "Nor will he be."

He swung his weapon in a blur of motion that defied vision. After thrusting Elera out of danger, Karl leaped back to avoid the trajectory of the blade ... and glanced down in surprise at the thin streak of blood soaking through his shirt.

Perhaps not so thin, he had time to think before Ronin swung again ... and again. The blood seeping from his wound was fast stealing what remained of Karl's strength. He stumbled and fell, hissing as steel scraped stone a hairbreadth from his skull.

Rolling quickly, Karl crouched with one hand on the ground and used the other to swipe at the other man's legs. But even as Karl jumped back to buy both distance and time, he staggered. He saw Ronin rise and leap, twisting in midair with his ax raised high ... and shouted in denial when Elera stepped in front of the blade.

But Ronin's ax struck steel instead of flesh, sending sparks flying into the air. Karl jerked Elera roughly out of danger, knowing she would bear bruises from his grip. *She should be glad of it*, he thought, considering the alternative. But it was not any blade of theirs that had blocked Ronin's ax.

"He has seven days," Tem said to Ronin, shifting his sword until he stood directly in front of them. Steel strained against steel as the two riders clashed. "Seven days free of harm from any rider, and seven days to accept the bond. Take his head at the end if you can, but so long as there is blood of a rider in my veins, you will honor the laws of seeking."

It did not seem to Karl as if he would. Ronin's eyes bulged

and the vein in his temple throbbed. His ax scraped the length of Tem's sword before knocking the rider against Karl and Elera. They each managed to keep their feet ... though certainly one would have died if it had been Ronin's wish to kill. He evidently meant only to remind them that his arm could not be so easily swayed.

"Seven days," he sneered, lowering his ax. "And not by your words, Tem, although I will remember your allegiance on this day."

He inclined his head toward the rock at their backs, indicating the snarling bull currently wedged between the cliffs. His hiss was directed toward Ronin, and his tail was poised to attack.

Ronin carefully reversed his steps until the dragon calmed. He tilted his ax toward Karl. "Seven days, *seeker*."

Thrusting through the men, he leaped over the fire and ascended the crumbling ledges of the cliff.

"See to your seeker, Elera," Tem said, once Ronin and his dragon faded into the night. "He needs assistance."

Elera was already inspecting the tear in his shirt. When she gasped at the severity of the wound, Karl grabbed her hands and shoved her back.

"Behave," she hissed, glancing furtively toward the hovering warriors. More than one set of eyes had narrowed when he pushed her. "Tem!"

With what little strength he had left, Karl knocked the rider away and walked off on his own two feet. On the cliff, the bull snorted, swiveling lizardlike in the air and winging his way over its edge. From there, his shadow quickly climbed into the stars.

When Elera attempted to sling her arm around his waist, he glared at her. "The men here would take my life for insulting you, but do nothing while one of theirs strikes you down?"

He'd meant it as a shout, though what emerged from his

lips was barely a whisper. He hadn't noticed that he was staggering until they entered the cliff passages, but he did recognize the fear in Elera's eyes.

He leaned against the rock wall and whispered, "You win. I'll take the help."

Tem knelt, set his shoulder against Karl's abdomen, and hoisted him over his shoulder.

"You've got a lot ... to answer for ..." Karl grumbled just before everything went black.

He woke in stages, moving slowly from one plane of consciousness to the next until finally he was fully aware ... and breathing the very scent that had haunted his nights for almost a month. He didn't open his eyes, but he knew well enough that it was more than just his wound lighting a fire below his stomach.

"I know you're awake."

Karl sighed, then winced when the small motion made his injury throb. He would have spoken but for the flask of water she brought to his lips. In small and greedy sips, he drank until the soft brush of fingers replaced the cool metal of the flask.

"Easy to take advantage of a man flat on his back," Karl murmured, opening his eyes. His gaze narrowed when he noticed the arrogance in her smile, but he did not object when Elera reached over and smoothed his brow. "Tell me what happens in seven days."

"Questions are a good sign of recovery. So is annoyance," she added when he growled, though her hand fell as her smile faded. "And it's five days now."

"I've been—"

"Lie back," she whispered, pushing gently against his chest when he tried to rise up on his elbows. "You'll pull the stitches. Twenty-three, if you must know, and a few more holding the muscle within together. You have good reflexes. Most men would have been halved by that move."

Karl sank back with a frown. "Not the first time he's used it, then?"

"Nor the last, I'm sure."

When she wouldn't meet his eyes, Karl hooked his finger around her chin and turned her face to his. "What happens in five days, Elera?"

"I'm sure you've figured it out by now."

"I'd like to hear it from you." When her eyes clouded, he raised a brow. "Perhaps I like the sound of your voice."

"No, you don't," she said with a grin. "The sound of my voice sets your teeth grinding. I should know; I've been talking to you for two days."

"Is that why my jaw hurts?" He sighed. "I thank you for your care, Elera ... and I suppose that's what this is. Of course, I wouldn't have needed it without your interference in the first place."

"Fair enough—"

Before she could finish, he pulled her roughly down next to him. She froze.

"Don't you dare ever"—he shook her shoulders, ignoring the pain that immediately shot through his midriff—"*ever* step in front of a blade meant for me. Promise it."

His eyes blazed with emotion, his fingers tightened their grip on her body, and still she whispered, "I can't."

He felt her start to tremble as she held his stare. Karl took a moment to harness his temper, easing the tension in his hands. By the time he released her, he was calm once again.

"You mated with me that first night?" When he saw the spark of amusement in her eyes, Karl's breath exploded out of him. "I speak not of the physical."

Elera relented. "I know what you meant. And yes."

"How?"

"Always the scholar?" She sighed when he frowned at her. "It's called the breath of fire, but I don't know if I can explain how it works. It's just there, like a heartbeat. My people have a connection with fire and all its properties. Have you seen the blue tint in the steel?"

He touched his stomach and shot her a wry look.

"Right," she said softly. "It comes from the heat of the blue flame our steel is tempered within, a flame we can manipulate so that our weapons are stronger than anything your own blacksmiths could create. And more malleable as well."

"And in mating?" Karl pressed, maintaining his focus.

"It is a sacred bond, this giving of one's breath to another. The moment of merging is overwhelming for the recipient, sexually inflaming ... and very difficult to resist."

"Difficult," he repeated dryly.

"Impossible, then," she said, her eyes growing sad. "It works only with a man or woman who has not yet known intimacy. But when enacted properly, it should begin to bind each pulse between us."

Lifting his wrist, and closing his fingers over her wrist in turn, Karl felt his pulse leap the moment he realized it was in sync with hers.

"We bond empathically with our dragons and physically with our mates. It is the way of my race," she said softly, when he looked at her for explanation.

"So you have left me no choice in this mating." Though his temper burned, Karl looked at her thoughtfully, remembering the warrior who had knelt before him. "The man mated to you rules your people."

Elera nodded. "He does."

He sighed. "Tell me the purpose of these seven days. I have only five left before fighting this Ronin of yours."

"He's not mine," Elera insisted, and looked away when he

hissed. "You have seven days to accept or deny my bond. That is your choice."

Hiding his surprise, he asked simply, "If I do not accept?"

"Normally you are free to return to the land below."

"Then this Ronin will force you to bond with him and rise to rule." He paused. "I do not think your man will be content to let me leave after having known you."

"He's *not* mine," she repeated, placing her fingers over his lips when he would have spoken. "Ronin has wanted me and legitimate rule of this land his entire life. With one stroke I have thwarted him of both." Elera shook her head. "The bond I gave you is unbreakable, at least for me. For as long as you live, I can have no other mate ... and so my world can have no other king. No, I don't believe he will be content to let you leave, regardless of your choice."

Saying nothing for a moment, Karl exhaled slowly, then once again closed his fingers over her wrist. "You will always feel this connection?"

She nodded.

"Will I?"

"You can feel it now only when we touch, and only when we touch will our hearts beat as one. If you accept my bond, you will begin to feel an echo beneath your own pulse. That will be mine. By the rhythm and strength of that echo my people can guess at the level of exertion ... or distress ... of our mates." Elera shrugged. "Even if you do accept my bond, you'll need time and practice to recognize the echo that comes with it."

"And if I do not accept, Elera?" he prodded. She had managed to avoid answering that question.

"The bond will never be complete, and only I will be bound."

He refused to reveal how her confession shook him, or dwell upon the meaning of his suddenly erratic pulse. Karl fisted his hands to hide their trembling and focused upon the immediate threat. "For your warrior to both have you and rule, he must first kill me." He looked up in surprise. "Your bonded mate must be a virgin."

"As Ronin is," Elera said, inclining her head. "He has abstained on the presumption that I would one day perform the rite with him. But Ronin is not the man to keep my people from their end."

"So you looked for another to take his place. Elera..." He covered her hand. "Why did you choose me?"

He watched her eyes rise to his hair. Watched them soften as she reached out and twirled a lock between her fingers.... He had no right to feel these stirrings when she touched him.

"Intelligence," she finally said. "And strength. There are none here with enough of both to—"

"Keep your people from falling. I remember." But for a moment he had glimpsed something more than just determination and desire in her eyes. "Very quickly you lose your faith in me. If your Ronin fails in his battle against me, what happens then?"

"He's *not* mine," she said, rising from his side and pacing to the terrace. "And you were not injured so terribly before."

True, he thought with a nod, though she couldn't see it with her back turned. "Elera?"

"You leave or rule my people as king." Looking at him over her shoulder, she added, "And claim me as your mate."

He studied the defiance in her face. "I have another option, even if you do not."

"You can't leave now," Elera said, shaking her head. "The laws decree that you must remain in Verteva the full seven days. Riders will be watching to make sure you don't run."

Karl's eyes gleamed. "So now I am a coward as well as a captive?"

"I didn't mean to imply that." Her shoulders bunched when she spotted the amusement in his face. "You wouldn't care if I had."

"It is for a man to decide what he is, not the words or implications of others." He grinned. "So these seven days are used to convince me of your appeal."

She glowered. "Not just mine."

"The appeal of this land and these people then, but from your point of view." Karl laughed aloud … until his midsection protested with a sharp burn. A chuckle caught in his throat. "I am flat on my back for your appeal."

"Are you?" Elera ran her eyes slowly along his frame.

His amusement fled. She was enjoying this. He tipped his head, conceding the round. "In any case, it was another option I spoke of."

Her brow furrowed, and he stared, patiently waiting for her to remember.

She paled. "You cannot mean to—"

"You made a promise, Elera. I will hold you to it."

"Give me the five days, at least." She rushed to the bed and dropped to her knees, looking anxiously up at him. "Let me show you my world, the dragons. You can't have come all this way just to …"

He kept his eyes devoid of emotion, knowing that it would frighten her more than any level of rage would have. Her eyes shifted to the wall, teeth emerging to worry her bottom lip.

"Thinking of a way not to keep your word?" Like his expression, his voice was without inflection. "There is none, I assure you, or I would have found it myself by now."

"Three days, then," she whispered, trembling when he did not reply. "But you came with Tem. That means you must care a little."

"I cared only to retrieve my blade, and I needed you here to do this." Grabbing her wrist before she could set her hand over his heart, Karl sighed. "You've no right to expect anything else. You speak of sanctity, but you took what was sacred to me. Not the blade, but my life's work. You took it with deception, trickery, and without a thought for my rights. And you did this simply for politics."

Tears hovered on her lashes, but she blinked them back. "I won't let him kill you." Her words were barely a whisper. "Please understand, I didn't want to hurt you. I ... You cannot end your life because of my acts. I will do whatever you ask to make amends, but give me the time to show you—"

"My honor is restored with my blood on my blade." Tearing his eyes away from hers, Karl stared at the ceiling in a gesture of dismissal. "I need but an hour alone to complete the ceremony...."

His cold control slipped when a single tear fell to his arm. Karl turned his head to call back his words, but she was already walking to a table in the corner of the room. From there, she removed his blade and carried it to his side ... whispering his name in a tortured apology before racing to the terrace. Leaping over the rail, rising on the neck of the bull, she ripped through the clouds without a single backward glance.

With his breath caught in his throat, Karl sat all the way up, nowhere near as helpless as he'd let Elera believe. He lifted his blade by its hilt and rose to his feet. He'd turned ghostly pale by the time he made it to her table, since walking required slightly more effort than sitting. He opened the drawer and placed the blade inside.

He'd never had any intention of using it. Perhaps when he had first set out after her ... Karl sighed. He might have performed the ritual the morning after. Perhaps.

But adventure had sharp and merciless hooks, and he was no stranger to their sting. The taste of a hidden culture, a strange world, immortal creatures that should not exist ... Karl had long since lost his desire for the blade in his hunt for knowledge.

Some of his interest was in Elera alone, though he didn't yet understand why. His creed taught him to care for the safety of others, but he hadn't felt so much fear for another person in all his years as an Initiate ... or such rage as he had known when he saw another man raise his fist to strike her down.

He should not have been surprised. Physical intimacy could create the illusion of deeper emotion, especially for one who'd never known a woman's touch ... and this woman had consumed his dreams for nearly a month. But she'd given him little real reason to feel anything other than contempt—

She brought you to a new world, gave you knowledge beyond your dreams, then stood between a blade and your neck and refused to surrender to a man she knew was wrong for her people.

Quashing those thoughts and the unfamiliar emotions that accompanied them, Karl staggered toward the bed. Her bed, he realized, noticing the feminine feel to the room despite its bold color scheme of red and black.

He stopped in front of a gilded mirror and stared at his reflection. No ... he'd had no intention of using the blade on himself. Nor could he fool himself into believing he'd lied to teach Elera the consequences of her behavior, though it was certainly a lesson she could use.

He could despise her methods, but he could not deny that she had acted to keep her people and her world safe. He had acted only out of temper, in order to exact a cruel retribution.

It wasn't the Mattaen way. And whether it was his training or his heart, it wasn't Karl's way either.

He looked at his reflection, then bowed his head in shame.

Ten

She was sobbing for the first time since her childhood. Deep, wrenching shudders that shook her shoulders and stole her breath. It was fury prompting her tears, rather than sorrow. Impotent fury that something so precious could be so carelessly thrown away.

Gasping as the bull suddenly swerved around the apex of their lands, Elera tightened her hold upon his crest. Despite her grief and anger, she thrilled to feel the power writhing within him.

So he needed only an hour? Elera snarled at the thought as the bull flew smoothly over the clouds. One hour to put an end to the vibrancy in his remarkable eyes, to cement her fate and the fate of her people ... to deny this world of dragons and breathtaking rites.

To deny her!

She would know the moment his life ended. It would hurt her, a physical pain ripping through her veins when what was bound between them ended. She hadn't told him about that, but she should have. If only to use his honor against him, she should have described every detail of the agony soon to be hers.

"Not against him," she whispered into the wind. "For him. The stupid, stubborn, narrow-minded ..."

The rest of her words were drowned beneath the bull's roar. She was transmitting her fury to him, and his pace had increased as a result. Subtle changes in the pressure of her legs calmed him, guiding him back to the manor.

Had she crooned over Karl these last two days just so he could finish what Ronin had started? Had she lost both sleep and weight this last month, feeling only a gnawing fear in her gut as she waited for him to arrive? Just so he could dismiss both her world and her? She had not!

In an effortless motion borne of instinct and practice, Elera leaped smoothly from the bull's back as he flew past her manor. She landed softly upon her terrace, even as the wind from his wings quickly faded back into the sky.

Stomping through the drawn curtains, she shouted, "Keep your Mattaen honor if you must, but you will not perform this rite in such a cowardly fashion! If you are going to take your life, you will have to do it with me watching...."

She paused, heart in her throat. Neither Karl nor his blade lay on the bed. Thinking she might have missed him on the terrace, she threw back the curtains and called his name.

There was still no sign of him.

"Elera?"

She whirled, swaying in relief at seeing him standing just behind the curtain. He raced through the archway and placed his hands on her shoulders and held her steady. A moment later, he lowered her into a chair.

"Drink," he ordered quietly, lifting a cup to her lips. He touched the tears smeared across her face and swore. "I was only using your bath, Elera."

Surprise had her focusing on the sopping red tresses falling over his bare chest. Her eyes flared wide when she noticed his chest was not the only part on display.

Following her line of sight, Karl shrugged. "I wasn't expecting you to return for a while. Not until the hour was up, at least."

She tossed her head. "Then you should know that while you do this thing—"

"I heard," he said, tracing his thumb over her bottom lip,

and answering the quick catch in her breath with one of his own.

Her eyes lowered to his stomach, but he grabbed her hand before she could reach out to touch.

"Just seeing to your wound," she quipped. "It's too soon for you to soak it in water. Not that it matters, I suppose."

Karl smiled. "I do know how to take care of myself, Elera. And I wasn't soaking, merely washing." His fingers brushed her hair, a quick and easy touch, before he rose and walked outside. "The blade is in your table. I won't use it."

"You'll give me the days?" Rushing to his side, Elera smiled up at him.

Her joy quickly faded when she looked into his eyes ... and realized that he'd never intended to use the dagger.

"I see. A ruse of your own. A punishment ... and I don't suppose I can fault you for it. Come." She took his hand, and this time ran her fingers over his wound without interference. "You shouldn't yet be on your feet."

She looked up when he didn't move, and bit her lip at the intensity in his stare. After only a moment, Karl allowed her to lead him to the bed. He sank to the edge and closed his eyes. Elera left him sitting there while she changed out of her riding clothes. Moving into the adjoining room that held her bath and toilette, she found a towel for his wet hair.

She stood between his legs and draped the soft towel over his shoulders, surrounding him with her scent. He opened his eyes just as she lifted it to his hair and began gently rubbing the strands dry. She pretended not to notice when his gaze lingered on the thin wrap she wore around her breasts and then traveled downward to examine the gentle slope of her stomach above her low-slung pants.

Karl's body stirred. Did much more than stir, actually, as it sprang abruptly to life. He tensed, then grunted when his wound twinged.

Elera lowered her eyes and tried to hide her smile, well aware of her effect upon him. She supposed it didn't help that she stood on her toes, arms wrapped around his head to reach his hair ... leaving her body within easy reach of his hands. Or his mouth, if he so chose. She finished her task as if unaware, and caught the water that had dripped to his skin with a last brush of the towel.

"Would you like me to braid it for you?" she asked finally, curling a lock around her finger.

She froze when he placed a hand on her hip. His fingers skimmed her waist, circled around to her back to stroke up her spine ... and finally brushed her nape to tangle in her curls.

His other hand was a fist on the bed, the knuckles white with tension

"Elera?" Karl whispered, pulling her close enough that she could feel his breath over her lips. When her tongue darted out to wet them, his fingers tightened in her hair. "How do I accept this claim of yours?"

She searched his eyes, stunned by the heat in them. "A kiss." Did he mean to accept their bond that very moment?

Karl cocked his head. "That's it?"

"All of this began with a kiss," she murmured.

"True enough. But there are many kinds of kisses, as some-one once told me." His words trailed off as he blew softly over her jaw, down the curve of her neck.

"On the lips," she added, shivering from the combination of his breath and hands. His tongue flicked out to tease the sensitive skin beneath her ear. "The breath we share on the first kiss you give me will seal our bond."

"I'll remember," Karl said, setting her abruptly back, though his hand remained on her arm until her legs stopped trembling. Finally he dropped to his elbows with a groan, and then to his back. "Food, Elera, if you have it. I will need my strength, and quickly, if I am to enjoy these few days in your world."

It took her a moment to respond, since her body still thrummed from his touch. But even as she realized he had manipulated her, albeit in a more pleasant manner this time, she also noticed that his own body was not immune to his methods.

She chuckled as she left the room. Once she passed through the door, Elera peeked back inside just in time to see his lips curve in a slow, satisfied smile.

The man ate enough to sate a dragon. Elera watched, equally amused and impressed by the amount of food he packed into his lean build.

Propped up at the head of her bed, Karl noticed her smile and winked before returning his attention to his meal. He drank from his cup and then dubiously peered inside it. She had laced his drink with healing herbs, and though she had tried to disguise their bitter taste, he apparently could still taste them. Before he had a chance to protest, she walked to the terrace and stared over the hills, seeking the bull.

A soft smile played on her lips when she spotted him napping in the sun. It was exactly what she would like to be doing. A female nuzzled his side, butting against him until he finally deigned to grant her a space beneath his wing.

She sighed when Karl approached and laid his hand on her shoulder. Lack of clothing apparently would not be enough to keep the man abed, though he had tucked a blanket around his hips. "You can't keep walking around," she said, turning to wrap her arm around his ribs.

"I can't afford to stiffen up either." Karl nodded toward the hill. "You haven't told me what you call him."

"I don't," she answered, and since he hadn't pushed her away, she settled more fully against his side. "It seems silly to try to name something that's lived so long. The men croon endearments, and I suppose I do too...."

The curve returned to her lips.

Karl stepped away, placing some distance between them. "Naming something implies a brand, or an ownership of sorts."

She smiled, nodding. "It just isn't done. Besides, I don't need it to call him to me."

He watched as she raised her hand. The bull immediately turned his head her way. "How do you do that?"

Elera shrugged. "I just want him and he knows."

For a moment, Karl watched the dragon settle lazily back into the grass; then he raised his eyes to the men lining the borders of her land. "Who are they?"

"Ronin's," she said, with another shrug. "And I don't mean to diminish your significance, but two-thirds of that number are always here. More so since I took the bull below without telling anyone what I was doing."

"So you received trouble for that on both ends," he said knowingly, though with little sympathy. "Elera?"

"Karl," she drawled.

"How loyal are they?"

"To the death," she answered abruptly. "As for honoring the outcome of another battle with Ronin, should you choose to stay ... should you defeat him in the first place ... should you—"

When she broke off in exasperation, Karl smiled. "Too many shoulds?"

Closing her eyes, Elera took a few calming breaths, and warned, "We rarely have an outsider for king. Without Ronin's death or willing yield, I don't know how many will bend their knee to you."

He stood silently for a while, staring thoughtfully at the low-hanging clouds. "Air doesn't seem as thin as when I climbed here."

"I gave you something to help with that."

Karl held her chin. "Don't. And nothing else for the pain."

He left her standing on the terrace alone. She watched as he collapsed wearily atop her bed. He groaned and then fell asleep the instant his head touched the pillow.

Elera groaned, as well, although her turmoil was due to the rider swooping down from the sky. Ronin landed on the grass below her terrace. He said nothing, but the visible working of his jaw struck fear in her as nothing else could.

A wary glance tossed over her shoulder assured her that Karl remained unaware … deeply asleep now, Elera realized with a soft smile. She should have known; the steady rhythm of his pulse echoed beneath her own.

The recognition threw her for a moment, though she should have been feeling his state of being in various ways for some time now … steady for sleep, erratic for exertion, fear, or perhaps the desire he tried not to reveal. She'd been trying not to notice, in case he decided not to stay.

She studied the way his hair glowed in the soft light of the lamp beside her bed. Would she feel him within her during the nights she'd spend alone if he left? She knew of only one man whose mate never made the journey to accept his bond … and he never spoke of it.

A low growl warned Elera she had lingered too long away from the man below her terrace. Ronin's face had reddened to the same shade as his tunic. She made no sound, knowing Karl was incapable of handling yet another physical confrontation.

After a few tense moments, Ronin brought his dragon to her hind legs and took to the sky.

Elera rubbed the chill from her arms as she watched the silhouette of rider and dragon disappearing into the setting sun.

* * *

Karl woke just before sunrise. His body felt weighted down from the altitude, and the pain from his injury had become a pulsing ache throughout his entire body. But his mind was clear, focused, as it could not have been with pain inhibitors.

Pain itself *was* a point of focus.

He shifted his weight, absorbing that pain rather than trying to fight it ... and would have rolled to his feet if not for the wrenching sight of Elera curled in a chair next to the bed. Still in her clothes from the day before, he noted with a wry grin, and snoring softly into her knees.

She'd been watching over him. Had done a fair job of it, if the shadows under her long lashes were any indication. A wave of tenderness washed through him.

When a rap on the door disturbed her, Karl stroked her cheek and murmured nonsense until she snuggled deeper into the chair and slept on. He didn't yet have the strength to lift her, but he tugged a blanket from the bed and tucked it carefully around her shoulders.

Tossing another blanket around his own, Karl crossed the room and swung open the door before Tem could rap a second time.

"You're up, then." With a glance at the sleeping woman, he nodded. "Let's go."

Catching the robe Tem tossed and wearing it in place of the blanket, Karl followed him down the corridors. Despite the sun blazing just outside the windows, most of the rooms were still cast in shadow. He knew the high cliffs and surrounding hills could account for some of that, but he also thought the gloom of the manor came from more than simple seclusion.

It came from limited comfort and even less decoration. No pictures, no ornaments, no tapestries of any sort adorned the manor. There was nothing but long cracks webbing patterns in the walls, the ceilings ... even the stairs, Karl noted, skipping a step that looked particularly unsteady. "I thought you said you wouldn't be my friend when I got here."

Inclining his head slightly, Tem walked out the ground-level doorway and entered the overgrown yard. The glaring sun had both men squinting. "And what makes you think I have been?"

"Answers in questions," Karl muttered, wondering if that was an idiosyncrasy of these people ... or just of Elera and her friend. He tried again. "You did have a hand in saving my life."

"I saved Elera's, friend, not yours." Tem looked back at him with a sigh. "She'll coddle you, as much as a woman like her is capable, anyway. And that's going to get you both killed."

He was silent for a while, leading Karl through a crevice dug directly into the cliff. The dank and enclosed atmosphere within aggravated the heat making their skin itch, but the crevice soon expanded into a spacious training chamber.

"I love her, and that's the plain truth of it." Tem shrugged, lighting torches on the wall to illuminate the weapons hanging alongside them. "If she were any other woman, I might have let that grow into the kind of love a man has for his mate. Instead I love her as if she were my blood, and a man wants to keep his blood safe, yes?"

He didn't wait for an answer, but pulled down an ax, grinning when Karl stiffened.

"You're not as bad off as she thinks." Tem nodded to Karl's stomach. "But you're not quite up to a defense yet, either. Leastways, not physically. Did she tell you how we make the steel?"

"Somewhat."

"Then she did," Tem answered with a smirk. "You've got to see it to understand. But this"—he hefted the ax—"is one of the choice weapons of my people."

He tossed it over, and out of reflex Karl reached out.

The curse hadn't fully left his lips for the stitches he was about to tear, when he caught it. He tilted his head, feeling only a pull in his wound, rather than the hot pain he had expected.

Karl flipped the ax in his hand. He noticed that while the blade spanned the width of his shoulders, it also weighed less than a child's training sword. He stared up at Tem. "Going to give me a lesson, friend?"

Tem measured him silently. "Mattaen are trained in warfare, yes?"

Karl nodded, wary.

"Then it's not a lesson you're needing, but an edge." Losing his smile, Tem straightened. "I'm going to show you every move Ronin has."

Deciding not to point out that he might be gone before that fight, Karl ran his hand along the blade.

"It's thin," he said. *Thinner than should be possible.*

"No less strong for it, though." Picking up another ax, Tem walked over so Karl could examine the differences. But this time he refrained from handing it over.

Karl nodded. "Heavier in the blade, giving it more impact on a swing. Isn't that the point of an ax?"

"Sure, and that's why Ronin's is heavier than this. But even Elera could swing the one you're holding. And has, point of fact." Tem tilted his head and compared the two weapons. "It won't shatter upon contact with the heavier, but—"

"The arm wielding it would."

"Aye, that's true enough."

Karl turned the training ax over in his hands. "Some might say that you are cheating by teaching me Ronin's techniques."

"Not to my face, they wouldn't," Tem said quietly, revealing a glimpse of the warrior within the man. "And it won't go beyond this room."

A bit of leverage for you in the future, should I stay and you wish a favor, Karl reasoned.

"Besides ..." Tem moved to the center of the room, swinging the ax to loosen up. His eyes dropped pointedly to Karl's stomach. "Some might say this just evens things out."

Karl's lips curved. "I can agree with that."

ELEVEN

Karl never attempted to participate with the lightweight weapon. Instead he circled as Tem mimicked some of Ronin's strikes and feints. More than half the man's moves were flawed, but an exceptional few roused Karl's warrior spirit.

There would be other attack positions, Tem claimed. Those Ronin kept to himself in his personal training, for he had the cunning heart and mind to go with the muscle of a true warrior king. And a true warrior king would know that someone was always plotting to overthrow him.

Still, the details Tem had stored of another man's fighting style were exceptional, giving Karl both pause and cause to reevaluate his original impression of the good-natured rider. As he absorbed the instruction and advice, he also studied the man giving them.

Afternoon heat replaced the slightly cooler morning air. The room became a torment, but even after Tem staggered under the weight of the ax, he did not cease his instruction. He merely tossed the weapon aside and picked up a set of curved and serrated daggers.

"He wears these—"

"I've seen them," Karl interrupted with a nod, narrowing his eyes when Tem flipped both daggers in his hands and the line of each blade curved into the opposite direction.

What was once a downward slant was now an upward angle.

"No trick of my hands," Tem explained, holding the blades

out so Karl could watch the alteration in slow motion. "Pressure in the weaker points along the hilt alters the composition of the steel, and allows it to shift into another position."

He demonstrated. Karl watched in astonishment when the metal lost its rigidity. A casual flick of Tem's wrist, a subtle change in the pressure of his fingers, and the steel sprang rigid once more ... with the curve of the blade pointing in the other direction.

"Quite an edge," Tem said. "You think you've compensated for a strike, the blade curves outward, and your neck is slit. Can take years to learn to compensate. Better take you less."

Karl accepted the proffered blades, fingers feeling for the subtle differences in tensile strength. When he found a pressure point and the blade altered slightly, Tem grinned in approval ... then jumped when he noticed a woman leaning within the entrance of the cave.

Elera stared at him for a long moment before shifting her dark eyes to Karl. "You don't need to be on your feet to learn to manipulate those. And you've missed two of the meals you claim to need so badly."

She said nothing else, merely tossed a bag of bread and meat at his feet. With a slow nod, she spun back around the corner.

"If she expected you to stop, she wouldn't have brought the food," Tem said, hooking the bag with his sword and rooting for something he liked.

The words brought an immediate halt to Karl's forward step. Disconcerted that he had moved to follow her, he accepted the sack of food ... and ignored the quick grin of the rider as Tem began instructing him on how to counter the twin-bladed attack.

Karl flicked his eyes briefly to the tunnel as he bit into the grainy meat. Elera's displeasure bothered him enough that his first impulse had been to follow her and set things right. He was fairly sure that irritated him, only … she'd looked all fired up, despite her cool tone and stare.

He was afraid it might be more than just an impulse to make amends that prompted him to go after her. That it might be something a bit darker, a need to bring her fire to the surface. To see her eyes glaze in passion, taste her curves, breathe her heat …

How could she compel him this way? He, who even among his fellow Initiates had been known for his icy control. He, Karl, who had rebuffed countless women with nary a second thought. How could one infuriating female dragonrider have brought him to this state?

Growling under his breath, he curbed his wayward thoughts before his body could respond accordingly. He forced his mind back to the *edge* currently being offered and struggled not to react when he noticed Tem smirking.

Night had just begun to fall when the pair left the crevice searching for food after Elera failed to appear. They'd heard the wings of the bull as he landed on the cliff shortly after her exit, and it occurred to Karl that she might have gone flying to work off some of the restless energy that still plagued him. He found a sort of justice in that … and ignored the leap of pleasure he felt at the thought of affecting Elera as strongly as she affected him.

The shadow of Tem's beauty hid the stars as she glided gracefully down, landing with a thump before the men. That quickly, Karl ceased to exist for the rider.

Only after the rider and his dragon had flown away did he allow himself the luxury of hobbling. He limped and shuffled along the lower levels of the manor until he reached the first staircase. Swallowing his groan, Karl stared up those marble steps, and was still standing at the bottom when he heard the bull fly past the manor.

By tracking the sound of Elera's steps across the ceiling, he knew the exact moment she discovered he wasn't yet abed. Her movements ceased, silence … and then a piercing shriek.

A man didn't have to be experienced with women to know the folly in revealing his current state of agony to this one … especially since he knew he had overworked his body. He turned on his heel and stumbled into an adjacent sitting room, where a fireplace lay barren. He sank to a chair with a curse.

He could do nothing about the sweat soaking his skin and only hoped she would attribute it to the humid night air. By the time he heard her at the bottom of the stairs, his hands were relaxed and he wore a placid expression. When she paused in the corridor before walking in the room, Karl planted a smile on his lips, turned his head—

"You stupid idiot." Closing the distance between them, Elera laid her hand on his cheek. "I can see it in your eyes."

The simple insult must not have been enough to satisfy her, because she also hissed a line of foreign expletives.

He glared at her. "Is that an actual dialect, or just another way to torment me?"

"Most of that was directed at the fool who kept you out so long," she snapped, and tilted her head to meet his eyes. "If you live through the next few days, I'll find plenty more for you."

Her gray eyes went soft as she smoothed his hair away from his brow … and that tender look slipped straight past his guard.

"Elera," Karl breathed, sliding his fingers through her dark locks, fisting his hand around her curls until her eyes shifted back to his.

"Plenty of that for you too," she whispered, wide-eyed. But she pulled away. "Later. Right now, I want you on your back."

He looked up expectantly, one copper brow raised in response to the erotic image her words produced.

Elera sighed. "I meant in bed."

She gasped when he pulled her forward, dipping his head to run his lips up the column of her neck. His teeth scraped the line of her jaw, and strength rippled in his shoulders when he felt her hands upon them.

"What have you done to me?" he murmured.

Elera shook her head and planted her knee between his thighs on the chair. When she shifted to give him easier access to her neck, her leg brushed the rigid length of him beneath his robe.

Karl pressed helplessly into the caress and growled against her throat.

His hand stroked down her back, traced the band of her pants, and he slid his fingers inside. The material was molded against her skin, and his fingers got stuck. But her soft moan against his temple had his blood rushing, yearning as she purposely shifted her knee.

Karl's pulse erupted in a fury of desperate need. Impatient fingers found and released the clasp at her hips, drawing her pants down, slipping along her soft skin. Finding her. Frantic now, he plunged two fingers into her scalding entrance, groaning as her nails bit into his shoulders. Her hips tilted, granting him deeper access, which he took at once ... driving reckless and hard, shuddering with power when she cried his name.

He flicked the pulse in her throat with his tongue, instinctively matching it to every stroke of his fingers. Elera's moans urged him to drive deeper, faster ... daring him to discover what else would draw his name from her lips.

He withdrew his fingers, coaxing a whimper from her mouth ... but he'd simply moved them to her breast. But he wanted flesh, not cloth ... and in one sudden move, he ripped the material of her wrap apart. Elera gasped as her breasts spilled free ... then moaned after he ducked his head and closed his mouth over a rigid peak.

He growled against her skin when her nipple hardened within his mouth, and he thrust his hand back into the heat between her thighs. It was addictive ... that heat, that slickness, that scent that grew stronger as her flesh began throbbing around his fingers.

He drew harder on her breast as lust rode him. His sex began pulsing in time with hers, and he twisted her body ... mindlessly lapping at her other nipple as his name spilled from her lips.

He pulled her closer when her cries started coming in broken gasps.... *Too rough ...*

Elera lost her balance and stumbled against him.

He hissed, his body stiffening ... and she pulled back at once. Her pants were tangled around her thighs, and she landed bare-bottomed on the floor in front of the chair.

He moved immediately forward, reaching down to help her. She must have seen the cold sweat washing over his skin and quickly gestured for him to step back.

Although the shimmying she did to pull her pants back over her hips did nothing to cool his blood, Karl sank back against the chair and fought to control his pain. It was no less than he deserved for starting a fire he had not the experience to control....

"You stupid idiot," Elera whispered again, slapping away his hands so she could lift his robe and see the damage.

Heat flooded his face when she swore. He knew full well the condition of both his injury and his member. But she merely traced soft fingers over the few torn stitches and the blood smeared across his skin, then whispered his name in regret.

"A minute ago I was a stupid idiot," he grumbled.

Gathering closed the torn edges of her shirt, Elera sighed. "That was for me, for letting you seduce me when you're too weak to do anything about it."

He made an affronted noise deep in his throat. But the sound rang weak even to his ears, and Elera smiled before cupping his cheek.

"I'm sorry, Karl. Take a moment to breathe, and then I'll help you get upstairs."

He did as she asked. After inhaling a few more times until he could work through the pain, he leaned heavily on her shoulders.

"Wouldn't think there was enough of you to bear me up," he rasped, pale again when they started climbing. By the time she got him to her bed, his hands were shaking and his eyes were closed. He groaned as he lay back, then hissed when cool water trickled over his wound.

At least she'd pulled a blanket over the member no longer covered by his robe.

He didn't make a sound while she restitched each thread, nor even when she rubbed stinging salve on him after. But he did curse when he felt the entire wound go numb.

"I said nothing for the pain!"

"Nothing that affects your mind," she said firmly, looking up at him. "And the numbing won't last long, just for enough time to let you get the rest you need."

When he continued to glare down at her, she climbed next to him on the bed and stroked his cheek.

"Your body can't heal if it's fighting itself, Karl."

She was right, he knew, and let the tension ease from his body. Turning his head away, he asked, "Are you to sleep at my side this night, then?"

"Are you asking me to?" Elera replied. When he swore in

response to her question-instead-of-an-answer tactic, she pressed her lips to his shoulder. "I would like it, if you will not object."

"I would welcome it." Lifting his hand to twirl the locks hanging over her shoulders, Karl answered the question in her eyes: "There is something about you, Elera. It pulls at me, even as I try to will it away."

When he tugged her closer, she did not object. Laying her cheek in the hollow of his shoulder, Elera shifted until she fit snugly against his side.

He wrapped his arm around her waist. Only when her eyes grew heavy did he whisper, "I still would not have kissed you."

She smiled against his skin, shrugged, and fell into sleep while he wondered how her breath against his neck could soothe him more than the numbing salve on his wound.

Elera awakened to the scent of Karl on her blankets and in her pillows. A purely feminine thrill washed through her. She snuggled deeper into her bed … enjoying the sensory pleasure of being surrounded by his scent.

He had held her in his arms all night.

Her lips curved. He had *wanted* to hold her in his arms all night.

She felt a small pang of regret after noticing he was no longer abed. But he was only sitting in the chair across from her bed, working the blades. She didn't need to open her eyes to know it. The soft sounds of shifting steel relayed his every movement. And by the sound of things, he'd gotten the knack for it.

"It is near noon, Elera of the dragonriders, and still you lie abed with that wicked smile upon your lips."

Elera opened her eyes to see the humor in his. With a sinuous stretch designed to seduce, she sat up and rubbed the sleep away.

"Have you been awake long?" she purred, hiding her grin behind her hand when he looked away to whisper some kind of chant beneath his breath.

After a moment, Karl held up the blades. "Long enough to get a feel for these."

He showed her, changing angles with pressure from his fingers.

"It's harder to counter an opponent's shift," she warned, but nodded approval anyway. "Are you hungry?"

"I am."

When his gaze fell to the swell of her breast, barely covered, since she still wore the shirt he'd torn the night before, she traced her curves right under his eyes.

His tongue shot out to lick his lips. When his eyes climbed back to hers, she smiled. "For food, Karl?" Sliding off the bed, Elera swayed close enough to touch him, though she did not. "Or for me?"

"For you," Karl admitted, seeming to enjoy throwing her off guard as much as she enjoyed teasing him. "But I'll take the food, as I'm likely not up to anything else just yet."

With a lopsided grin, she lowered her eyes to the arousal tenting his robe. "As usual, you underestimate your abilities."

His cheeks bronzed, though his lips still curved. "Food, Elera. And after, perhaps you could show me something of this world of yours."

"I'll see to your wound first. After the meal," she amended, listening to his stomach rumble.

She was gone and back while Karl stood on the edge of the sunken tub in the second of her adjoining rooms. He seemed to be considering whether or not his injury could withstand a soaking.

"Probably not," she said. "Give it another day, maybe two. I'll help you in the meantime."

"I don't need you to," he said quickly, nodding gratefully when she handed him fruit and bread. "Do you live here alone?"

After she realized he hadn't meant to dismiss her, Elera halted her retreat and returned to sit with him by the tub. Longingly, she watched his fingers unravel the braids and coils in his hair. "I live with my grandfather. Warwick."

His fingers stilled. "Father of your father?"

"Yes, my scholar." Elera smiled softly, knowingly. "The father of a dragonslayer. I did not lie."

She could see he wanted to argue the point, but he let her remark go unanswered. "And how does a dragonslayer come to sire a dragonrider?"

"My father came here to kill, and loved instead."

His fingers resumed their work. "Loved the dragons?"

"No," she said wryly. "Loved my mother. She rode the bull, as well, but was already mated. Bonded by force … a virgin whose mate did not need her consent as he forced his breath upon her in order to rule."

She could see Karl frown beneath the tresses hanging over his face. "What about the choice?" he asked.

"The breath between two members of my race bonds both immediately and forever … just as I am bonded immediately and forever to you. The only condition is that the recipient of breath be a virgin."

"Then why did Ronin not force his breath on you?" He sounded confused by what would have been a grave error in judgment. When she lifted a dark brow in amusement, he added with a sigh, "I assume you were a virgin at one point in your life, Elera."

"I assume so." She inclined her head in amends for her teasing when he grumbled. "The breath does not bond anyone who has not yet seen twenty years of age, which is when my people reach physical maturity and pass from childhood to adulthood. Ronin would have known to wait until then before making the attempt. But by then there had been a boy...." Her eyes softened as she remembered. "We were both very young."

She shrugged and resumed her story. "My father fell in love with my mother despite her bond, took her to his bed ... and when they were discovered, she was executed, and he shortly after."

"Elera," Karl whispered, shocked.

She shook her head, smiling sadly. "I had obviously been born by then. It's how the riders found out."

His hand grasped hers, brought it to his lips. "You have the look of your father?"

"I'm told so, though that was not the reason for their discovery." She looked away. "My people cannot mate among themselves and bring forth issue. That is one of the reasons why men find mates from below and send them on the same path I sent you."

"Elera ... no woman could travel the path I did," Karl rebuked ... and frowned. "How do the riders know where a sacrifice is being made? Or when? You could not have expected that I would be at that village...." His voice grew higher with each new question.

"Did you think it was coincidence that you stumbled across a sacrifice in that village?" Her lips curved into a smug smile as she handed him some lather for his hair. "We initiate the ritual by allowing our dragon to mark the area. The villagers recognize the marks and the sounds of the ground rumbling beneath the dragon as it prowls, and if they have the fifty *tarlae* and want to save the girl, they contact the slayers as soon as they identify the signs. It took more effort with you. I saw you in the barrens and had to follow you to find the village where you would pass—"

"I heard no ..." He gave her a disgruntled look. "Why the ruse? Why did you not bargain with me before I reached the village?"

"I had considered it ... but bargaining with an Initiate when there were no consequences to his refusal might not have worked so well in my favor." The corners of his lips curved slightly, and she exhaled in relief before continuing. "It will be difficult enough for my people to accept an outsider as king. I thought it best to keep to the traditional laws of seeking ... and the ruse and journey are both long-standing traditions."

"What of the men, Elera? How do they know which woman will be sacrificed?"

"Sacrificial virgins are pledged at birth and marked shortly afterward to signify that they are to remain untouched. By that mark, a rider knows who the sacrifice of each village will be ... and can decide whether he wants her or whether he should keep searching—"

"Based on appearance alone ..."

"Sometimes," Elera quickly added, unwilling to have him think her shallow. "But men who care for intelligence and character as well as beauty have walked away from their prizes before."

Karl seemed to be considering, and she sighed as he cupped water from the bath and let it run over his skin. "If no slayer is called?"

"It is the rider's choice. He can claim to be passing by and demand his payment anyway, or he can take her while the village is distracted by the dragon and perform the rite elsewhere in the barrens ... and they believe she was taken away to be devoured, or devoured on the spot."

"Which keeps your ruse alive," he said softly. "You do not give women the same choice as you gave me, then. If she were ever to return to her home ..."

"Every seeker has earned the choice. But what would they return to? Poverty and families who fed them to a beast ... and might not welcome them back anyway?" Elera shook her head. "Few women ever leave, and none in my lifetime ... although some choose not to make the journey at all—"

"Such as those who were raped?"

She started—the man did not forget a word—but reluctantly nodded. Many of the women came despite the rape, she knew. Some had never seen the men around them behaving any differently and thought it was normal.

"As for those who do choose to leave our land or choose not make the journey at all ...?" She shrugged. "Too many people have supposedly *seen* virgins devoured to believe the tale of a girl they would think mad ... or worse, unacceptable to a dragon. They would cast her out. The others ..."

"If I did not believe an entire village, Elera ... I can see how they would not believe one girl. They are told of this place after the breath, then?"

"I don't know what they're told, or how much help they are given, Karl. The rules of seeking forbid the riders only from leaving evidence of our people—"

"Like the map you left me."

She scoffed. "That was nothing without my words to accompany it. But the journey is a test of strength, and my people need to see strength in you. As for the women, if they aren't strong enough to make it here, bearing the feminine equivalent of what you faced, they aren't strong enough to bear a child of riding heritage."

"It takes more than blood to beget strength."

The quiet words were the last Karl spoke for the remainder of his bath. But he did brush his lips over her forehead, perhaps in sympathy for the pain she could never fully mask when thinking of her parents. He also allowed her to take the towel to his hair and skin when he stood clean and dripping on her floor.

"Did your father never kill a dragon, then?" he asked, pulling her up when she would have knelt to dry his legs.

"My father killed the dragon of my mother's mate in a rage over her execution. Then he brought me to Warwick, went back, and challenged the rider himself." Her hands trembled. "He lost."

"And you?" Karl pressed.

"I shouldn't have been born. We aren't fruitful without the bond." Taking a deep breath, she looked up at him with a shrug. "But I was the daughter of a rider, no matter the circumstances of my birth. My place was here."

"How was it that they allowed your grandfather to come here and care for you?"

"No one else wanted me. Warwick was a warrior in his own right, fierce enough to handle this world and the temperament of its people," she said with a grin. "With the exception of the granddaughter who had her every whim granted with a simple tremble of her lips."

Karl leaned down with a chuckle, and very nearly touched his mouth to hers. He drew back at once, sighing over the flash of pain she had not managed to conceal. "I didn't do that to hurt you."

"I know," she whispered, as if his confession didn't make his rejection worse. She had never known anyone to fight his natural desires as much as this man. "Do you still want to see the land?"

Karl nodded. "But on foot, rather than from the back of the bull. What?" he asked, when her hand shot up to cover her sudden smile. "Don't tell me it isn't done, because Tem let me ride—"

"Stop," she said, setting her fingers over his mouth to ensure he did. "I'm sorry. I should have explained. I didn't realize you had been thinking … Dragons don't tolerate same-sex riders. The bull has never been touched, nor ridden, by any but a woman."

"When you say don't tolerate, you mean …?" Karl tilted his head. "So I can never ride him?"

She heard the disbelief in his tone, but also, surprisingly, the disappointment. Elera grinned. "You just said you didn't want to."

"I know what I said," he grumbled, leaving the bathing room and looking around the bedroom for his robe.

"Here." Walking to the bed, Elera tossed him the men's clothing she had procured. "The pants are soft and low enough to stay away from the wound, and the vest can be left open. The air will be good for it, anyway."

And her day would be pleasant, since he was no chore to look upon. Perhaps he guessed that she had chosen this outfit as much for her own pleasure as his comfort, since he frowned … then glowered after he slipped into it and looked down. The white silk pants hung well below his navel, revealing the enticing twin lines leading to the soft bulge below.

"You have a beautiful body, Karl," she said throatily, allowing her eyes to roam over the length of him, then wincing when she saw the angry red line of his injury. "You should wear white more often, to contrast the color of your hair."

Karl laughed aloud as she bit her lip sheepishly. "I know little of the ways of being a mate, but I still believe such comments are best left to my lips, and not yours." He chuckled again. "Next you will be adorning me in fine jewels, hoping to find my favor."

Elera tossed her head, wondering if he realized he'd just spoken of them as mates. Her heart had certainly given a quick leap. "I already have your favor, or you wouldn't have to fight so hard not to kiss me."

"You might be right," Karl said softly, surprising her again.

He held out his hand. When she took it without hesitation, his fingers curled firmly around hers. "Show me…" He tilted his head. "What is the name of your land, Elera?"

She smiled ruefully. "Verteva. My world is named Verteva."

"Then show me Verteva, Elera. Show me why I should love it."

TWELVE

Perhaps it was the call of the land, or the allure of the woman at his side, but Karl soon forgot his pain and simply enjoyed the journey. The constant change from grassy terrain to naked rock was erratic, but fascinating. Smaller homes lay nestled along the edges of cliffs, while larger dwellings were hewn directly into the rock. Lining the horizon were the grand manors Elera claimed could not be reached in just one day, at least not on foot. Their extravagant crimson banners stretched high into the sky, designed with black emblems standing bold against the red.... He saw weavings representing weapons, dragon wings and claws, cycles of the moon, and flames rising in odd patterns. Elera's banner appeared to hold the only full image of a dragon ... the bull depicted in flight.

"Royal Houses," Elera explained, glancing up at him. "Very old, very rich ... although each belongs to the dragon first, and the rider second."

"Dragons determine royalty in your world?" he asked, then realized he should not have felt surprised. It seemed dragons determined most things here.

"They do ... but there are many more people in my race than there are dragons to ride. Royalty can slip out of one family upon the death of the rider ... or the dragons can choose from the same family for generations. It keeps my people from becoming..."

"Arrogant ...?" he offered in a bland tone, then grinned when she ducked her head.

"Complacent," she insisted.

He chuckled as he searched the horizon.

"Ronin's House isn't visible from here, if that is what you're seeking."

With a shrug, Karl glanced back at her manor. The bull's manor, he corrected silently. He wondered how it could be in such a state of disrepair, if the woman within was the deciding factor for rule of this world. But he said nothing, nodding instead to the riders leaving their duties to watch him walk by.

"They're afraid to welcome you," Elera said softly, when none returned his gesture. She nodded toward their escort following too closely behind.

"I'm not blind, Elera." He touched her hair before sighing up at the sky, where dragons dove and soared in carefree frolic.

Verteva was a marvel of odd, slanted landscapes, of elaborate manors boasting red and black crests against white slate walls. The highest cliffs soared well beyond the clouds; the lowest dipped under the horizon. And nowhere could the eyes look without seeing a dragon, whether napping on a hill or playing in the sky.

Karl noticed Elera's scrutiny and shook his head. "It's easy enough to be captivated by the beauty of your world, especially for one such as me."

Continuing to walk slowly because of his injury, he listened as Elera pointed out some of the dragons' favored nooks in the nearby cliffs. She giggled into her hand when the bull sprang from one and chased three females off their perches. Puffing his chest, the dragon spread his body over the crest of the mountain ... then rolled to his back and allowed his females their revenge when they returned.

Karl's laugh earned more smiles than just Elera's and even a grudging smirk or two from his escort. This was what Ronin saw when he swooped down from the sky and leaped from his dragon's back. He sent her away with a slap to her hide, then stumbled with a grin when she nudged him in rebuke. The softness in his expression vanished as soon as his eyes met Elera's.

"The day appeals to you," he said, in what seemed to Karl to be some sort of traditional greeting.

"Or the company," someone mumbled bravely from within the gathering crowd.

Karl and Elera had walked as far as the central marketplace, one of four such places in Verteva. Occasionally, merchants put on shows of combat to entertain people passing through. Today, however, the show seemed to be the battle for Elera's hand.

Ronin sought the foolish speaker out, glaring through the crowd. After seeing the warrior's face flush with temper, Karl instinctively set Elera behind his back.

Ronin glared at him now. "Three days are left of your protection, stranger, not Elera's. I will do with her what I wish, and when I wish it."

Karl said nothing. He held his ground with his fingers wrapped tightly around Elera's arm. Only by breaking his own laws and bringing harm to the seeker could Ronin get to her now.

"Enjoy the taste of her while you have it," Ronin said bitterly, swallowing this temporary defeat. "She'll be beneath me in four days. Sooner, if you let her out of your sight, and suffering for every touch she's given you instead of me." With a careless shrug, he strolled onto the main path of the marketplace.

Seeing the fear in Elera's eyes, and knowing it was mostly for him, Karl fought back his rage. He leaned down and murmured in her ear, "A hardship assuredly, to keep you at my side for three eternal days."

He clutched his chest as if in agony, and winked when she glowered at him. But her lips were twitching, which eased some of the tension in his shoulders. He did not like seeing her in distress.

"I still have the bull, you know," Elera said softly. "He'll come if I'm threatened."

Karl was doubtful. "He didn't the night I came here."

He dropped the matter when he noticed her discomfort, but a shadow fell across their easy mood for the remainder of their day.

All the walking was finally beginning to take its toll on him. Though he kept quiet, he did glance at her in exasperation as she led them up a steep incline.

Is this not the same woman who tended to me gently in her bed just yesterday, while scolding me for being off my feet at all?

He smiled then, inwardly rebuking the pride that kept him from telling her of his discomfort. "Elera."

"I know," she said, lifting the hand that hadn't left hers since the incident with Ronin. Her lips brushed his knuckles before she smiled, pulling him faster. "But I want you to see something before we head back."

Karl sighed. They were almost at the top of the ridge, so he ignored the fire in his gut and jogged the last few feet. Hearing the roar of rushing water, he softened at the realization that she could be feminine enough to find a waterfall worth sharing. Then he reached the top of the ridge, stared over its edge ... and completely forgot his annoyance over the torturous climb.

"Tell me," Elera whispered when she heard his soft gasp.

Helplessly, he shook his head. No mere waterfall this, but a cascading pool completely surrounded by cliffs and smaller falls. Merged into the cliff itself were the ruins of an ancient ivory manor. A half-crumbled balcony jutted out of the ruins far above the lake below, but was mostly hidden by the dark waters falling from a mouth in the overhanging ledge.

Karl followed the flow of the pool with greedy eyes, and

found a second drop in the water some distance away. Now it was him leading Elera, walking along the ridge until he stood in front of this second set of falls.

"Majesty," he whispered, watching as the lake below branched around protruding rocks to form a handful of smaller streams. Those eventually fused back into a single body of water that was surrounded by silver-embedded stones. And amidst the water, the cliffs, and the multiple veins of silver ... dragons dove.

Piercing the surface of the water, they emerged long moments later with wings outspread, only to soar behind the clouds before diving to repeat their game. Others swam up the streams before wallowing beneath the falls or lounging on the banks to catch the fading rays of the sun.

In a daze, Karl followed Elera along what might have once been steps in the cliffside. By the time they reached the banks in this web of falls, the surrounding cliffs and ridges had completely hemmed them in.

"This is a sacred place," Karl said softly, pulling her to his side.

Smiling, she knelt at the edge of the pool and cupped a handful of water. When it flowed from her hand in twilit shades, he dropped to his knees with another gasp.

"I thought it was a reflection of the dusk, or maybe the color of the ground beneath the pools," he whispered, letting the dark liquid pour between his fingers. "The water is black?"

"A reaction from the silver that seeps into it from the caverns."

"Silver," he repeated, pulling his hand out of the stream to follow a vein along the bank. He glanced at her. "I do not think, Elera, that you have any need for the silver *tarlae* that you demand."

She grinned, but shook her head.

"You are wrong, scholar. This silver is forbidden. It feeds them," she whispered.

Karl turned his head toward a dragon flying directly up the stream of a waterfall. "Explain," he demanded.

She grinned at his impatient tone, and shrugged. "If they were carnivorous, Karl, I don't think there would be any creature left in the world. We also think it sustains their longevity, but this is only a theory."

With a nod, Karl watched the beasts for a while. "They absorb it?"

"Straight from the water by their scales, and that's all anyone knows. That manor"—she nodded to the ruins in the higher cliff—"once belonged to our earliest ancestors, or so the legends go. From before we rode, in the times when all we did was care for the creatures we once deified. Only a chosen few were given leave to dwell so close."

"Leave?"

Elera smirked. "Or at least they were fast enough to keep their heads upon their shoulders."

"Ah," he said, flashing his teeth. "Do you have writings describing when your people started to ride?"

"No ... but we know it was only after we began bonding with them that we could ride them." Elera smiled and lifted a finger to her eyes. "Our proximity to them changed us enough that they could tolerate our touch. Or so we think."

Changed them ...

His smile slipped as he glanced to the various shades of dragons swarming in the sky and along the banks, thinking of the various shades in all the eyes of the people he had seen that day.

He looked into Elera's. Not just gray, he realized with a feeling of unease ... the exact gray of the bull she rode. His voice was quiet. "Dragons choose you by the shade of your eyes?"

"Somewhat..." She hesitated, and he could tell that she was uncertain. "The gray in our eyes shows that we have the physical means to bond with dragons ... we call this riding blood, though as I said, not everyone has a dragon to ride. But while the shade of gray might determine our ability to connect with a particular dragon, many in my world share the exact shades ... so dragons must also choose us for other reasons. Perhaps it depends on our first meeting."

This connection between dragons and riders was more esoteric than Karl had first believed. He stared curiously at the females lounging about and asked softly, "Do they reproduce?"

"Always the scholar?" Elera looked and sounded amused now, and he inclined his head in acceptance of it. But she shook her head. "I have never seen a ... a baby dragon, or egg ... or anything else that writings say they have."

The dragons that had altered the physiology of the people who rode them did not reproduce. The people could not reproduce among themselves....

He would think on it. The puzzle appealed to him.

But the sun had lowered as they stood talking, and the fire from its passing set both the falls and their path aglow. The dragon that had earlier flown up the stream now glided sleekly beneath the water. Her wings spread, a darker stain against the black; then she broke the surface at barely an arm's distance from where he and Elera were kneeling. She disappeared behind the clouds before he could reclaim his stolen breath.

"We are allowed here now, yes?" Karl whispered, cautiously searching the surface of the water for some clue of what lay beneath.

"Yes, my scholar," Elera murmured. "We are allowed to be here, swim here, ride here ... anything you might think to do besides take the silver from the ground."

To prove it, she slipped over the edge, clothing and all.

"Elera," Karl breathed, for despite her assurance it did not sit well with him that he could not see through the black depths.

She swam out farther, treading water. In the next moment, her body rose unnaturally, sending Karl lurching to his feet. Before he could leap in, the crest of a dragon appeared out of the water below Elera's thighs ... followed quickly by a set of tame orange eyes.

It was the bull, and perhaps *tame* was not the word that should be springing to mind. At least those eyes were not glowing with fury.

"You knew he was there?" Karl called, backing away only slightly when the bull's tail and wings emerged as well.

Elera laughed. Of course she had known. At the pat of her hand, the bull lowered his head to the bank and held still while she climbed down. When she came close enough, Karl snatched her into the circle of his arms.

"I'm sorry," she said, looking anything but. "Couldn't resist. There's nothing else in the water except the dragons themselves. You have my promise on that, at least."

His fingers traced the drops of water running down her shoulders and back. When she closed her eyes and arched into his touch, the only promise he cared for was in the humming response of her body.

"You're stunning, Elera," he whispered. He wondered if she knew what this uninhibited offer of passion did to him—to a man who would have *never* possessed something of his own after joining the brotherhood ... who had never once thought he might *want* to possess something in his life. For this beautiful creature to tell him that she belonged only to him ...

He had watched her as much as he had watched her world this day, had listened as she spoke of the dragons and the family she had lost. It was more than desire, he admitted, that compelled him. He was coming to care for her ... deeply so, and in so short a time that his mind was still attempting to understand these unfamiliar emotions.

The bull chose that moment to snort, drawing both their gazes just before he shook his massive body. Karl flipped his damp hair from his face, then watched in awe as the beast ascended to the sky with scarcely more than a whisper on the wind.

Elera giggled into his chest, having turned to keep his wound dry after realizing the bull's intent. Her laughter trailed away when his arms tightened around her. He pulled her closer, wanting her to feel the unmistakable shape of his arousal against her stomach.

His groan was lost somewhere between pleasure and torture as she shifted enticingly against him. When her tongue licked a line up the center of his chest, his hands wrapped around her arms. Instead of pushing her back, he lifted her to her toes.

"You tempt me," he whispered, close enough now that his breath warmed her lips, "more than any trial ever set in my path."

She sighed, and he inhaled. It would be easy for him to lean in and brush his lips across hers ... to forget about what might come next. But it was not his nature to act without thinking, especially when he was still struggling to understand these strange new emotions. He needed time....

Slowly, and with greater torment than he'd ever thought possible, Karl set her back upon her feet.

"We should head for your home." His stomach clenched when her eyes widened with hurt from his rejection. Had she brought him here hoping he would claim her? "Elera ..."

"No," she said stiffly, turning back to the steppes. "In this instance words are better left unsaid."

He tilted his head, considering his options, but in the end he nodded. "As you wish."

★ ★ ★

It was night by the time they made it back to her manor. With little shame, Karl accepted Elera's help in ascending the stairs to her room. He eased onto the bed. When Elera stepped away, he caught her hand.

"I'm only going to change my clothes," she whispered, meeting his eyes for the first time since his rejection at the pool. "I will sleep at your side if you still wish it."

Karl released her with a nod, and pretended not to see the sheen of tears pride had her blinking back. But he could not keep the catch from his breath when she stripped before him, nor hide the tremor in his body when she donned a transparent slip and stepped into the thin stream of moonlight. "Elera."

"I would rather you say nothing at all, Karl."

"As would I," he said softly, holding out his hand. When she took it, he brought her fingers to his lips. "But I must, even though many men have likely said the words. You are every bit as enchanting as the world you love."

The compliment shocked and pleased her. He could see it in the softening of her eyes, the trembling of her lips. He suspected this side of his nature confused her, since he would not take what she so freely offered.

"I don't understand you," she whispered, confirming his thought. She allowed him to pull her onto the bed and nestle her against his side. But her body tensed and she seemed to struggle with words. "Can you not forgive me, Karl? Is that what stops you from accepting me?"

He kept his surprise carefully concealed when he glanced down at her. "The Mattaen do not teach their Initiates to hold grudges, Elera."

"So the Initiate forgives me," she whispered, closing her eyes for a moment before she lifted her chin. "What of the man?"

He traced the line of her jaw. "Does the woman ask for for-giveness … or does the rider who hopes for a king?"

"I …"

Elera looked disconcerted … and he knew then with cer-tainty that she had not considered separating her personal needs from the needs of her people. But he did not want to frighten her into ignoring her needs altogether, so he did not push her further.

Covering her mouth with his hand in an attempt to stem his sudden desire to place his lips over hers, he whispered, "If forgiveness is what you seek, Elera, then know that you have mine. But no … it isn't what stops me from accepting your claim."

He settled back onto the pillows when her eyes clouded, and tightened his arm around her waist.

She bristled as he tugged her closer. "I don't know how you expect me to get any sleep curled up against you, when all I can think about is—"

Karl dragged her hand down his body and closed her fin-gers over his blunt arousal.

"Sleep may elude us both, Elera," he murmured, pulling her hand back up before she could caress him … though his body all but wept for this reminder of her touch. "But since I can't keep you in sight with my eyes closed, I must have the feel of you to know you're safe."

Even though his lids were already heavy, and falling despite the call of his body, he did not miss the quick flash of anger causing her gray eyes to storm. He fell asleep with a pained grin on his face … and the music of her whispered curses in his ears.

Karl was standing on the terrace, staring out at the sun rising over the peaks of the cliffs, when he heard Elera stirring in her bed. From the corner of his eye, he saw her reach for him in her sleep. He could not suppress his grin when she bolted upright and tumbled to the floor.

She might be angry, perhaps even hurt, but not so much that she did not fear for his safety. Or perhaps it was something else. He remembered what it felt like to wake alone after a night spent in another's arms. With a sigh, he shifted on the terrace to purposely draw her eyes, then pretended not to notice when she glared up at him.

Her lips parted in surprise when she noticed the meal he'd fetched sitting on the small table. He waited for her to join him, then handed her a sweet-smelling tart. "Tem was here," he said, staring when a spot of pastry clung to her lower lip.

Elera slowly licked it off and glanced innocently up at him, then spoiled her chaste look by chuckling. "I can't stay angry at you, Karl, no matter how many reasons you give me. What did Tem want?"

"He's waiting in the cavern. I said I would join him."

"So why haven't you?" she asked, turning her head to look at him.

"Didn't want to wake you," he said simply. In truth, he'd lain awake more than half the night while she stirred restlessly against him. "And I can't go without you."

With a flick of her fingers, she dismissed his concern. "Ronin won't try anything. Not here in the manor …"

She stumbled over her words, a mistake she did her best to conceal by biting into the tart.

So the warrior had trespassed here already. Karl covered her hand with his. His other was curled into a fist, carefully hidden beneath the table. "I cannot train if I am worrying over you."

"Why would you worry over me?" she argued, but did not pull away when he took her chin and tipped her head.

Karl held her eyes. "You will come?"

Answering him with a careless shrug, Elera finished her meal in silence and brushed the crumbs from her fingers.

"Will you wear this?" he teased, fingering the wispy material slipping off her shoulder.

"Too easy. To distract, then best you," she explained when his brow furrowed. "Don't object. If I have to spend the day in that hot, smelly cavern, I get to join in the fun."

He let her examine his wound before they left, knowing she would be pleased. While his ache was dull and throbbing, it no longer writhed with hot claws of fire.

His body was healing.

Tem somersaulted backward, not an easy task in a room that size, and deftly kicked the blue blade out of Elera's hand. Flipping the weapon still grasped in her weaker hand, she spun, raking its edge near enough to Tem's chest that his shirt tore open. Beneath the material, a thin line of blood welled up.

She stopped in concern ... and lost her final blade beneath Tem's hold on her wrist.

"That's cheating," she said.

"Is not." Retrieving her blades, he tossed them back. "You're softhearted, and a bit of blood always gives you pause. It's just good practice, getting you to work on your weaknesses."

Karl chuckled from the corner of the room, having watched their byplay while practicing blade manipulation. "You let her cut you to distract her from cutting you? Good ploy, rider. I wonder if that will work for me."

Though Tem only grinned, Elera took his comment in a different vein. "You think I can't cut him unless he allows it?"

Most men would have recognized the danger in answering her question incorrectly, and chosen their words wisely. But since she was sparring with Tem, Karl simply shrugged.

The rider groaned. "I'll thank you later, seeker, if you live three days instead of two."

But though his words were directed toward Karl, his eyes locked warily upon the woman already purposefully circling him.

Holding one blade out before her and the other in an arc over her head, Elera smiled. And attacked.

Karl forgot his own studies to watch the artistry in their battle. It was easy to see that they had danced to this tune many times before, although to an unlearned eye, their near misses seemed intentionally lethal. But the pair moved as one, lunge and retreat, feint and dodge. Steel scraping steel until the sound mingled with their deepening breaths.

Her motions were liquid, Karl thought, as she slipped effortlessly from one stance to the next. His lips curved. She was better than he'd expected.

Much better.

Perhaps that explained the sweat beading Tem's skin in his effort to keep pace. Why he used the bands on his wrists to deflect and parry, rather than the heavier and slower blades in his hands. And why his breathing quickened to a sharp rasp.

When Tem's counterstrike put Elera on the defense, Karl stiffened. He could no longer tell if the man was holding back or even checking his strength. A shiver of fear ran the length of his spine.

"Enough," he said, softly at first. Then again, with more volume when neither heeded his call. He hissed when Elera dipped her head back to avoid the swipe of Tem's blade beneath her jaw.... *Enough!* Karl darted across the room, his own blade slipping between Tem's steel and Elera's throat. In unison, the pair froze. They slowly shifted their attention to the man entering their fray.

"I would have curved the blade, seeker," Tem said cautiously, indicating with a shift of his eyes that very motion already under way. His steel would never have grazed Elera's skin, and his eyes clouded with insult at any insinuation otherwise. He stepped deliberately back, obviously relieved when Karl directed his fury toward Elera.

"No more," Karl snapped, more harshly than he'd intended. He slapped the blade from her hand and stepped forward to bully her back against the wall.

The edge of her second blade tapped his chest.

Normally, he might have been amused, tolerant enough to allow her the liberty. But his blood was thrumming against his temples, and his temper slipped from its carefully tended chain.

Batting her blade aside, grazing his palm in the process, Karl knelt and tossed her over his shoulder. "No more," he repeated, setting her roughly atop a ledge in the wall. He shook her when she glared mutinously from behind the disheveled curls falling into her face. "*Maybe* Tem would have stopped the blade ..."

Tem hissed his displeasure from across the room.

"... but another with less skill could not. No more."

"A shame, then," Elera said, shifting deceptively in his arms, "that you have not accepted my claim. Even his mate is bound by law to obey the edicts of her king."

That said, she hooked her foot behind his knee and shoved his chest. Not hard enough to send him to the floor. Just hard enough to knock him back and give her enough of a lead to escape unhindered from the cavern.

THIRTEEN

Pressing one hand over a few torn stitches, Karl glared after Elera's back. The bulk of his anger fell on Tem after the man shook his head in amusement.

"If you fall for the ploy of those words, seeker, I will lose all faith in your dubious abilities to lead my people. Not that I don't want you to accept her—Wait," Tem shouted, chasing him down the corridor. "She'll have called the—"

Leaping through the overhang and into the open field beyond, Karl didn't bother stopping. He snarled every curse that sprang to mind when the bull swooped away with Elera on his back.

"—bull," Tem finished lamely, coming to stand at Karl's side. Moments later, half the contingent of Ronin's loyal riders followed the bull into the sky. The rest remained cemented along the borders watching them. Tem hissed in disgust. "Ronin's going to figure out what I've been doing."

Karl never took his eyes off the sky. "Call your..." Biting back *beast*, he said instead, "... dragon."

Tem frowned. "Even Ronin's riders couldn't catch Elera now, much less me if I—"

"She doesn't go anywhere alone!" Sprinting up the hill to keep sight of her fading figure, Karl shouted back to Tem, "Do it!"

Tem started laughing, wisely retreating when Karl advanced with clenched fists. His beauty swooped down, landing protectively between her rider and the man intent on causing him harm.

"Perhaps you should not delay so long in accepting Elera's claim," Tem said, climbing to his dragon's back. He smoothed her scales in a long caress. "You might get better results."

"Ungrateful autocratic ass," Elera yelled to the night sky, clinging to the bull as he soared and dove in an attempt to channel the fury being transmitted from his rider. "Give him just a hint of rule and watch him change to a tyrant!"

Dipping her head to feel the wind whipping through her hair, she glanced over her shoulder and laughed mockingly at the guards she'd left far behind. She narrowed her eyes when she saw Tem pursuing also, and pushed the bull for greater speed. He plummeted over the edge of their world, twisting to fly through the honeycombed matrix of their vertical foundation.

By the time they soared up and over the opposite edge of their land, night had fallen in dark rivulets across the sky. The bull's breathing was as labored as his rider's. Exhausted by her emotions, yet elated by the ride, Elera relinquished control and trusted him to see her home. Of course he saw her to Tem first, waiting just over the crest of their land.

The bull slowed his pace so the female could fly alongside them.

"Elera?" Tem's voice breached the expanse between their dragons.

Sighing, she lifted her head and edged the bull close enough that neither would have to shout. It was a while before words would come to her. "I didn't know you held back when we sparred," she said finally. Cursing herself, she tried again. "I didn't know you held back *so much* when we sparred."

Tem awkwardly looked down, then changed topics. "That isn't what upset you."

She considered ignoring him, but eventually surrendered. This was Tem, after all. Her childhood friend with whom no experience had gone unshared. Hadn't she been treated to firsthand explanations of his youthful sexual romps? Hadn't she also been blackmailed with any number of her own misdeeds if she ever told a soul of his first *disappointing* few?

Tossing him a rueful grin, Elera inclined her head. "I am ... on edge. It is difficult waiting, wanting him as I do."

Tem stared at her, his face blank. Elera sighed. There were times when it proved more tiresome than not, having a friend who knew you so well. "I *do* care for him. And yet I don't know if he hesitates for lack of wanting me, or lack of wanting to rule."

"Or something else entirely," Tem offered with a wink. "Who would not want to rule this world, or you along with it?"

"You."

He laughed. "If I had ever thought you might obey me, I might have considered—"

Tem chuckled, veering to avoid a clash with the bull.

Elera let him draw close a second time. "Tell me how every rejection can have me wishing I had never set out on this path to begin with, while at the same time I am relishing every stolen moment...." Her eyes glazed in memory, then narrowed. "I want to rake out his eyes!"

"Frustration." He nodded, before teasing, "You are not used to going so long without a man in your—"

"I am," she growled, glaring at him when he laughed. "Just not when the object of my desire is lying pressed against me every night. I will remember this humor when you have to wait for your claim to be accepted. In fact, I think I will whisper horrible things in your choice's ear, just to prolong—"

This time he roared with laughter, urging his dragon to a faster pace when she did the same with the bull. "I think, Elera, that I will be a happy—and unbound—man for many years to come. Who in the whole of the world could ever make me laugh as you do?"

"Unbound because of your annoying mouth," she muttered, cringing when he smirked. She sighed, seeing the shape and colors of her manor on the horizon ... a speck still, but nearing fast. "I'm afraid, Tem. And I weary of it."

Her unexpected confession washed away the last of his humor.

"He won't lose." Tem held up a hand to ward off her objection. "You chose well, blood of my heart. Ronin's cause is lost."

She nodded, if only to signify that she'd heard his words. But she waited until he veered toward his own manor before whispering, "If he doesn't accept, his strength will matter for naught. For there are none to rule us after."

Karl waited on the lower-level terrace, shrouded by overhanging boughs and vines. When he heard the bull return, his shoulders loosened, his fists unfurled ... and the fury in his eyes doubled.

It would be unwise to face her in such a state, he knew. So he stood in place long after he heard her steps on the balcony above, and even longer after the bull soared back into the sky.

"My granddaughter displeases you?"

Karl spun, unnerved by the man's silent approach. He schooled his face to show nothing more than faint interest. "Warwick, then?"

With a nod, the man stepped out of the shadow. "An old warrior needs the comfort of a seat."

Unwilling to offend, Karl had no choice but to sink into a chair opposite the old man's.

"So?" Warwick prodded.

Karl frowned, having forgotten the question. Recalling it,

he sighed. "At times, she does." When Warwick stared, he amended reluctantly, "She is a challenge. It is not displeasing. Infuriating, perhaps, but no … not displeasing."

"She has great passion," Warwick said, snorting when Karl flushed. "I wasn't speaking of that. She is my granddaughter, and such is best left unknown to me." When color began to rise in Warwick's face, he cleared his throat. "For life, seeker. She has great passion for life … and for dragons, and for this world."

"Will you sing her virtues to me, elder?" Karl asked, deliberately shifting his eyes to the other man's. "What makes you so certain I am worthy of her?"

"Assuredly you are not," he said stiffly. "But she is my granddaughter—"

"So you have said," Karl interrupted, but he dipped his head in response to the reproving look that followed.

"And you are her choice."

Both men fell silent, until Elera could be heard descending the stairs. Karl ran a hand over his face. "Your granddaughter is asking me to accept much more than just herself."

"Aye, she is," Warwick agreed, rising to his feet. "But sometimes you have to take the step in order to see the path."

Karl froze. "That is from the scrolls of the Initiates."

"Is it?" Warwick scratched his head, shuffling his feet with a simple smile upon his lips.

Karl glowered. "I see the intelligence in your eyes. This facade of senility is beneath you, elder."

Letting his smile fade, Warwick straightened to a height that would once have rivaled Karl's. "Be cautious of the eyes, seeker, and ever wary of the wisdom that makes them miss much more than they see."

"For the wise are oft misguided by their own arrogance?" Karl relaxed as he completed the riddle. "Clever, but not of the Initiates."

"A bit beyond their ilk, I think." And with his wink, the lightness of their mood was restored. "In any case, I prefer the former."

He left Karl wondering what an old man might consider beyond the Initiates, only moments before the sound of Elera's steps preceded her entrance onto the terrace. She stopped just short of walking into him as she rounded the corner. Of course, he'd moved to the corner first, to ensure their proximity.

He studied her carefully, noting the shadows of fatigue under her eyes despite the flush of passion over her skin. He had been terrified, knowing she flew alone after Ronin had promised to harm her in just such an instance. But after a few hours of pacing and ranting, he'd calmed enough to consider trying a different approach with her. Cool indifference might accomplish what temper and passion had not.

"You are well, then?" he asked, satisfied when her eyes clouded. Without waiting for an answer, he stepped past her in the archway and headed for the stairs.

"Karl?"

He stopped and turned, raising a brow before politely inquiring, "Yes, Elera?"

"I …" She tilted her head uncertainly. "You're not angry?"

"I was wrong to order you about. Certainly you have dealt with greater dangers than this one warrior." He nodded his head in dismissal, and watched her eyes flare.

"Karl?" she called again, following him when he turned and climbed the stairs.

"I'm tired, Elera." Entering her room, he slipped out of his vest and pants. "If you need something, surely it will wait till morning?"

Her eyes roamed hungrily over his body. Elera frowned. "You *are* angry."

"If I am—"

"You're angry, and you make your displeasure known by ignoring me." She grinned when a muscle in his jaw ticked. "Karl, that's a very … um … womanly thing to do."

"Then why don't you do it to me," he snapped, "and I will have peace the rest of this night!"

Her laughter gave way to shock when Karl crossed the room, slung her over his shoulder, and dropped her onto the bed.

"You prefer a more heated approach?" he rasped. His lips pressed against her throat as he followed her down.

"Karl…" She gasped when he ripped the wrap off her breasts. Her back arched when his mouth closed hot and hungry over her nipple. Using his hair to pull him closer, Elera cried out at the friction of his thigh between hers.

Before she could reach down his body and close her fingers around him, Karl imprisoned her wrists above her head. All the while he suckled her breasts, laving the valley between as he switched from one nipple to the other. When she lifted her knee to his waist, he tugged her pants down as far as he could. Slipping his free hand between her thighs, Karl cupped her warm, slick folds.

"There is nothing cold here," he growled, sliding a finger deep inside her, shuddering when she clenched around him. "Nor here."

His thumb circled her nub, moving faster when she started writhing against his hold.

By the order, this is a mistake. It was the last clear thought Karl had for a while, lost in the taste and scent and heat of woman. His mouth continued to suckle her breasts, his tongue flicking her rigid peaks until they glistened in the moonlight.

His fingers stroked into her with an unhurried rhythm. He could bring her fast to her peak. Knew exactly where to touch and when to stop, having absorbed these teachings as thoroughly as he applied the skill to Elera now.

But he wasn't thinking of his studies when he touched her. He was thinking of the sighs she made when his fingers traced her weeping flesh. Of her cries as he drew hard on her breast. And he was responding to every shiver, every writhe, every catch in her breath, with instinctive adjustments in pacing and pressure until she moaned, shuddered, and he felt her release against the fingers still stroking deeply inside her.

Only then did Karl remember himself. Even though he could not stop until she lay limp and sated under him, he did pull back the instant she whispered his name.

Eyes closed, he turned away to mouth ritual words of control ... repeating them until he thought his body might implode from hunger. If he had ever needed the strength of his training, it was now. Slowly and with great agony, Karl willed his desire back....

To no avail. It took four tries to slow his blood and force his body into a trancelike state of relaxation, but by the time Elera called his name three times, all evidence of his arousal had vanished. He could do nothing about the sheen of sweat coating his skin, and hoped only to keep the rasp out of his voice.

"Karl?" One hand pressed to her pounding heart, Elera sat up.

He stood and stared down at her. Saw the uncertainty in her eyes when she noticed his seeming lack of interest, and very nearly gathered her up to soothe the flash of pain that quickly followed.

"But you didn't ...?"

"No," he said, and knelt on the bed to hold her chin in his hand. "I asked only one thing from you, Elera. That you not put yourself in danger. Considering how much you ask from me, it should not have been so hard for you to bend on this small matter. But you refused."

He said nothing else, since further words would serve only to soften his rebuke. With a gentle brush of his thumb across her trembling lips, Karl grabbed a blanket and retreated to the terrace.

She did not chase after him, though he could see that she wanted to. Watching from the corner of his eye, he stretched out on the marble floor as she tugged her pants over her hips and slid from the bed.

She hesitated when he did not turn his head toward her, and in the glow from the lanterns, he saw her teeth come out to worry her lip. He closed his eyes when she slumped back onto the edge of her bed.

Sleep did not come to her quickly, but when he finally heard the steady sound of her breathing, he sat up and stared as she lay curled beneath the blankets.

It wasn't that he felt less angry, he thought, staring up at the stars as a soft breeze blew across the terrace. But most of his anger was directed toward his own lack of control.

It was the vulnerability in Elera that truly filled him with remorse. Her uncertainty had kept her from venturing onto the terrace for fear that he would turn her away.

But he could offer no reassurances or his lesson would have been for naught. He never wanted to have to commit to such a course of action again, or to see so much pain in her passionate eyes. Not to prove a point, not to keep her safe, not even to stake his claim.

Remorse kept him from sleeping. When Tem crossed the grounds a few hours later, he gave up on rest altogether and went in search of the rider.

From the secluded caverns facing Elera's terrace, Ronin crouched to watch and wait as dawn began to peek over the horizon. He could no longer get to her in the manor, not with the seeker always near, but he knew her claim was not accepted ... for he'd watched from this perch every night since the seeker's arrival.

And his eyes were exceedingly keen.

He had seen the hands of the seeker crawling over Elera's flesh. Had also seen the seeker retreat by himself to the terrace, until Tem had arrived a few hours later to practice swordplay.

Ronin allowed fury and lust for the woman who dared to defy him to fill his mind. He could not act, not when the bull paced a hill less than a hundred yards away. The dragon had interrupted his last trespass on these grounds after only a few minutes.

If he were to slip over Elera's terrace and take what she had denied him—with the seeker and her friend less than a scream away—he might not make it back out … especially if the bull's bellows brought the seeker, the friend, and possibly even old Warwick running to her aid.

Location was the key to circumventing the bull.

His pulse leaped when Elera stepped onto her terrace, drawn by the bull's rumble. But more than vengeance or even sexual fulfillment, Ronin wanted to rule, so he did nothing more than tilt his head, call his dragon … and leave the cover of his crevice to take to the sky.

Elera stiffened on the terrace, and Ronin curled his lips. Let her doubt that the seeker had the strength to protect her. Uncertainties would only heighten her fear. . . .

FOURTEEN

The sun was just rising when Karl searched Elera out. He frowned when he saw the extra layer of curtains darkening her rooms, and tasted just a moment of alarm upon noticing the locked terrace doors.

He relaxed when he heard the sounds of her bath running in the next room. Walking quietly to the doorway, Karl peeked into the room ... and lost his breath at the sight of her standing naked and wet in the sunken bathing pool.

The graceful line of her back captivated him, as did the slow movements of the cloth caressing her skin. She sighed as the steaming water lapped beneath her breasts. Karl watched her in silent thrall, lingering over the alluring curves of her body.

Was he supposed to resist her? Was he supposed to *want* to resist her? She did not love him, and in truth he did not expect it from her in such a short time.

But sometimes you have to take the step in order to see the path. It was not a popular saying among the Mattaen ... although the Initiates were more daring because of their youth, and tended to apply it too often. But even the Mattaen understood that *sometimes* the greatest knowledge could be obtained only with the greatest risk.

Karl grinned crookedly. The saying had never been meant to help a man in his position ... but he thought it applied. He also suspected the old man had known exactly what he was doing by mentioning it.

Elera had risked her life and her future in order to save her people ... taken the first blind step without ever knowing what would come.

If she could dare so much, how could he not have the courage to risk his heart?

He removed his clothes and dropped them in a pile on the floor. When Elera leaned backward in the tub to wet her hair, he crouched behind her and lifted the dark strands from her neck.

"You once asked if I would allow you to wash mine," Karl said as he eased into the water at her back. "I ask you now for the same courtesy. I am well enough," he assured her, removing her hands from his injury and tucking them back beneath the warm water.

She turned to face him, and he stared at her pale curves, now visible through the surface of the water.

"May I?" he asked again, lifting his eyes to hers.

With a silent nod, she shifted back around and surrendered to the sensation of his fingers gliding through her hair. "I don't understand you."

"So you've said." Karl's lips curved as he reached for the soap. He slid his lathered fingers through every lock of her hair, gently massaging her scalp until that dark mass was piled atop her head. Unable to help himself, he lowered his lips to the exposed nape of her neck.

"Karl ..."

Though her voice was laced with longing, he felt her hesitation before she leaned into his touch. Knowing she thought of the night before, Karl wrapped her in his arms and gently folded his body around hers. He couldn't help but have a physical reaction to the curves and scent of this woman, but he did nothing more than whisper in her ear, "I love you."

Her breath caught on a cry.

"As I loved nothing in all my days below. Say nothing," he murmured, sensing her intent. He kept her facing away from him long after he loosened his hold to rinse the lather from her hair. Even when the suds had dissolved from the water, his fingers continued to comb through her curls. "I wasn't meant for it, Elera. And I don't know if it is enough."

"To stay with me?" she whispered, reaching back to twine their fingers together.

Karl rubbed his chin over her head. "To rule with you."

He let her turn then, but merely lifted her to the edge of the tub. Moving close, he cupped her cheek. "Today is my last day, for tomorrow I must choose or leave. I would spend the hours of this one in your world ... alone."

He could see by the look in her eyes that she wanted to object. He felt her tremble as she tightened her grip on the panic showing beneath her lashes; then he stared in surprise when she nodded acquiescence.

"Elera," he whispered, raising her hands to his mouth. "Will you stay here, with Tem at your side, and keep the bull on the grounds so that I know you are safe?"

Some of her fire returned when she heard that condition ... and also a rueful look that gave him a moment's pause. After some internal struggle, she nodded again.

"And ..." His lips curved when her eyes narrowed. "Will you return the favor and wash my hair this morning?"

A reluctant grin lifted the corners of her mouth. "You ask much of me," she said, already unthreading the braids in his hair, sighing when his knuckles skimmed her jaw. "But Ronin's guards won't let you leave the grounds alone."

"Elera," Karl chided softly. He lowered her from the ledge and knelt in the bath so she wouldn't have to reach to stroke her fingers through his hair. With a sigh, he embraced rather than fought the burn of his body for hers. "Let me worry over such matters."

★ ★ ★

Tem was sitting in the courtyard, snoozing into his chest as Karl left the manor. But he was still attentive enough to lift a hand when Karl passed under the trees to duck into the caves beyond. Tem glanced at the riders watching the grounds from the cliffs.

They didn't budge.

The seeker who had once planned to enter the brotherhood that could bring destruction to their world now slinked around Verteva unattended ... and with nary a whisper to alert even the dragons standing guard.

Tem grunted, and dozed on.

It wasn't sight of the world or its people that Karl wanted, though his nature forced him to observe as he traveled. With only seven days to make his choice, he had to judge this world by the only people he had known during his stay. Tem for his good nature and fierce loyalty, and Elera for her spirit ... and the compassion she hid deep in her heart.

Then there was Ronin, though Karl knew little of the man except his thirst for power, and the loyalty he inspired through fear and might. The warrior wanted Elera as more than just a means to the throne, despite her thoughts to the contrary.

But people were people no matter their geography. Many had faults, few had virtues, and there were none who did not possess a little of both.

Karl ducked beneath a rocky overhang as two riders flew overhead. One of them carried a child on his lap. Laughter tumbled down from the boy in the sky, followed by his squeal after the dragon plummeted sharply in play.

He didn't doubt that he could live here, content to unravel the mysteries of these people, enthralled by their culture alone. But studying and ruling were two different matters, and he was not arrogant enough to believe that he could successfully combine the pair. Or that he even had the right. There were more dangers in this world than just the struggle for power.

He had trained for the upcoming battle to help even the odds, but also to observe the people doing the training. The furtive glances between Tem and Elera when his status in the Initiates had come into conversation had not gone unnoticed. Nor had he overlooked the elusive manner of the elder, Warwick. The man was far too intelligent to be unaware of his own references to the Mattaen.

Oh, there were many secrets here ... secrets he feared could stretch his beliefs, possibly even shatter his ties to the world below. It was this fear driving him to reaffirm the beliefs that were true to *him*, and not just to the creed to which he had adhered. A man who did not know himself could bring naught to his mate but weakness. Karl had been weak when he had given in to desires that had *nothing* to do with Elera's breath.

He had wanted her from the first moment he saw her, and he had to come to terms with that. He had known she was holding something back and still risked his place in the brotherhood to gain experience as well as knowledge. Perhaps he had not known himself as well as he had thought, and so had failed to realize what he had truly desired. This not knowing had been his true failing.

He would not dwell on it.... Dwelling on past mistakes brought weakness; learning from them brought strength. He had to accept what had happened and learn from it. Because he was staying.

He had wanted to stay from the moment Elera had stood bravely between Ronin's battle-ax and his neck, though he'd known he *would* stay only when she trusted him enough to let him go his way this day. While Karl might never have expected to take a mate, now that she was here, he would bring what strength ran in his blood to their bond.

It was strength and acceptance he sought on this solitary day. As he reached the ridge leading into the silver valley, Karl could think of no better place to renew his beliefs than in the ruins of a long-forgotten world.

"I can't just wait," Elera snapped, pacing the courtyard while Tem leaned casually against the stone wall. Despite his easy stance, his eyes were cautious, for she had been pacing and ranting all morning.

Knowing better than to point this out to her, he said simply, "I won't stop you from leaving, Elera. He's not king yet—"

"And if ever he is, your loyalty switches from me to him?"

Tem flinched, and tried to think of a way to avoid such an awkward subject. He grinned when he found what he thought might pass. "If he is king, then loyalty to one is loyalty to both."

Elera's eyes narrowed. "That's the most ridiculous thing I've ever heard!"

Perhaps not as clever as he had thought. Deflated, Tem took a step away from the wall, wary about having his back pressed against something when she was eyeing his throat so intently. Her sudden slump had him rushing to her side.

"Ronin was here," she whispered, after he tilted her chin in concern.

Tem kept the fear from his voice, asking, "He hurt you?"

"Don't be stupid," she snapped, though her tone lacked fervor. "He was only watching, but Karl didn't know, and I didn't tell him."

Tem nodded. "So that he could have his day."

"Yes." Covering his hand, which had risen to her cheek, she whispered, "And now I think I should have, if only to warn him to be on guard."

"He's going to be on guard, Elera." Tem stepped back with a sigh. "You want to go after him?"

"I told him I would stay here with you and the bull," she said, then lifted a brow. "Maybe you?"

"I gave my word to him when we sparred this morning, to remain in the manor until he returned." With his back to Elera and his face to the cliffs, Tem considered his next words very carefully. "Bull's got a strong will, and a fierce need to keep you safe. Couldn't really be your fault if he got confused while you were grooming him and, say, took flight and brought you where you wanted to be? It's presumptuous to think such a creature could be bound by his rider's word, when her heart wills her somewhere else."

Fully expecting her to dismiss his suggestion, Tem turned about. What she did instead was press her lips fast to his, and smile wide enough to rival his own grin.

"I forget how often you break the rules, and no one notices," Elera said, slapping her hand against his chest.

But he caught her arm before she could spin away. "Wait until dusk, Elera. At least then, you can still argue that you gave him his day."

And perhaps Karl will be back by then, Tem thought desperately, already regretting his impulse to help her. It was a knee-jerk reaction, one that stemmed from a lifetime of troubles shared. Still, if something happened to her on his suggestion ... if anything went wrong, he wouldn't be able to stomach it—though Karl and Warwick would ensure that he didn't suffer for long.

"It's only a few hours," he coaxed, sensing her indecision. "If Ronin knows Karl left, he will have done something by now. And if he doesn't know, he won't know to do anything unless he returns tonight."

Elera sat at the table with a sigh, staring at the sun as if she could will it down. "I'm not going to be very pleasant company for those few hours."

"What?" Tem staggered as if in shock, winking when her

lips twitched despite her glare. "I can see that you are humbled by my bravery." *Or my stupidity*, he thought, glancing toward the sun as if he could force it to remain in the sky.

Watching from within the manor, Warwick snorted. He sent his compliments to the seeker playing master to the pair of dancing puppets outside.

Feeling not nearly as certain of his mastery, Karl watched the sun dip below the crest of the land. He stood just inside the terrace of the ancient manor, having climbed the wall just slightly off to the side of the waterfall. The route directly beneath the falls would have been faster, but a single misstep on the slick rock would have sent him plunging to the jagged stones at the bottom.

Stepping back from the falls, Karl returned to the room behind the terrace. Here, earth, stone, and silver veins merged with the cinder-block and marble walls. The roar of the water bounced off the walls, locking the room in total seclusion, a feeling enhanced by what had once been a doorway leading to the rest of the manor. It now stood buried under the countless rock slides of the ages.

The sun glistened over the silver in the walls. As would the moon, he knew, when it filtered through the falls.

He decided that this room—void of any furnishings or tapestries—was as magical as the valley itself. Of course, he'd acquired a few essentials from the marketplace to make sure of it, then carried them up the wall in a pack on his back.

Now he waited expectantly for the one thing needed to complete this night. And as the last ray of the sun flitted along the silver in the walls, Karl smiled.

Even over the water's roar, he recognized the hum and beat of the bull's approach.

* * *

Elera frowned astride her dragon's neck, peering over his crest to study the darkened valley below them.

"I thought we were finding Karl," she whispered, rubbing his scales and leading him in a slow circle. He knew what she wanted. It wasn't the first time she'd had the bull search for someone by offering him the person's scent. But perhaps he was choosing to ignore her in favor of something he wanted for himself.

It wouldn't be the first time he had done that either, and often she enjoyed wherever they wound up despite her original wishes. But this was no such time.

Elera's tension manifested in her stiffening legs, which set the ridge of his spine bristling. She knew he would never lose control by extending it with her sitting atop him, but empathy was strong between them, and she felt more than just annoyed by this delay.

She felt afraid. Enough that after the bull landed on the cliff above the ruined manor, she shimmied off his neck and circled to his face.

"Karl," she said, gripping the sides of his snout and forcing him to breathe the scent of the man's shirt. When he tossed his head, sending her sprawling to the earth, she shrieked, "What's gotten into you?"

His answer was a gentle nudge after she regained her feet. Unfortunately, *gentle* to the bull meant a hard shove between the shoulder blades to Elera. She windmilled her arms to keep from tumbling over the edge of the cliff and into the falls below, then stumbled in surprise when someone shouted her name.

"Karl?" Elera dropped cautiously to her knees, peering over the edge. "What are—"

"Get away from the edge!" he hollered from his perch on the terrace, waving for her to get back.

"But how did you get down there?" she shouted ... and even through the dark, she saw him fist a hand in his hair. A score of curses competed with the sound of the roaring water.

He yelled back, "I didn't get down; I got up. Now will you get back!"

Elera nodded, but she couldn't be sure he saw. The falls had doused the light from his torch.

"Where is the bull?"

"With me," Elera called, shooting the dragon a reproving look when he butted her again.

"If you get him to fly you to the banks below, I'll lower a rope and pull you up!"

"Why go two miles when you can go one?" she muttered, and climbed atop the bull's head. Instead of sitting, she stood, holding on to his crest for balance, and sent him soaring over the edge of the cliff.

Karl had expected her to do as he'd asked and was completely unprepared for her reckless leap onto the terrace as the bull passed over it. He stumbled backward from the momentum that had launched her into his arms, and closed them around her so he could take the brunt of their tumble.

"Are you mad?" Running his hands over her body in search of injuries, Karl glanced up and then noticed the curve of her lips. She saw him take a deep breath as he hauled them both to their feet. "I would have pulled you up the cliff, Elera. Are you certain you're not hurt?"

"I'm sure," she said. He was still holding her in the circle of his arms, his busy hands running up and down her back. Concern flitted across her face. "Are you?"

"Lost my breath. And now I think you'll tell me what has you breaking your word to seek me out."

"The day's over," she whispered, and felt the heat rise in her face. The excuse had sounded better when she'd practiced it with Tem an hour earlier. "And I didn't mean to leave … but the bull was restless … and sometimes he just goes where he wants…."

She was supposed to have said that in the opposite order, and certainly not with a stammer. But Karl was slipping his hands through her hair, pulling her head back, and she forgot what his question had been to begin with.

"Elera …" Dipping his head to inhale the scent of her neck, Karl flicked his tongue over her skin.

They both shuddered.

"I was worried for you," she whispered finally. "And there's something I—"

She gasped when he dropped to his knees and pressed his lips against her belly. His strong arms wrapped around her waist to draw her close. Feeling the shudder rip through his shoulders, Elera twined her fingers in his hair to hold him.

"Wait," he murmured. Rising reluctantly, Karl took her hands and led her away from the falls. "Come; I have something to show you."

With a secret smile, she followed him into the room off the terrace. He looked so pleased that she decided not to tell him that she'd been here before, always with the bull's help. She knew to expect the glimmering veins of silver that set the room sparkling. She'd experienced the absolute feeling of isolation behind the thundering falls.

But nothing could have prepared her for the glowing candles arranged carefully about the wall. Or for the soft fleece in the center of the room, covered with and surrounded by the longbow blossoms she'd admired along their walk. Their sweet fragrance saturated the air, a seductive contrast to the wilder scents of earth and dragon carried on the cool breeze.

Karl had been watching her carefully, and now he gave her a rueful grin. "You've been here before."

"Not like this," Elera whispered. "Never…"

Brushing his thumb up the side of her neck, he leaned low enough that his breath was hot against her ear. "Never with a lover?"

His hand splayed possessively across her stomach, fingers tightening until finally she shook her head.

Lifting a brow, Elera shot him a curious glance over her shoulder… then narrowed her eyes. "You knew I would come looking for you."

He shrugged, pressing a soft kiss to her shoulder. Moving his hands up her stomach, he traced the line of her wrap, teasing the curves beneath. "I was fairly certain I could count on the pair of you to wriggle free of your promise to stay away."

"But we—"

"Without technically breaking your word," he interrupted, and finally did chuckle. "But I bet it was still daylight when you and Tem cooked up your plan."

Lowering her eyes, Elera pivoted in the circle of his arms and wisely changed the topic back to what was of interest to her. She wondered if he could feel her heart racing against his chest. "Do you want to be my lover, Karl? Is that why you waited for me here, like this?"

"Your lover?" Karl's body went rigid. "Would you let me? Without the kiss, without the claim?" He tucked his finger beneath her chin, and she struggled to meet his eyes as he spoke. "Would you let me have you, come inside you, bring you pleasure as I take my own? All without any assurance that, when tomorrow comes, I will choose to stay?"

She hesitated, sadness and doubt warring within her. She could not refuse him, not with her blood rushing in her ears and her body aching for his. But she had so hoped he would have decided to stay with her by the time they came together, that she could have felt treasured and accepted as Karl pressed his lips to hers ... embracing her as his love and as his mate before making love with her once again.

He had clenched his jaw during her silence, and she traced her fingers along the tight muscles as he studied her. With a rueful look, he parted his lips as if to speak. She laid a finger across his mouth, bit her lip ... and nodded.

FIFTEEN

Karl whispered her name as hunger raced through his blood. For a moment, he held her tight, molding her skin and scent to his frame as he attuned his mind to the sound of the rushing falls. Exterior focusing was a simple trick to distract the body from pain... he would use it now to distract his body from its rising needs.

He wanted her so much he shook with it, but he would not rush this night. He would touch Elera for as long as it took until every doubt he'd seen in her face disappeared.

Her sigh was soft against his skin as his hands started roaming, cupping her bottom, grazing her thighs, caressing the dip in her waist.

Keeping his eyes on hers, Karl backed her into the room, stopping when they stood in the center of the blanket. He eased the wrap from her breasts, letting it glide from her skin and float to the floor. He said nothing, speaking with only his eyes and fingers and lips as he trailed a path from her jaw to her neck, down through the valley of her breasts.

Her hands fisted in his hair when he knelt to caress the skin below her navel. He drew back and stared up at her, using deft fingers to unclasp the band at her waist. Karl tugged the material down, leaving it to gather at her ankles.

She wore nothing underneath, and bit down on her bottom lip as he brushed the tips of his fingers across her darker curls. His touch roughened, grazing down her thighs, the backs of her knees and calves. By the time he lifted each of her feet, removing her boots and pants, she was gripping his shoulders for balance.

Only after she stood soft and naked did Karl lean back and let his eyes devour every sweet inch of her skin.

"Karl," Elera whispered. Her cheeks grew pink.

He stood ... hands circling her throat, delving into her hair. He bent his head to scrape her jaw with his teeth, as she so often did with him.

When she swayed, Karl steadied her with his hand on her elbow. He took a step back to remove his clothes while Elera watched him with wanting eyes.

As bare now as she, he closed the distance between them. His breath caught when her hands roamed reverently across his chest. He dragged one to his lips, smiling sinfully as he gently bit her wrist. He remembered his quick shock of pleasure when she'd done the same to him on their first night together.

Elera gasped as she remembered also, and then grinned at him.

"I like this sound you make, Elera." He mimicked her words of that night, bending his knees and scooping her into his arms. "I long to feel it against my skin...."

He lowered her to the blanket, trying to be gentle. But she twisted against him, lips pressed to the hollow of his throat as she moaned. The sound skimmed across his skin, set his pulse skipping ... and he forgot to be gentle.

His hands tangled in her hair as a surge of possession swept over him. *Anything* ... he thought as he lay next to her, over her, pinning her thighs beneath his own. He could have anything, *everything*, with this woman ... and he would.

Moving one hand from her hair, he cupped her breast. His breath grew rough when her nipple instantly became hard beneath his palm.

His touch softened then, to circle, tease, and pluck. Elera

moaned his name, hands flexing in his hair, her thighs scissoring as she strained for release. Shifting his weight, Karl cupped her other breast. When she arched her back, his hands reached beneath her, lifting her until his mouth could close greedily over one upthrust peak.

She cried his name, and Karl's vision went dark. The flavor of her skin, the bite of her nails as her hands lowered to his shoulders ...

He shuddered, moving off her legs to slide his thigh between them. He rasped his tongue across the tip of her nipple.

"Karl, please!"

She twisted in his arms, and he felt her shudder when his lips closed fully over her, drawing hard. *Too rough*, he thought, but she wasn't complaining. His hand glided down her hip, gripping her thigh, caressing that soft inner skin as he stroked slowly back up. She was hot and wet when he found her. Karl trembled as he traced her folds, fighting the urge to plunge into her, to feast upon the madness that would come when he took her.

His tongue left her breast, licking lightly underneath before moving to taste the skin above her thundering heart. Pinning her atop the blanket with one hand on her chest, Karl scraped his teeth down her stomach ... nipping at her navel, grazing the soft slope beneath. All the while his fingers traced and teased her folds.

Only when his breath poured hot against her inner thighs did Karl stroke his fingers inside, growling when she lifted her hips. He looked up for a moment, felt the breath explode out of him when he saw Elera writhing beneath his hold. Her eyes were closed, her lips parted, and her breasts glistened where he had kissed them.

Karl applied pressure with two fingers, feeling a cold sweat wash over his skin when she cried out and tossed her head.

His thumb slid against the swollen nub between her folds, softly at first ... and harder when she bucked against his hand.

Blood thundered in his ears. He flicked her tender flesh again, circled it, moaning himself when he saw sweat beading across her skin. He wanted to watch her fall into that deep, dark pleasure. Knew he could have her there in three breaths if he tried.

But there was more to this than simple pleasure. Karl pressed his lips to the inner skin of her thigh. He couldn't seem to stop shaking from the effort of holding back—the rush of his blood had long since overpowered the rush of the falls in his ears—as he rose slowly along her body. His skin brushed over hers, sending the blood surging through his veins. But even after her legs curled over his, he held back. Even after she tilted her hips, moaning as the tip of his shaft slid between the soft folds of her entrance ...

He waited still, though it was costing him. His breath came in rasps, heating the column of her neck, the fullness of her parted lips as he leaned close.

"Elera," Karl murmured, locking her in place by tangling his fists in her hair. When she writhed beneath him, he growled, "Elera!"

Her eyes popped open, then widened when she saw his lips so close to her own.

Here was the look he had wanted to see: hope washing away her doubts, the sheen of tears as she realized that he had brought her here to be so much more than just her lover. He saw something else flash in her eyes, something soft, yet potent ... but he could wait no longer.

He shifted slightly, dragging his shaft along the heat of her ... and again, until they both trembled and moaned.

"I am yours," he whispered against her mouth, his mind calm and quiet now that the moment was here. Her fingers tightened on his arms at the barest press of his lips to hers. "And you are mine...."

His mouth closed hungrily over hers, claiming her even as he surrendered to their bond. As he swallowed her cry, he thrust deep inside her. Karl stilled for a moment, remembering her discomfort the first time he had pressed inside her.

She squirmed beneath him when his tongue stroked hers, thrusting possessively within her mouth. And he could no longer hold back. He moved his hips urgently against hers, too long denied this dark bliss and scalding heat. His arms tightened around her as he continued to surge inside her. Their cries mingled.... The taste of her lips was every bit as addictive as the heat between her thighs.

Pressure built between them, escalating as the sweat on their bodies heated.... His arms were shaking when Elera screamed her release into his mouth.

Thank the stars. It was his only coherent thought as he held her close and pulsed hard and unendingly inside her.

Of all the things he might have expected to see in the aftermath of their lovemaking, her silent tears were not one of them. But he could feel the moisture on her cheek when she buried her face against his chest. Her shoulders shook.

"Elera?" he whispered, skimming his lips over her cheeks. "This wasn't meant to make you cry...." His hands tightened in her hair as a thought occurred to him.

"You didn't hurt me," she whispered quickly.

"Ahh," he murmured, lowering his lips to hers once more. "You weep in awe of my tremendous skill."

She might have tried to snort in response, but the endearing sniff that emerged instead made his chest tight. He stirred inside her, seeing her shoulders square and her chin lift, defiant and desperately trying to conceal the soft emotion swimming in her eyes.

"Kiss me again."

A whisper of a demand, but a demand nonetheless. Karl obliged with a grin, gently this time, until her tears started anew.

"Elera," he chided, brushing her cheek with his fingertips. She wasn't listening, and he could think of nothing else to do but deepen his kiss until the hitch in her breath came from desire, rather than the emotions overwhelming her.

But since he *was* still inside her, holding his weight on his elbows to keep from crushing her, his own breathing became labored when he felt her body pulsing around his shaft. His member grew hard and full in her warm embrace.

"Please, yes, again..." She moaned and wrapped her arms around his neck as he rocked slowly and gently within her.

Perhaps if he had not been so caught up in her, Karl might have wondered more at the warning rustle from the bull outside the manor.

Instead, his lips found Elera's, and thought was lost.

Ronin climbed over the crumbling rail of the terrace, listening to the hot roar of blood in his ears. He'd had several near-lethal slips on the slick rock below, but those couldn't explain the surge of adrenaline that left him unaware of his surroundings. Rather, it came for the sound of Elera's cries drifting out of the room... along with the throatier moans mingled with them. Both sounds had long since ceased.

Not even a murmur could be heard from within.

Of course, Ronin would not have known otherwise. The roar in his head drowned everything out, including reason and thought... leaving only instinct to guide him silently across the terrace and into the room.

Now he stood and stared down at the man who had dared to defile Elera. Shifting his eyes, Ronin let them crawl over her curves, curled still against the seeker's body.

She was so soft ... soft and sated by another!

Blood seeped into his vision, shading the room in red. Without ever realizing he'd reached for the battle-ax slung over his shoulder, it was in his hands. His forearms bulged as he tightened his grip on the hilt of his weapon. He crept silently forward, only to stop within a foot of the interloper's head. But his charcoal eyes never once left Elera. She would die first, he decided, unaware that he whispered the words aloud as he raised his ax above his head. He would then fight the man who had taken everything Ronin would have claimed as his own.

He would relish every drop of blood spilled by his ax, savoring the seeker's horror when finally he fell atop the ruined body of his lover. They could remain here, bonded in blood, while Ronin ruled this world in their stead.

It was the whisper that woke Elera. A whisper of sound, a shadow across her face. Her eyes blinked open just as the unmistakable whistle of a blade slashed down toward her.

The ax pierced the blanket to embed itself deep within the marble beneath, but only Karl would feel the bite of its blade as it glanced off his bicep. He'd used his shoulders to shield her as he kicked the weapon off its trajectory. In the same fluid motion, he rolled beyond its range with her crushed tight against his chest.

Her confusion quickly gave way to fright. That was Ronin bellowing in rage, and Ronin yanking his ax from the floor to swing wide....

She grunted, shoved suddenly against the wall with enough force to see stars. Though she would remember well the wind from Ronin's blade whispering across her face. Just as she would remember Karl facing off with the greatest warrior in all Verteva, with neither weapon nor clothing at his disposal.

In true berserker style, Ronin swung again. Karl dodged,

having nothing on hand with which to counter. He stood between her and the warrior intent on shedding her blood, refusing to give any ground that might allow that ax to come so close to her again.

She could see blood now, red tracks spilling down his arm and dripping from the fist he had formed. But Karl looked steady, slate-hard, and keen to strike back.

He found an opening in the rider's swings and hammered a fist into his stomach. Ronin retaliated quickly. But his footing was off, and his elbow merely glanced off the edge of Karl's jaw, instead of crushing his nose.

Still, Karl's head snapped back, and Elera hissed in dismay when she saw the blood spurting from his mouth. She frantically searched for a chance to enter the fray. But as long as they fought in such quick, close quarters, she could do naught but distract her mate and get him killed.

So she watched and waited—then screamed when Ronin charged forward with the same strike that had nearly halved Karl on his first night here. Forgetting cool strategy, Elera rushed at Ronin with all the rage and fear boiling in her blood. She would not lose her mate now!

Karl cut her charge short with a simple flick of his hand, and sent her tumbling to the fleece.

Karl! Heart in her throat, Elera glanced up in alarm . . . and watched in awe as her mate flipped backward and over the blade that didn't draw even a drop of his blood on this, its second attempt.

He'd moved with the same speed that had assured Tem of his victory. His speed gave Ronin pause. Doubt flitted over the warrior's face. With a step in reverse, he studied the man Elera had brought to usurp him.

"Mattaen." His eyes narrowed, gleaming as they shifted toward her and he noted that she was no longer protected behind the shield of her lover's body.

Ronin's lips pulled back in a snarl. Sheathing his ax over his shoulder, he lowered to a crouch and released the blades strapped to his arms.

"Do not!" Karl roared, diving headlong into Ronin and knocking the blades away from her throat. One embedded itself deeply into the wall beside her head, and the other Ronin managed to keep as he and Karl slid across the floor.

The ax got lost in their tumble, but Ronin was already slashing with his blade. By the time each man leaped back to his feet, she imagined Karl had a new appreciation for the gift of Tem's *edge*.

Still on the floor, she grabbed the lost blade by its hilt, straining to free it from the wall. But she kept her eyes on the men disappearing into the darkness beyond the room. Sounds of their battle drifted in from the terrace ... a scuffle, a grapple, the sharp crack of stone.

Elera grunted, falling back as the blade loosened unexpectedly. Sparing no thought for her bruised backside, she leaped to her feet and raced through the archway.

The entire terrace plummeted away beneath her feet!

She managed to spin and grab hold of the stone, pulling herself back inside the room. She looked carefully over the edge and found Karl clinging to a teetering slab of marble. Water battered his back, and also Ronin's, where the rider hung just as precariously a few feet away.

"Stay there!" Karl shouted, recognizing her intent.

When Ronin shifted his weight to try to swing his leg over the edge, the entire slab dropped another few inches. He lost his hold, found another before he fell, and hung now with only a few fingers supporting his weight.

Elera rammed the blade deep into a crack in the floor at the edge of the room. Reckless now, she swung her leg over the broken terrace. Holding on to the hilt of the blade for stability, she began lowering her body so that Karl would be able to grab her leg and pull himself up. But the terrace shifted with her every motion, forcing her to maintain a painfully slow descent.

"So help me, Elera—" He broke off with a curse when she slipped, though she managed to tighten her grip on the blade before continuing to stretch out her body. "Drop one inch lower and I will mottle that ass in more shades of black and gray than all the dragons in this world!"

She knew exactly what waited at the bottom of the cliff, so despite her fear, she tossed him a cheeky grin. "Can't do it if you're dead, now, can you?"

Her words ended in a shriek when the terrace jerked. This time the marble screeched steadily against the stone beneath as it gave way beneath the weight of the water, the men ... and her constant movements atop it.

A final jolt cast Ronin directly beneath the falls. Even he did not have the strength to resist their force. He screamed Elera's name as the thundering water ripped him away from the terrace and drove him down.

She didn't have time to dwell on the betrayal in his tone. Sharp edges were biting into her stomach, scraping her thighs and breasts as the terrace continued to shudder. Throwing caution to the wind, Elera held the blade with just one hand ... and dropped. Karl was probably going to give her every single one of the bruises he'd threatened, but he reached up just as the terrace broke away.

His fingers found her calf.

She would bear bruises from that alone, but Karl must have realized that she couldn't support his full weight for long. He kicked off the tip of the plunging wreckage, swung fast for momentum ... and let go of her to fall free.

He slammed into the side of the cliff, and she breathed a sigh of relief when he found purchase in the rock. His grin was pained when he glanced up ... and she had to smile herself as she realized he was ogling her naked body ... even though he hung precariously off the dangerously slick rock. Something like thunder rocked the cliff just then, sending him fumbling for better purchase.

"Elera!"

"What?" she called, struggling with her weakening grip on the hilt of the blade.

"Do you think that's the bull climbing up?"

The bull chose that moment to plunge his claws into the rock beside Karl's head. Ignoring the man to see to his rider, the dragon climbed with wings spread wide, unhindered by the water rushing over its sleek body.

"I know I'm not supposed to ride him," Karl shouted from beneath a belly of scales, "but do you think he would let me hang off—"

"He'll kill you!" she cried out in terror, hearing Karl's stubborn grumble. "Don't touch him!"

"Elera?"

She dropped onto the bull's crest as soon as he was near enough, and hung her head over his neck. "I'll find something to lower—"

"Yes, that's good," Karl shouted up at her. "But perhaps as an alternative to using your body as the rope this time"—he raised a brow—"you could use the *actual* rope I brought along with me."

Sixteen

By wrapping the rope around a protruding rock, Elera gained the leverage she needed to support his weight as he climbed to the room. No sooner had Karl's feet found solid ground than he crushed her against him. The rope slipped unnoticed over the edge.

"You're bleeding," she whispered.

He pushed her back with rough hands. His eyes lowered, narrowing over every abrasion, bruise, and smear of blood marring her skin. Some of that blood was his, he reminded himself, easing his hold on her arms.

Elera tilted her head. "Still going to wallop my—" She squeaked as he pulled her hard against his chest.

"Don't joke. I almost lost you. And yes," he said, when she melted against him. "Every shade of every dragon. I promise it." He felt her lips curve against his skin.

He glanced over the edge of the terrace. It was disturbing to feel those garnet eyes upon him, but Karl refused to loosen his grip on Elera. The beast was going to have to become accustomed to seeing him touch her.

"Even Ronin couldn't have survived a fall like that," she whispered, squirming in his arms until he sighed and let her go.

"No," he agreed, and glared at the bull. "I thought he was supposed to protect you?"

"He does, but Ronin—"

"Was going for you." Lifting her chin when she averted her eyes, Karl added, "I was just in the way."

She was shaking with the cold aftermath of adrenaline, and did not object when he grabbed the fleece and wrapped it around her shoulders. "I'm going to have to go get the rope," she murmured.

"It's not the first time the bull stood by when Ronin threatened you," Karl said, refusing to be distracted. "I want to know why."

"Why does it matter?" Elera studied his face, then sighed. "The bull knows we mate. The riders, that is. So he knew I'd eventually take one, if only from the example of all the women who rode him before me. But he's also the sole bull in a race of females. He doesn't hurt them, but he *will* mate with whichever he wishes, whenever he wishes."

She pressed her fingers over his lips before he could speak. "The bull can't sense emotions in anyone but me ... but like most animals he can smell strong emotions. Ronin felt as much lust as anger toward me. Passion and violence are often mixed in our culture, and because the bull understands male dominance in sexual relations, I think the scent of lust confuses him. Enough to make him hesitant to interfere in what might have been a legitimate mating."

"Rape," Karl corrected, brushing his fingers through the tousled mass of curls hanging down her back. His eyes grew soft. "This isn't how I envisioned our night together."

"Karl ..."

"It's nearly at an end, anyway. And yes," he said, overriding the words he sensed hovering on the tip of her tongue, "I do know we need to make this public. But this night, Elera, was meant for us alone." So she would never doubt it was she he wanted, and not her kingdom.

Startled by a sudden thud outside the room, Karl shoved Elera protectively behind his back. The ripple in his shoulders eased when Tem peeked around the wall.

"Well, now," Tem drawled, eyeing the wreckage below and

the state of ruin within. With a wink for Elera and a smirk at her naked mate, he leaped down from his beauty and stood with his thumbs hooked lazily below his belt. "Looks like I am late to the party."

Karl searched through the rubble to find his pants. When his gaze fell upon a mangled feminine wrap, he murmured, "Better late than early in this instance."

Elera's cheeks bloomed as Tem's laugh echoed through the room.

Karl insisted they search through the wreckage, hoping to find some evidence of Ronin's death. But even knowing the current had probably dragged the man's remains over the falls at the end of this pool, he could not fight a lingering sense of doubt when they found nothing. Only after seeing the exhaustion in Elera's face did he call an end to their search. They flew home, Elera on the bull and Karl doubling with Tem.

Karl scooped her up and carried her to her bath, where he tended every scratch and bruise, all the while whispering words in a language she did not recognize. His eyes never left her as she tended to his shoulder, murmuring in sympathy over the condition of his fingers, brushing her lips over each abrasion.

After they were both washed, each wound gently and thoroughly cared for, Karl pulled the curtains closed. Tugging Elera with him onto the bed, he closed his eyes and stole the few hours of peace remaining to their night.

Something was fluttering up her neck.

Still half-asleep, Elera batted at the distraction before snuggling closer to the warm body covering her. She heard a soft chuckle, and a set of lips replaced the fingers that had tickled her. "Mmm," Elera murmured, leaning into the soft touch. "Karl?"

His teeth tugged playfully on the lobe of her ear. "Did you expect to wake with another?"

"I didn't expect to wake yet at all," she grumbled, though she wrapped her leg over his hip in a sensual invitation. "You could love me again to make up for waking me.…"

"Tempting," he whispered. He tugged her into a sitting position instead, keeping his hands on her shoulders until she caught her balance.

Her blurred vision cleared, and from what she could see, the man had business on his mind. Elera tilted her head. "Spanking time?"

Even though his lips curved, Karl shook his head. "Answer time." When the color faded from her face, he touched her cheek. "You and Tem and Warwick have all made references to the Mattaen, and even Ronin yesterday—"

"Karl, I don't think this is the time."

He caught her hand before she could rise from the bed. "I'm not facing your people half-aware, Elera."

"They're your people now too," she said softly, staring at the bed, the floor … anywhere but at him. He remained silent until she looked at him and said his name.

"I'm a part of you, Elera, and you of me." He tucked a raven lock behind her ear. "My heart hasn't gone any farther than that. I'm staying," he assured her, "and I'll do whatever is necessary. But I don't have any desire to rule here, and you've the right to know that."

"In time?" she whispered.

"Perhaps." Karl inclined his head. "I can promise to try, Elera. Nothing more."

"Warwick thinks I could rule"—she lifted her chin—"if not for the customs that require our leader to be a man."

He cocked his head. "You would use me as a figurehead?"

"I didn't mean that," she said quickly, blushing when he winked. "I just meant you're not alone. I can help."

He cradled her face in his palms. "Help now then, by speaking honestly."

"You'll be angry," she whispered, looking away.

"Enraged, assuredly," he answered, and pressed a quick kiss to her lips. "But I have been angry with you on countless occasions, and still I am here. Start with your father, Elera. The puzzle begins there, I think."

She took a deep breath, attempting to conceal her surprise. "I am reminded why I chose you," she murmured. She squared her shoulders. "May I get dressed first?"

"Elera."

She sighed. "As you wish. In the beginning..."

With a sigh, Karl leaned against the bedpost and crossed his arms indulgently.

"I jest," she said weakly. "We don't know the beginning beyond what I told you about the ancestral ruins. The puzzle doesn't start with my father, Karl. He just picked it up somewhere along his path."

"And where did his path start?"

She had postponed this moment as long as she could, but now there was no choice but to tell him the truth. "It started with ninety silver *tarlae* and a black blade of honor."

His jaw tightened, yet he hesitated only briefly before nodding. "He was an Initiate. That explains the reaction I got from Tem when he learned of my past. If an Initiate came here to slay the dragons, it stands to reason that any Initiate since would receive a poor welcome."

"Karl, you asked only where his path began," Elera whispered, shaking her head and fisting her hands to keep them from trembling. "My father never fell from it."

Even as his eyes lifted from her fists to her face, his body froze. Karl shook his head. "No, that's impossible."

"The Mattaen have always known of us. Maybe ... maybe they forgot for a while, until my father took his vows and found the scrolls more than half a millennium old in the tombs. He came to hunt dragons, as the Mattaen had once before."

Karl said nothing to contradict her. He simply eased from the bed to stand before the terrace with his arms folded across his chest. "Your father was a Mattaen monk, fully ordained."

"Yes."

"He would have broken his vows to have your mother, and you."

"Yes."

Karl's jaw clenched. "Did he come here alone?"

Elera shook her head until she remembered that his back was to her, then whispered instead, "He brought seven other men."

His jade eyes shifted, staring at her with far more patience than she would have thought him capable, considering her tale.

"Monks," he corrected quietly.

"Monks," she repeated with a nod. "Those who'd trained with him to resurrect the sect of slayers among their order."

"So the Mattaen train monks to slay dragons?" Karl asked, trying to keep his voice neutral. "This is the point of the order I was to join? To slay immortal creatures?"

"Not the point, no. But a part, yes." Sliding off the bed, Elera stepped tentatively toward him. "My father said the old slayers were a secret sect … one that was disbanded and eventually forgotten after our people forged a truce. Most of the monks who took their vows after the fighting ended never knew of us. They, at least, were honest … are honest," she corrected, seeing his back stiffen.

"What was the truce?"

His question was as abrupt as his tone, and Elera decided not to close the distance between them just yet. "The Mattaen would build the realm, which they did, and the riders would be forbidden from taking their mates from within it. As compensation, we were given free rein within the outskirts."

"That is a ridiculous truce, and over a small matter—unless you were truly destroying entire villages when they denied you your *prize*."

"Some were."

Taking a deep breath, Karl glanced at her over his shoulder. "This does not endear your people to me."

"Our people. Every history has its darkness, Karl." She said it quietly; she was beginning to recognize the temper he held in careful check. "The Mattaen are no different."

"Every race blames another for the darkness in themselves," he countered, then sighed. "Go ahead, Elera. Finish your tale."

"No, you're right." Without touching him, Elera stared out the terrace at his side, and explained, "Before the war, before the truce, it *was* a Mattaen who killed the first dragon to die in millennia; but it was done to save a village that had refused to relinquish its virgin sacrifice to the rider. While my people never started this war with yours, yours cannot be faulted for acting on behalf of the innocent. Initially."

"Initially," Karl repeated, waving his hand for her to continue. He stared out the window at the bull, who was on a nearby hill, basking in the warmth of the rising sun as three females frolicked atop him.

"Humans are mortal, and meant to die at some point or another. But the dragon ..." She shrugged. "This was a creature that would never have died of natural causes. A creature meant to see the ends of eternity. The dragons were deified by the early riders. Anything done to preserve our race so that we could continue to care for them was justified, including making an example of any village that thought to refuse the virgins the riders needed to procreate. I do not pretend that it was right; I'm just explaining the standards of the time."

"Your people went after the monk who killed this first dragon to die?"

Elera shook her head. "That dragon's rider slew the monk in that day's battle, and then killed himself. Our riders mourned for a long time. If the dragons had not also been in mourning, I think my people would have ridden and slaughtered every Mattaen and Initiate in the land. As it was, the bull refused to allow anyone to ride him or his females for years. More than one man lost his life trying. During this lull, the Mattaen formed the slayers … and they came for us."

She walked away to pace the room. There was understanding, even respect in her voice for the men who came in the name of the innocent, but it was the righteous outrage of a rider that flashed from her eyes.

"It was a slaughter. Four dragons were lost before we even knew the slayers were in our land. Two more dragons fell in the following battle." She shuddered, paling even as she said the words. "Every monk who set foot on our soil died, killed by the hands of the riders or torn apart by our dragons. And though it seemed for a time that the bull would wage war on rider and Mattaen alike, he relented and we rode again."

"How long did the war between rider and slayer last?"

"Decades, and with great losses on both sides," Elera whispered. "Is it a surprise that after so long a war, who started what faded quickly in the wake of who struck last?"

Karl considered. "The Mattaen offered a truce."

"They did not," Elera rebuked, and felt slightly vindicated when his brows bunched. The man placed far too much value on his *revered* Mattaen code. "They had no need of a truce; they were winning. But my people had a king for the first time in many years, though he was a man chosen from below by the bull's rider. It was he who went to the Mattaen and negotiated the truce. I think it was because he wasn't one of us, and yet came to love this world anyway, that his words carried weight."

"I am not he, Elera."

She said nothing, and he sighed.

"Part of this truce disallowed the destruction of entire villages?"

"Of course," she said lightly, though she couldn't quite manage a grin. Discussing this part of her history soured her stomach. "In return, we forbade them from kidnapping our people."

Surprise flicked over Karl's face. "Why would—"

"The steel," she explained. "They wanted the secret of the steel in our blades, and so took our people ... and I don't mean warriors ... to learn the craft."

Warriors would have died on the torture bed rather than manipulate the fire and allow the enemy to create weapons to be used against the dragons. But women and youths? They would have tried to resist, but the Mattaen had learned their secret in the end.

Elera inclined her head. "They cannot manipulate the fire without a constant supply of our people, which means their *knowledge* is useless."

"There were true abominations on both sides, then." Karl closed his eyes. "Are you expecting this war to come again?"

"I ..." Elera hesitated. "When the bull lost my mother, he left us for years, disappearing into the barrens, perhaps, or even beyond them. My people believed that he would never return, and since my mother's mate had also disappeared, we had no one to lead. Feudal warring broke out between us."

She looked away from him.

"Ronin was the one who changed all that. He came into power at the age of twenty, and if nothing else, he did unite our people. Perhaps with fear and brutality, but he did what was needed at the time." She shrugged. "I was eight when the bull returned, sitting at the top of a northern cliff with a bloody lip and a black eye. They used to torment me because of my father."

Her eyes glazed a little as she sought the bull.

"All of a sudden the ground trembled, and I felt a hot breath … I'd say on my neck, but the bull's mouth was easily as big as me back then…. I knew who he was, of course. I just didn't know if he saw my mother in me, or my father. I knew if it was my father, I was dead. So instead of running, I reached out to touch him, and he let me." She sighed wistfully. "A few hours later, I was flying over Verteva with the taste of blood on my tongue … mostly because I had bitten it. I fell half a dozen times before learning how to plant my feet."

"And just like that you were a rider?"

Elera tossed him a glance. "He chose me. And he deposited me here, in the manor that had crumbled from lack of care." She grinned. "You should have seen Warwick's face. All of them, actually, when the girl they'd tormented became the rider of the bull. But with rank came Ronin's interest."

Karl's eyes darkened. "You were a child."

"For a while longer, yes. But he was always watching." Moving back to his side, Elera stared up at him. "I don't want you to mistake my words, Karl. I'm not saying Ronin wasn't the man we needed to come together. But he was not the man to lead us into the future. I do believe war is coming again. So did Ronin. He would have taken his army into battle and spilled the innocent blood with the guilty. Dragons would die again—"

"So you expect *me* to war on the Mattaen," he snarled, as his temper finally snapped. "To spill the blood of those who have been brothers to me, and by revealing the faults only I know they have. You think me such a traitor to honor?"

Elera held her ground in the face of his anger, and even raised a hand to his arm. When he stepped away, she let it fall back to her side. "I'm not asking you to lead a war on the Mattaen, Karl. I'm asking you to find a way to stop it from happening."

SEVENTEEN

"How long do you think it will take before this land falls to the oceans below?"

Elera flinched. Karl had been silent for so long, she'd expected to hear nothing more from him until he had mulled everything over. "Decades still. Maybe sooner, maybe longer. There are degraded sections in our base that continue to recede with every passing year. Eventually, we'll be too heavy to sustain elevation."

"And what happens to the dragons if the silver pools are gone?"

"There is another place below."

Though she had tried to conceal her tension, he heard it in her voice. Karl glanced at her over his shoulder. "A natural place?"

"In deep caves, and …" Again, Elera hesitated.

He prodded, "And?"

"And all below the realm," she finished, staring back at him. "I expect that's why the Mattaen chose that area. Your brothers never had any intention of living in peace, only of prolonging it until we fell of our own natural cause."

"A good strategy," Karl murmured, "and in harmony with the teachings of the order … I do not understand how the brotherhood could have forgotten this war when your people did not—"

"We couldn't forget … even if we forgot the dragons, the Houses that once belonged to them are crumbled in ruins throughout my land to remind us."

He nodded, seeming to ponder before he asked, "Do you know how to access these caves? Where in the realm—"

"I've never been to the realm, Karl." When he gawked at her, she shrugged and continued, "The village where you got the map is the closest I've ever been."

Karl left the terrace to come and stand before her. "Your mother's mate ... he took his life with the loss of his dragon?"

"No one knows. He journeyed by foot to the realm, intending to line the wall with the blades of all eight monks who had entered Verteva. It was meant to be an insult and a warning to any who might think to follow. He never returned; we don't know if he succeeded. But if he did, the Mattaen have had twenty-four years to plan their strike."

She reached out to touch him, but he backed away. "What makes you think I won't help them instead of you?"

"Others will think this when your past comes out," Elera answered softly. "But you would not have accepted my claim so lightly."

He relented and drew her close, then pressed his lips to hers. Both of them were trembling by the time he pulled back to rest his brow against hers. "Will you give me a lock of your hair?" he asked.

"I ..." Elera frowned in confusion. "If you like."

Letting his hand slide through her curls, Karl explained, "The men of my father's people always kept a lock of their mate's hair woven into their own. I would do the same."

"Who are they?" she asked, watching his fingers after he sliced through a lock of her hair and began weaving it into his own. "Your father's people?"

"Were," he corrected, knotting the black and red strands together. "My father's people were of the outskirts, not within sight of the realm, but not far from its boundaries. A raid from a rival clan destroyed almost all of us. Those of us who survived ran to the realm, hoping for a safe haven. I earned my entrance into the Initiates a few years later."

Rising to her toes, Elera brushed her lips over his. "I'm sorry for you. I didn't know raiding still went on in the outskirts."

"The Initiates do what they can to stop it, and a few other atrocities."

He had seen to it that they did, Elera thought, and smiled. But his eyes were troubled once again. "Karl?"

"Is there anything else I should know before we face your people?"

"Probably, but now you know as much as I do." She tilted her head. "You're not angry, then?"

"I am." He traced her cheek with his finger. "I can be angry, Elera, and still love you with every breath in my body."

"As I also—"

Karl's fingers pressed against her lips, cutting short the words he had yet to hear. "I do not think you can. Not yet, and not with the influence of politics and war on your choice. I will have no untruths between us, Elera. It is enough that you are mine."

She left him then, because he seemed to desire solitude. She didn't try to correct his assumption ... not because he was correct that she didn't love him, but because he wasn't yet ready to hear it.

For such an intelligent man, he was certainly lacking in intuition. From the moment she had looked into his eyes as he had prepared to take both her body and her bond, Elera had known she loved her curious, passionate mate with every fiber of her being. How could he not have seen it?

He stood watching the sunrise, aching at the thought of what he must do. It was not the thought of betraying the Mattaen as a whole that had his hands fisted at his sides, but the thought of betraying the Mattaen as one.

Simon.

Tenacity had always been Simon's greatest strength, and that trait would eventually see him successful in his search for the dragon scrolls ... whether he believed Karl's story or not. But now that success would lead Simon to the slayers. If this war truly began again, could either brother ever know what lay in the other's heart?

Steps, Karl reminded himself, fingering the red-and-black lock in his hair. His first step was to see to these people. But already his mind was spinning, working ... and he knew his second step would be time, and the buying of it.

The sun had begun to descend behind the cliffs by the time he and Elera stepped into the inner circle of the gathering grounds. The bull rode the wind above their heads, where a gale was brewing, turning the sky as gray as her eyes.

Elera looked back and smiled at her grandfather as he walked in their shadow. Taking his hand, she pulled him to her side.

"There is respect in him for those like me," Warwick said gruffly, when she glanced at Karl to see if he would object. "He would not set me back."

"Then my choice was even more well placed than I had planned," Elera said formally, and ruined her tone with a hard hug to both.

Over her head, he and Warwick exchanged troubled looks. People were already waiting on the grounds ... riders and their families, men of riding blood and ability but with no dragon to complete them. Tem waited in the center of the gathering circle. His golden hair was pulled tight against his nape, his arms were banded with steel, and his chest was armored. He wore ax, sword, and blade, and his hands held the banner of his House.

The heads of thirteen separate Houses formed a rigid line behind him.

"Do they always do this when a claim is accepted?" Karl murmured.

"This is part of the ritual when a king is accepted," Warwick answered. "I've never seen such a display, for there has been no king in my time here. But it is written ..."

He didn't finish, for Tem stepped forward. His gray eyes were clouded, but his smile seemed genuine. "We've been waiting all day, seeker. Anytime you want to kiss the woman, feel free"—his grin peaked—"before my bloody arm falls off from holding this thing."

Karl glanced up at the tapestry, impressed by its intricacy. "How many Houses are there in Verteva?"

"Forty-nine riders for forty-nine Houses," Tem said, sobering somewhat. "They won't all come, seeker."

"Karl," he corrected absently, eyeing the ledges of the cliffs that surrounded the grounds. Many more people were arriving, though some chose to watch from afar.

"We haven't had a king not of these lands since ..." Tem struggled to remember, and shrugged. "It's been a long time. Ronin was not the only man who would have objected."

"Blood will be spilled over this?"

"Yours, if you don't stop thinking and start kissing." Aggrieved, Tem shifted the weight of his banner and looked to Elera for assistance.

She smiled at him, then gasped when Karl spun, lifting her with one arm around her thighs and claiming her mouth in a passionate kiss.

He vaguely heard the people cheering and then the more elusive sound of wings whipping in the wind. But Karl continued to deepen his kiss, desperate to consume her, until the feel of her hands fisting in his hair stole his breath.

He drew back, ignoring their audience to gaze into her eyes. His lips curved when he saw the dazed look on her face and felt her wobble when he set her back upon her feet. Karl leaned close to her ear and whispered, "So there would be no mistake in *my* claim."

Warwick was the first man to bend his knee before the seeker.

"That isn't—"

"It is," Elera said, placing her hand on Karl's arm when he moved to pull her grandfather up. "It must be shown, and first by the blood nearest me."

Tem knelt next, unusually solemn.

Here was a man to trust with one's life, Karl thought, standing silent and straight as the entire gathering performed the rite. Women, children, riders . . . all knelt in respect. Elera moved before him, meaning to do the same. He held her elbows, forcing her to remain on her feet.

"But—"

"Never." His voice was as firm as his hands. "You stand at my side, and nowhere else. I will not yield on this."

Elera nodded uncertainly . . . and sighed when he kissed each of her hands before returning his attention to the people. "Now you ask who objects," she told him.

She'd leaned closer to whisper her instruction, and Karl grinned at the still-kneeling crowd. "My mate asks . . . who objects?"

Elera opened her mouth, then closed it after she heard chuckling from the crowd. "Now you say, 'If any do object, let them—'"

"Now she says, if any do object, let them . . ." He cupped his ear, making a production out of waiting for her next words.

When they came, his eyes flared wide. "I do not think I can repeat those words, mate."

She snorted, then laughed herself when he caught her up in a quick kiss.

"I do not know your ways," Karl called aloud, placing Elera at his side to address the crowd without humor. "Nor your land, nor you. I do not presume to think I can lead anyone I do not know, or that I would deserve fealty from those who do not know me. So knowledge is the place that we will start." He grinned down at Elera. "If there is no one who objects."

Tem stood then, shouting loud enough that even the dragons in the sky paid heed. "I do not object! I, Tem of the House of Pryor, honor the rule of the bull rider's mate, as is our sacred custom. As is the will of those who ride now, and of all those who rode before us. The House of Pryor opens its doors in allegiance to the seeker made king … Karl of the House of the Bull!"

He clapped Karl on the shoulder.

"My blood for yours," he added softly, with a wink for Elera. "Even though I know you do not seek this path."

"True." Karl inclined his head, clasped the other man's arm … and grinned. "But your blood is a good incentive."

Tem flashed a wicked grin and stepped aside. The riders came forward now, introducing their Houses, their wives and children. The elders among them greeted Warwick with as much dignity as Karl, pleased that the new sovereign had not set his mate's grandfather aside.

After the words of fealty came music and dancing, and a feast that put even the festivals to shame.

"It is almost as if they knew I would not object," Karl whispered, when a lull in the festivities gave him a quiet moment to speak with the woman at his side.

Elera flashed him an arrogant look. Swaying close enough

to touch him, she pursed her lips and waited for his kiss. Yet he hesitated ... his breath mingling with hers, his shoulders rippling with tension. He stared at the ridges of the surrounding cliffs.

Elera turned to follow his line of sight ... and gasped. The riders loyal to Ronin lined the cliffs, with the wings of their dragons aggressively spread. Not just the riders stood atop those ridges, she saw now. Around them stood the dragonless army that Ronin had built from the weakest servant up. And as formal war attire shone in the last of the light, not a single word was spoken.

He felt Elera take a tentative step backward. Laying his hand over her shoulder in reassurance, Karl took a steady breath ... and waited. Everyone inside the gathering grounds eventually noticed the pair's distraction. Eating and dancing came to a halt as all eyes lifted to the army above.

"They cannot object," Warwick said, standing to his full height at Karl's side. His back creaked a little with the effort. "Objections needed to be stated when the question was posed."

"Then why?" Elera whispered.

"Ronin," Karl answered, jerking his head to the rider approaching from the sky. "Not so dead as we might have wished."

Her hands started to shake, and Karl brought them to his lips until their trembling eased. He could do nothing to ease the fear on her face. His eyes narrowed, honing in on the rider swooping as low into the gathering grounds as his dragon was capable.

"He still can't object," Elera whispered.

"No," Karl agreed, brushing his knuckles over her pale cheeks. "He cannot object. His intention, I think, for he would not have been victorious had he done so."

The same law that would have forced their challenge despite the injury Karl had sustained would have worked against Ronin today. Now he was the one torn and bruised.

"By coming late, he suffers no defeat and maintains the illusion that he was not here to voice the objection he feels." Karl glanced briefly at Elera. "You underestimate this man's mind, I think."

"Intelligent in war," she said softly. "Not in peace."

Sometimes the former was all it took to achieve the latter, but Karl said nothing, and instead watched Ronin drop from his hovering dragon. The man stumbled on his landing, but moved quickly to stand before the couple.

His animosity seemed to emanate from him in waves, but his torn and battered body would leave little doubt in the minds of the people that he had already placed an earlier objection. More important, that he had lost it.

"Ronin of the House of Samson honors the House of the Bull."

The House, not the man at its head ... but Ronin wasn't finished. "Yet the House of the Bull has been led astray, first by the mother and now the daughter."

He paused, relishing the fear glittering in Elera's eyes. If he was surprised that she did not object, he hid it well ... and didn't see that it was Karl's hand tightening on hers that compelled her to silence. His past would have to be revealed at some time, and while Karl might have preferred that it happen later, it was just as well dealt with now.

Hiding his smirk, Ronin leaped atop a boulder and pointed with his ax. "The seeker being given your fealty is of the Mattaen, come to slay as they have in days long past. I say he dies before being given the chance."

Silence swept through the gathering as all eyes turned to Elera and her choice for king.

"Strike him down," Tem said, stepping between the couple and the warrior.

"Tem…"

Ignoring Karl's warning, Tem continued. "You could not last evening when it was still forbidden. Do so now, if you dare."

"I objected to the loss of my woman last eve, perhaps out of turn … but if I was defeated, then I should not be here now," Ronin shouted aloud. "It will not be my blood, but yours, Tem of Pryor. I say Tem knew of the seeker's lineage. I say it must be Tem who fights the challenge, or Tem who dies a traitor at this Mattaen's side."

Tem winced, realizing belatedly that Karl had tried to warn him of this trap.

"What says the rider of the bull?" someone shouted, and it was here that Karl saw the prestige Elera had, king or no.

But she was trapped and knew it well. To deny Ronin's challenge would condemn both men, and perhaps also herself. To accept would lose her one. She looked at Karl, saw no help in his eyes, and turned to Tem.

"You must accept, child," Warwick said from behind her, too softly for anyone to hear except Karl and Elera.

She took her place at the edge of the challenge ring. "Karl of the House of the Bull is no Mattaen," she called out as thunder cracked the sky. "He walked as an Initiate, with no knowledge of this world or the race of dragons until my interference in his life. He came here to seek, as is our way, and not to slay. Karl of the House of the Bull will fight to defend that truth, and his life, and his rule."

She took a breath before turning to the friend who'd guarded her heart all their lives.

"Tem of the House of Pryor is now, and has always been, loyal to Verteva. By the strength of his arm and the purity of his challenge, he will reavow his loyalty to blood and dragon. Name your terms."

"The terms are to the death!" Ronin shouted amidst the roar of his army on the ridge.

"The terms are decided by the challenger, not he who suggested the challenge," she snapped, and Karl had the satisfaction of seeing Ronin's face purple. She jerked her head toward the circle of challenges, where Tem waited, already tossing his formal attire aside.

Only cloth would stand between the coming bite of steel to flesh.

Karl caught the blue-toned blade Tem tossed to him, and entered the ring.

"First blood," Tem said quietly, and Karl knew most men would think Tem's terms as weak as his chosen weapon. But he was grateful when some of the fear left Elera's eyes.

He had done no more than nod when Tem flipped the blade in his hand, spun, and swiped. The wind of it whistled passed Karl's throat, close enough that it might actually have drawn blood. When he landed on his hand, having dropped back to avoid the slash, he fingered his skin just to be sure.

Tem was already tossing the blade to his other hand, dodging the kick meant to knock him off balance ... and slashing again. Countless attacks, all fast enough to send sparks streaking across the silver in his blade.

If not for the reflexes Elera so admired, Karl would have been sliced to ribbons in those first precarious seconds. But he found his bearings quickly enough, then countered with a few lightning-quick swipes of his own ... and marveled that Tem had the speed to evade each one.

They rarely crossed blades, content to feint and weave as they sought first blood. By the time the rain started falling, each was drenched with sweat and breathing hard.

"You held back while training me," Karl accused, though his tone rang with approval. He rolled to the ground, spun, and swept Tem's legs out from under him. His blade scraped the earth a hairbreadth away from the other man's flesh.

"A bit," Tem admitted, regaining his feet with a grin. "But the blade is not Ronin's strength; it is mine...."

He lunged, slicing through the material of Karl's shirt. When he saw Tem's crestfallen expression, Karl simply laughed and knocked the rider back to the ground with a boot to the chest.

Stripping out of his shirt, Karl swiped a hand across his stomach and held it up for all to see. Tem had confided that his people had never regarded him as a formidable warrior— at least, not a warrior of the same caliber as those in Ronin's army. They hadn't understood that Tem could never have joined the army, not when his oath would conflict with his love for Elera. But with both men holding their footing in the muddy ground and pelting rain, and the crowd watching in amazement, Tem's status as a warrior renowned for the blade was surely set in stone. The rider did not hold back, despite their friendship, which confirmed his loyalty to his people. Even beaten, his blood and heart would be proven pure.

If Karl was defeated, Elera's people would believe he was a Mattaen slayer. He would die that night, perhaps torn to shreds by dragons, and Verteva would have lost its king more quickly than it had gained one.

Suddenly, all motion ceased within the darkness of the ring. Karl and Tem stood with their blades hanging limply at their sides, each measuring the mettle of the other.

When lightning lit up the sky, one blade dripped with blood.

The king had prevailed.

EIGHTEEN

Tem held his hand over the diagonal slash across his chest. Though the warrior had not desired any other outcome, he grimaced when he saw the blood smeared across his skin.

"I'll have to work on that if I am to best you another day," he grumbled, but winked at Elera, standing pale against the shadowy cliffs at her back.

Tem bent his knee for the second time that night.

As the crowd knelt with him, Karl stepped forward and pulled him to his feet. He looked over the wound, wincing inwardly. He would have to work on his mastery of the blade, for he hadn't meant to cut so deep.

"Have Elera see to that," he said now, quietly.

"If you held back," Tem growled, noting both the tone and the look of regret, "We'll continue this challenge with terms of death and not first blood."

Karl grinned. "I might have held back if you'd given me the chance to think of it, friend."

Tem rolled his eyes when Elera tended to her mate first.

Her wet hands moved like ice over the healing wound along his stomach. But Karl knew their trembling came from more than just the cold rain.

"You did well thinking on your feet," he whispered, tipping her chin to his mouth. "See to your friend now."

She turned then and saw the deep slash across Tem's chest. She glared at Karl, obviously preparing to deliver a lecture, when the soldiers on the cliff suddenly raised their voices.

A gesture from Ronin's hand quieted them. "I did not think you would lose, seeker," he whispered.

"No," Karl agreed. "You thought Elera would."

Ronin swept his eyes skyward and proclaimed, "Ronin of the House of Samson accepts the outcome of the challenge. I offer my ax and my warriors to the seeker turned sovereign." Looking back at Karl, he added quietly, "Such a king might do well with a strong army at his back."

It was a clever speech, Karl realized. The man had made it clear to all who listened that this was Ronin's army, offered out of generosity rather than fealty.

The rider's eyes gleamed, and Karl knew exactly what would happen if Ronin ordered an attack; the men on the ridge outnumbered the riders in the circle thrice over. But Ronin would lose standing with both sides for dishonoring the rites of the people and opposing their rightful king.

They would have their own battle. Perhaps not tonight, but soon. This was not a man who would renounce his cause so easily … or forget his revenge on the woman who had refused him.

Karl's hands fisted at his sides, but his words carried steadily over the howling wind. "A wise ruler would have no need of an army, though he would keep one nonetheless." Looking at Ronin now and not the people, he added, "I will take this army from you, Ronin of the House of Samson. With both hands, I will hold it firm."

Looking less confident, Ronin knelt, barely brushing his knee to the earth before lifting his hand to his men. They knelt as one, each shouting the name of his House … though not to whom he swore it. It was another slight, for they could be paying homage to either Ronin or him.

Knowledge of this shone in both their eyes as Ronin looked at Elera and said, "May your mating bring you as much pleasure as your mother's brought her."

Tem's fist shot out before Karl's could, connecting with Ronin's jaw and sending the man sprawling onto the dirt. "Verteva is united. Let us celebrate in the way of warriors this night," Tem shouted, planting a hearty grin across his face to ease the wariness of the crowd. "Challenges aplenty, and to the victor go the spoils!"

He grabbed a nearby woman and kissed her jovially on the mouth before setting her back on her feet. She shrieked when his hand slapped her backside, moving her out of the battle circle, but humor flashed in her eyes. When several other women sidled closer, Karl could see that the good-natured rider was a favorite among them.

Tem took a swig from a flask and beckoned Ronin forward. When the crowd cheered, Karl realized that Ronin was left little choice but to draw the ax he could barely lift.

Ronin grinned at Tem through a mouthful of blood. "You might not taste my steel this night, traitor, but you would do well not to forget that it beckons for your blood."

Tem's *spoils* seemed more than happy to care for the gash on his chest, and Elera was free to walk with Karl for the remainder of the night. The rain abated shortly into their celebration, allowing the crowd to feast and brawl until sunrise.

"In case I forgot to mention it," Elera whispered, tucked against his side as they walked the long path home, "you did well, also."

She stumbled, giggling into his shoulder when he swept her into his arms.

Karl's lips twitched. "I thought you did not like the drink." He had tried it, and the stuff did indeed scorch a fiery path down a man's throat ... though to his credit, Karl had managed to keep the tears from his eyes after that first gasp.

"Fire-brew," she corrected. "I was forced to toast your prowess many times. It was my duty as your mate."

"Mmm," Karl murmured, listening to the way she slurred her words. "I did not see the strength of its effects on you earlier."

Sighing, Elera nuzzled closer when he jogged the steps of her manor. "Hits me late ... and"—she hiccupped, giggling again—"and fast."

The world spun for both of them when she twisted in his arms, facing him head-on with her legs wrapped around his waist. "Elera ..." he called, smiling softly, waiting for her eyes to focus.

"I want you," she whispered, sliding enticingly against him.

When he spotted Warwick out of the corner of his eye, Karl winced. The old man raised his eyebrows in amusement when he heard the words and saw his granddaughter's condition.

"Elera," Karl said firmly, and again in despair when her hands started roaming between their bodies.

Forsaking his attempt to assure the elder that he was not going to take advantage of her, Karl raced up the stairs....

Elera did not seem amused, however, when he finally reached her room and peeled her limbs away, holding her wrists to keep her hands safely on the bed ... and off him.

"I'm not very drunk," she protested, and ruined her denial with a hiccup. Her squirming made him ache to bury himself in her soft heat.

"What if I were to tell you that the night of acceptance had to end thus, or it would be null?" she whispered.

"I would remind you," Karl whispered in her ear, wincing when she arched her back and brushed the tips of her breasts against his chest, "that your claim was accepted last night and fully ... consummated, as it were. Besides ..." He shifted his gaze to the golden beams streaming through the curtains. "This night is already ended."

She fell limp beneath him, and Karl brushed his lips across her forehead.

"Before you sleep"—her soft snore drifted to his ears—"I would have one more lock of hair from you, my mate."

Elera murmured incoherently into his chest. He would answer to her later if she noticed the missing tress. With a sigh, Karl reached for her blade on the bedside table, and let the thin lock slide between his fingers. After tucking her under the covers, he moved to the bedside table and removed his own black blade.

Karl sliced a lock of his hair to weave with hers, then wrapped the braid around his Initiate's blade. With a final glance at his sleeping mate, he locked the terrace doors and stole silently from the room.

The bull lifted his head, watching him racing across the grass and up the cliffs. But after a yawn that displayed his impressively curved teeth, the beast burrowed back into the muddy hill.

Uncomfortable with leaving Elera alone in the best of circumstances, Karl moved as quickly as he could. He kept his eyes on the sky, but no riders hovered around her home tonight. Ordering every dragon and rider away from her grounds had been his first sovereign decree ... much to Elera's humor and Ronin's temper. No doubt some secretly remained stationed about the cliffs, but they would not have seen him leave.

The rain was falling again, drizzling over his skin, soaking through his hair until it was plastered against his face. A dragon's paw engulfed in flames stood stark against the crimson of Tem's banner as it waved over the foremost cliff. This was his destination.

He narrowed his eyes when he heard feminine sounds of pleasure drifting down from an upper terrace window, then sat on the ground and settled in for a wait. It seemed like an ideal time to try to feel the echo Elera had mentioned, and so he lifted his wrist and concentrated.

He felt nothing. Not by clearing his mind, by closing his eyes, or even by attempting to meditate. He sighed, thinking that perhaps the noises from the room above had distracted him.

They went on for a long time, and he was struggling to contain his impatience when Tem finally emerged onto the terrace.

The rider threw back his head to catch the rain, and Karl moved. He was leaning against the rail by the time Tem opened his eyes. They flared in alarm, annoyance, and finally the recognition that the seeker turned king stood ready with a task for him.

"Already?" Tem asked, glancing back at the woman sprawled fast asleep across his bed.

Karl inclined his head, skimming his eyes over the stitches marching across Tem's chest. "If you're well enough."

"I am." Snagging a pair of pants from within the doorway, he slid them up over his legs, then stared into Karl's eyes. His normal humor was lost beneath the weight that came from having his sovereign's trust. "What is it you would have of me?"

Karl held out the blade wrapped in his and Elera's hair. "Deliver this."

Tem didn't ask what it meant. He covered it with a cloth and reached for his shirt. "Where?"

"To the Mattaen temple," Karl said, and watched Tem hesitate. "Wait on the stone wall surrounding their grounds at the exact place that the sun strikes on the fourteenth hour. There will be a monk by the name of Simon who will come there to meditate. Give it to him, say nothing, and leave quickly. He will understand."

"You would betray us?" Tem asked quietly.

Karl answered just as softly, "I hope I betray none, though it may be that I toe the line with my former brothers. Can you get through the wall of the realm unnoticed? And out?"

Tem studied him for a long moment. In the end, he nodded.

"Leave now," Karl ordered, noticing the woman beginning to stir within. "Journey safe, and return soon. Elera will have my head for sending you without telling her first."

Tem chuckled with little sympathy, and lifted his hand to the dragon waiting atop the roof of his manor. When he saw Karl's surprise, he smirked.

"She would have attacked anyone else." After grabbing a travel bag, Tem swung over the edge of the terrace just as his beauty dove beneath it. He hovered there with her for just a moment. "If she didn't like you so much, you would not have earned my trust so easily."

Karl watched the pair fly off, impressed as always by the ease of Tem's bond with his dragon. The woman within was nearly awake. By the time she stumbled onto the terrace, muddled with drink and lovemaking, Tem had disappeared under the wave of the horizon ... and Karl was halfway across the grounds, heading toward home.

NINETEEN

He approached the bed, relieved to see that his mate was safe and still sleeping. Karl leaned forward and allowed the water from his wet hair to drip onto Elera's cheek. She burrowed deeper into the blankets, murmuring as the bed dipped, then gasping when two hands roamed suddenly from her belly to her back.

"You're freezing," she said, pretending to struggle as he drew her up. "And my clothes are gone."

"They were wet," he said, dipping his head to sip at the tender skin along her collarbone. "And you're right: I am cold."

He said it with a grin, feeling her nipples tighten when they brushed against his icy skin. The slur in her voice was gone, so with his hair dripping over her face, Karl tossed the blankets aside and closed his hungry mouth over one rigid peak.

Elera stopped fighting to moan instead, sighing in disappointment when he released her.

"You are not feeling ill?" Moving up her body, Karl brushed her hair back from her cheeks. He lowered his head and lapped droplets off her skin.

"I'm not sober enough to be sick yet," Elera whispered, managing to wriggle her thigh free of his and swing it over his hip. "If you've any commands for me this morning, my king…"

"A gasp," he growled, tugging her head back to scrape his

teeth along the column of her throat. As ordered, her quick intake of breath filled the room. Karl grinned. "A moan."

She cried out when he slid his tongue over the tip of her breast.

After his teeth took the place of his tongue, he teased, "That gasp was out of order.... Ah, that's better," he encouraged at her moan, finding her heat with the hand he slipped between her thighs.

"You're toying with me," she rasped, arching her back as his mouth trailed down her stomach.

"Trying to." His lips curved beneath her naval, skimming over her darker curls before he moved between her inner thighs, eager to reach the sweetness waiting there.

"Karl..." Elera whispered.

"It is forbidden?" He hesitated, for he knew it to be taboo in some cultures, this tasting of a woman to bring her to pleasure. He'd read it. But he'd also read that others allowed it, and that the act was overwhelming for both the woman and the man. Karl had wanted to try it the night in the ruins, but, unsure of customs, had not.

Now he waited for her answer.

"Nothing is forbidden to you," Elera said, lifting her head to gaze down at him. Karl looked up at her, his face cradled between her thighs, his hair brushing against the sensitive skin there....

Elera squeezed her eyes shut.

"I would like to, if you do not object," Karl rasped, already feeling the rush of blood beneath his skin ... and hers. A blush spread across her breasts, and suddenly he could smell her arousal. She was growing damp from his breath alone.

Lifting her hands above her head, fisting them in the pillows, Elera whispered, "Do your worst."

"Is it to be a battle, then?" he asked, watching her closely.

"Do you remember what it felt like when I took you in my mouth?"

His eyes burned hot, all humor forgotten. "No mercy, then," he whispered. Karl tugged her close and took his first taste with a long, slow lick. He couldn't be sure which was more intoxicating ... the wild, sweet taste of her, or the wild, sweet sounds she made while he lingered, stroked, and brushed his tongue across her swollen nub. Her hips arched when he took it between his lips and suckled.

Elera cried his name, and the frantic movements of her hips told him she was close to her peak. Her hands left the pillows and delved into his hair—to pull him away or draw him closer, he didn't know. Nor did it matter what she wanted. She was his mate now, and he would pleasure her until he was satisfied that she could stand no more.

She whimpered when he released her. He moved down to lick the center of her folds, eager to taste more of the dark, musky flavor. When her frantic movements pulled her away from his mouth, he growled and then used his hands on her hips to hold her down as he flicked his tongue over the ultra-sensitive point concealed within the nub itself.

"Karl!" Elera's eyes went dark as the sensation took her. From his position between her legs, he watched as she surrendered to pleasure with long, throaty cries of release. As her thighs trembled against either side of his head and her damp folds pulsed around the fingers he'd pressed deep inside her, Karl lost control.

He slid up her body to plunder her mouth, groaning against her lips as he shifted his weight between her thighs to drive full and deep inside her. She gasped, and he paused, nearly mad with the desire to take her but unwilling to cause the slightest hurt. Her wet heat tightened upon his shaft. The muscles in his shoulders and back rippled as he struggled for control. He had to remain conscious of the harm he might inflict in his inexperience. He hooked his arm around her waist and pulled them both until he was kneeling and her legs were wrapped around his waist.

"Ride me," he demanded hoarsely, placing her hands upon his shoulders.

His lips found hers the instant she tilted her hips to take him inside once more. She set a soft, slow rhythm designed to drive him mad. He tightened his fingers in her hair, dug them into her thighs as his hips thrust hard to match her rocking.

Elera alternated the rhythm: fast and shallow, then back to slow and deep. She grinned when his eyes caught hers as they both gasped for air.

"Who toys with whom now?" Karl rasped, twining his fingers in hers.

Elera pressed her breasts into his chest, and he was lost. Karl reared back, then plunged deep inside her with one desperate stroke. He flinched when she made a small noise and caught her bottom lip between her teeth.

"Forgive me," he whispered, terrified that he had hurt her yet shaking with the effort of holding back. She slid slowly up the length of him until only the head of his shaft was nestled inside her. Her soft hand caressed his cheek just before she slammed back down onto him.

Before she could repeat the motion, Karl dragged their locked hands to her bottom and held her immobile.

"It is the power of it," Elera whispered, clenching her inner muscles around him, "and not the pain that takes my breath, my scholar."

He wrestled with that for a moment, but finally shuddered. Moving his hands to her hips, he raised her up and then drove deep inside her, grinding her mound against his body. Both of them cried out as he raised her back up so that she could plunge down again.

Her sounds of pleasure grew louder, and he soon forgot his

consideration. He took her with rough, frantic greed, pistoning into her until he felt her muscles clenching rhythmically around him.

His fingers tightened on hers hard enough to leave bruises. He wasn't sure how much longer he could maintain his rhythm before he came. "Elera, now …"

She screamed as he thrust into her once more, sobbing his name before tumbling off the edge of her second release. Her shuddering climax brought on his own.

Burying his face in her neck, Karl roared her name.

"Drink this," he whispered, rousing Elera from her sleep. She had succumbed shortly after their lovemaking, and he smiled as she groaned and attempted to bat him away. "Elera, I command it."

She snorted, and followed the sound with a second, much weaker groan as he tucked his arm beneath her neck and slowly raised her up. "Warwick says it helps with the aftereffects of your fire-brew. Now drink."

He held the goblet to her lips the moment she parted them to argue, so Elera had little choice but to do as he commanded. Eyes wide, she cupped her hands over his and swallowed every last drop. Her face turned pale.

"Going to be sick …" she whispered.

"No, you're not," he said firmly, holding her close and whispering words meant to distract her from her nausea. When her color returned to normal, he kissed her hand and laid her back down.

"I do not think you should partake of this brew…." He frowned suddenly, staring at the hands he held, noticing the bruises around her fingers and between her knuckles. Faint, but put there by him, he realized.

Elera attempted to draw her hand from his grasp. "It's nothing."

"Only because you have greater pains in your head," he rebuked, brushing his lips over her knuckles before tucking her hands beneath the blanket with the rest of her.

"Karl?"

"Mmm?"

"Would you like to see how the steel is made?"

"I would like that"—he traced her jaw with his finger—"when you have rested some more."

Elera glanced questioningly at him when she tried to see the sun and then realized that he'd closed the curtains.

"Well past midday," he said softly, "but you slept little, Elera. I would not steal you from your bed."

"Our bed," she corrected, pressing her hand to her forehead as if she were attempting to will away her dizziness. "Unless you would choose another room?"

He stared at her, insulted that she would suggest it. "I will not sleep parted from you, whether that is custom or your preference."

"I meant another room for us," Elera said quickly, unsuccessfully trying to hide her smile behind her hand.

Pretending not to notice her amusement, Karl tipped his head toward the terrace. "The bull watches this room from the hill. I have found no fault here."

The blanket had fallen away from Elera's breasts, and he spent several moments enjoying the view before he dragged his gaze upward and saw her pressing her hands against her temples. "A cold bath and I'll be well enough," she said. "If you don't want to wait, I'm sure Tem would be happy to show you—"

"I will wait for you," he said. Perhaps he was a bit too eager, but she wasn't likely to notice that in her condition. He rose from the bed to open the curtains just wide enough to let a small amount of light into the room. "Elera?"

She squinted up at him through her fingers.

"Why, if yours is the most prestigious House in your world, is it crumbling around us?"

"It stood empty after my mother's death, when there was no rider to tend it." With a shrug, Elera swung her legs to the floor, gratefully nodding when Karl put out his hand to steady her. "Ronin also put a stop to the mandatory collection of silver *tarlae* from the riders that would normally provide for its upkeep."

The *tarlae* earned for the slayer services, Karl thought wryly. "As further incentive for you to accept his suit?"

Elera shook her head, then winced. "To better arm his warriors, which you'll understand when I show you how the steel is made. But first I must bathe."

Her teeth were chattering by the time she emerged from the frigid pool. He leaned against the wall, watching her with the tolerant expression that the righteous reserved for the overindulgent.

She glared at him until he pulled her dripping wet against his chest, kissing her until her legs grew weak.

"We'll eat and then go?" he whispered against her lips.

Elera clutched her stomach. "Ah ... no. Not yet. I'll be fine until later, or I'll eat something as we travel."

He released her so she could dress. She chose a wispy two-piece outfit that made him want to forget about the steel and return to bed. The silver pants rested low on her hips, fluttering softly against her legs from the breeze coming in off the terrace. A single strap wrapped around her neck and back to secure the top, leaving him free to admire her bare skin. Even the lower curves of her breasts were revealed by the flimsy material, which parted in an upside-down vee to show her navel. As she moved into shadow, metallic threads sparkled within the fabric.

Elera's lips parted when he skimmed the length of her spine with the tips of his fingers. Gripping her waist and setting her on the edge of the bed, Karl took the sandals she had found and slipped them over her feet, slowly lacing them up her ankles.

"Shall I tell you to wear this color more often?" he whispered, tracing her calves beneath the legs of the pants. "That it sets off the mystery of your eyes, enhances the fire trapped in your hair?"

Elera cast her eyes skyward, sighing heavily. "If you must."

With a grin, he moved from her legs to her waist, skimming his palms over the visible curves of her breasts until her nipples poked against the shirt.

"Karl..."

He pressed his lips gently over hers, inhaling her sigh before drawing them both to their feet. "Let's go."

The people who had supported his bond with Elera the night before stared at him now with suspicion as the two of them walked to the village. Riders especially avoided his path. If not for the sadness Karl could sense building in Elera, he might have accepted this as inevitable until the people knew him better. As it was, he marched directly to... the name of the man's House escaped him for the moment... and offered his hand in greeting.

He ducked to avoid a tail lash from the man's dragon and kept a smile on his face.

"She is of sweet temperament, but not overly friendly with newcomers," the rider apologized. He nodded his welcome to Elera, who stood silently beside her mate.

"Truly?" Karl said sweetly. "I would not have guessed."

Pride shone from the rider's eyes, even while he tried to nudge the female into the sky. She didn't budge.

"It shames me to have forgotten your name," Karl said, frowning at Elera when she snorted over the man's supposedly casual attempts to send his dragon away.

"Dane," he replied. "Of the House of—"

"Seers," Karl finished. "I did not have a chance to ask if that was a true title or not."

"Figurative," Dane admitted, with the hint of a smile playing upon his lips. "At least for as long as I can recall. My mate, Kiera."

He nodded toward the extremely pregnant woman carrying what looked like a bundle of weeds and waddling down the path toward them.

"I wasn't present for the ceremony last eve," she said, smiling as she neared the group. Her cobalt eyes widened with surprise when the new king's hand on her arm waylaid her ungainly attempt to kneel.

"I will take it in spirit," Karl said solemnly, lips twitching when she whispered soft thanks beneath her breath, then blushed that he had heard it.

It did not take her long to recover, and she did not seem to notice that his eyes lingered on the tattooed ring of flames encircling each of her wrists.

The mark of a sacrificial virgin? He caught Elera watching him carefully, and knew it was so.

"I suppose Dane has tried to tell you of his beast's sweet temperament?" Turning to her mate, Kiera threw an armful of crushed flowers and vegetation at his feet. "All lies!"

"Kiera!" Dane reprimanded, smoothing the snarl from his female's snout. "You will hurt her feelings."

"I will hurt you if she tramples my gardens again," Kiera snapped, before turning her glare on the dragon. "I am having a daughter, so you can relinquish any notions you may have had of stealing the favor of my child along with that of this buffoon!"

"Kiera …" Stepping between his dragon and his mate, Dane cleared his throat nervously. "She doesn't take kindly to such a tone—"

"That's right, take her side as usual." Kiera's fist slammed into his stomach, stealing his breath along with his placating words. She nodded toward Karl and Elera, tossed a final sneer to the dragon ... and primly waddled back to a manor rising out of the nearest cliff. Dane was left worrying over which female in his life to see to first.

"I would take the pregnant one," Karl murmured, amused when Dane shot a wary look to his dragon. She tossed her head and took to the sky.

"They have not yet worked through their jealousies over my attention." And with the sigh of a battered and war-weary man, Dane inclined his head at the two of them, turned, and bolted after his mate.

"Is that a common problem?" Karl asked, after Elera took his hand and pulled him along the path.

"The females already compete for the bull's attention," she answered, chuckling when Dane scooped his pregnant mate up and smothered her shrieks with his mouth. "They do not enjoy competing for their rider's as well. Kiera's been here for only a few months."

He missed a step. "She made that journey *pregnant*?"

"She did, and she'll give birth to a son, despite her wish." Elera smiled. "The House of Seers has never had a daughter born to it. My people believe this son will be strong like his mother and perhaps even the one to bring the gift back to the House."

He stared curiously after the couple, who were now walking hand in hand. There was a loud thud a few yards ahead, and he turned to see a rider from Ronin's army leaping from his dragon's back. He gave Karl the barest hint of a nod, then retreated into a cave carrying two halves of a broken sword.

"Good timing, then," Elera said, dragging him in with her. "You can see the steel made *and* repaired."

The cave was dark, the air within moist with sweat and

heat. Even before they made it to the central grounds, Karl's shirt was slick with sweat. He scowled when he saw that Elera and the other riders remained unaffected.

The cave veered to the left just then, diverting his attention as it opened up into a larger cavern divided into multiple workstations. The stations stood in a circle around a mound of silver artifacts: *tarlae*, ornaments, medallions ... and an excessive amount of ladies' jewelry.

Karl raised his eyebrows.

"What do you expect?" Elera teased, following his gaze. "The strongest men in the realm are the Mattaen and their Initiates ... and they are forbidden. When faced with a strong and exotic stranger, such as the men here, what's a woman to do but throw herself blindly at his—"

"These jewels are *gifts* from women who try to seduce them?" Karl stared sternly down at her.

She widened her eyes and responded, "Gifts given in secrecy have the greatest sincerity."

More than a few patrons glanced over when their newly appointed sovereign threw back his head and roared with laughter.

"I don't believe that was the intended use of the saying," Karl whispered, tucking a wayward lock of hair behind her ear, and recalling the postings in the realm warning of thievery. "But I give you definite credit for creative interpretation."

Elera led him down a steep incline in the cavern walls. She would have rolled her eyes when he jumped the last ten feet to help her down, but the courtesy just seemed natural to him. She wondered if he knew how these simple niceties softened her; then she caught him watching her with a knowing curve to his lips and realized he knew exactly what he was doing.

He curled his arms about her then, shielding her from the wayward sparks of a nearby steelsmith's fire.

She sighed. "Don't do that."

"Don't do what?" Karl asked, distracted when the orange flames turned an incandescent blue.

"Don't place your body between me and the fire," she said, reaching around him to pass her hand through another flame.

Karl pulled her hand back at once, cursing as he anxiously examined the burn. It remained an angry red for the span of three breaths before fading into her skin.

"I told you we had a connection to fire, and so we do," she explained softly. "It cannot harm us."

"The burn was there, Elera, no matter how fast it healed."

"It didn't heal so much as it was absorbed." She nodded her head at the rider who had come in with the broken sword. Both his hands were in the fire, holding the shards until the flames turned blue and tinted the steel the same color. After he pulled back, the burns on both of his hands had vanished by the time he started hammering the shards together.

His eyes, a pale shade of gray, now held the same blue tint as the fire he worked.

"It doesn't hurt?" Karl asked, glancing down at her hand once more.

"We feel the burn—or I do, anyway," she said, struggling to explain. "And the pain is there, but it's … muted. Do you understand?"

"No."

Sighing, she added, "It's seductive, the heat of the burn, and it puts the pain in the background. With a bit of practice, we don't even notice it anymore."

When the rider shouted a chain of colorful expletives, Karl crossed his arms and glanced imperiously down at her.

"That was a liquid-silver burn, and definitely not seductive or muted. Not anything but an instant and searing sting … er," she corrected, listening as those curses grew more imaginative, "perhaps *sting* is not the proper term."

"Perhaps," Karl said dryly. "You add silver into your steel?"

She nodded. "The way we alter the properties of the fire allows the silver to merge into the steel. Our manipulation, the fire, and the silver are all essential to grant our blades their malleability and strength."

With a chuckle, she stood on tiptoe to kiss away his frown as he pondered her words.

"It is not so hard to forge the steel as it is to make certain it adjusts properly to pressure," she added as they walked slowly around the chamber. "Which is why, when a warrior has mastered a particular blade, he tends to repair it rather than replace it. It still takes getting used to, but not as much as a new weapon."

"Do all warriors create their own?" Karl asked, stopping at various stations to admire a few projects under way.

She shrugged. "Their weapon of choice, usually. The rest they take from supplies, or purchase with silver. Ronin's army will have been responsible for the bulk of that allotment."

She nodded to the mound of silver in the cavern, then wondered how long it would take for the people to stop referring to Verteva's army as Ronin's, when she herself had yet to do so.

Probably when it stopped *being* Ronin's army, she decided as Karl moved slightly into the path of an approaching rider. Not enough to stop him, but just enough that the man had to look up, acknowledge his presence with a nod, and shift to walk by.

"You say you don't want to lead," Elera said softly, once the rider had gone, "but you certainly have a way of making your presence felt."

Karl lifted her hand to his lips, but quickly turned down another passage when something caught his eye. "You also make regular steel?"

He examined the pieces of steel cooling in a tray, and Elera shrugged. "We don't need malleable steel on a projectile weapon."

"Like your arrows?" he asked.

"Piytin makes them for me," Elera said, nodding to a man lifting a second casing of arrowheads from the water. "And there's no charge for a nonmalleable weapon, so they're popular during training, or as secondary armaments."

"Seems like a great deal of preparation for a war you don't want," Karl said, offering his arm for the steelmaker to clasp when the man turned to greet them.

The steelmaker grinned at them both. "War tends to come faster when it isn't wanted. And anyway, what else should a group of rowdy warriors hope for but to see a good battle before they die in their beds?"

Karl inclined his head, then stared in surprise at the man's brown eyes. "You're from below?"

"Born here," he answered, and pointed a finger to his eyes. "My mother's eyes, my father's size ... but none of the rider in his blood. Happens sometimes. Aren't enough dragons to go around for all those of riding blood anyway, so it hasn't hurt me any. Despite what some like to say when they think I'm not listening."

She noticed the last was spoken with a bit more volume, and aimed at the two smiths working a few stations down. One of them shouted something about Piytin's six daughters being the source of his pain, rather than his lack of riding blood.

Karl frowned down at her. "I thought you said your people could not mate among themselves and produce issue?"

"If he doesn't have gray eyes, he has not been changed by being near the dragons and has no connection to them. But if his mate has riding blood—"

"She does," the steelmaker interjected with a bawdy grin.

Elera grinned. "Then she could perform the breath on him

and they could have children. The rest of my people who are of blood but without dragon also mate among themselves ... but for love alone."

Karl looked disconcerted ... but she knew that if it were easy for her people to have children, they would have outgrown their land long ago.

Those of riding blood who had no dragon to help them gain a mate from below prized men and women like Piytin.... The number of children they tended to produce supplied their race with enough numbers to keep their population healthy.

She saw the moment Karl realized the unique position these people held in her race ... so long as they remained virgins until bonding. His eyes softened and some of the tension he tended to hold in his shoulders eased. He approved of the balance, she realized.

"And what be your weapon of choice, newcomer?" Piytin reached over a ledge and pulled down a spiked mace. "This is my personal design, make, and choice."

Karl stepped closer, intrigued. "That's the tinted steel?"

"Aye, it is." He handed it over with a proud grin and then watched with Elera as Karl balanced its weight and studied its triangular spikes. "You extend the length of the spikes by changing pressure on the chain, and also by the force and spin of its release. Damn near art, you ask me, but hard as a rider's ass to learn ..." He cleared his throat, noticing Elera's less than amused expression. "I meant to say, it takes a lot of practice to develop the technique."

Reluctantly, Karl handed it back. "You find a rider to manipulate the flame for you when you do a weapon of motion?"

"Aye, most often Elera lends me her hand."

Busy chuckling over his pun, he missed the sharp look in Karl's eyes. She didn't, however, and lifted her chin defiantly. Was she a weak and silly female of the realm to cry over a bit of pain, or the rider of the oldest and most awesome creature in existence?

The angry gleam in her eyes quickly turned to surprise when Karl said, "Perhaps she would be willing to help you in the creation of a similar weapon for me? If you have the time, that is."

"And you have the silver," Piytin added. "Choice weapons are costly."

Karl grinned. "I'll get the silver, though the mace is not my choice, at least not yet. We'll see how it fits."

"The mace will take a while, but I could make your weapon of choice in the meantime," Piytin offered hopefully, rolling his eyes when Karl tapped a finger to his temple. "Not that, I suppose, but a blade, surely. Initiates always carry one, don't they?"

"I'm not an Initiate anymore," he said, and Elera could see he was taken aback by the easy acceptance in Piytin's tone. "Still, I'd be interested in a blade from you, steelsmith. Let me know the cost." He turned then, and sprinted out of the cavern.

"Let us know when you plan to start," she called over her shoulder, jogging to catch up with Karl. "He'll have to call on you for the blade, to keep the alterations in tune with your natural—"

She gasped when Karl slung her over his shoulder and vaulted up the rock. He set her back on her feet so he could start dragging her out of the cave. It took longer than it should have because he made a wrong turn and wasn't paying any attention to her directives.

The moment they exited, she demanded, "What was that about?"

Karl lifted his shirt over his head and dumped what little water remained in his flask over his pink, sweat-slicked skin.

"Oh," Elera said, then shrieked when he pulled her close to

claim her mouth in a fiery kiss. By the time he let her up for air, she felt as hot to the touch as he did.

With a sigh, Karl ran his hands over her arms. "It twists me up, Elera, seeing your hands in flames, knowing your skin is burning. I'm never going to feel any different, and I'm not apologizing for it."

"It doesn't affect me like—"

Silencing her with a finger over her lips, he added, "But I'm giving you the benefit of the doubt. I'm going to watch you help with the mace, and I'll try to understand."

She took a moment to consider, then slowly nodded. If he had been unwilling to try to understand, or if he had forbidden her from working the flame altogether … well, that would have been an interesting moment.

Karl's satisfied expression told her he knew her thoughts and wasn't overly concerned by them. With a sigh, Elera let him draw her close for another kiss. The man might not have the *desire* to rule, but he surely wasn't lacking in arrogance.

TWENTY

From his position atop the cliff overlooking the steelmakers' cavern, Ronin narrowed his eyes as he watched the lovers. He thought of how often Elera had denied him, of how often he had denied others who had offered in her stead! Yet the woman he had taken to his bed the night before could stir nothing from him. Not in all her attempts, or even his own ... though no one would know of his failure but him. He had killed her in his rage.

A subtle increase in the pressure of his thighs signaled his dragon to take flight. The couple was strolling toward the market.

He was going to take her.

The thought brought a sneer to what could have been a proud and intriguing face, if not for the cruel calculation that too often twisted his features. Ronin had never cared for his appearance. He'd stayed away from women for nearly four decades, and all to gain a throne slipping like quicksilver through his fingers.

He would rule through might rather than right. Leaning low, Ronin stroked the scales on his dragon's neck until her flight leveled and his hair streamed out behind him.

He whispered an assurance in the ancient tongue: "It will be well."

Elera and Karl spent the rest of the day walking through cliffs and valleys, visiting the nearby Houses. The riders greeted them with the attention due their rank, though rarely with any sincere warmth. It would take many days to see every House, she'd told Karl, since they were spread across the entire land of Verteva.

Looking up at the angry clouds forming in the sky, Elera sighed. "A gathering at our own home would accomplish this in one step, you know."

She sounded exhausted, and he looked at her in concern. "You're tired. I hadn't meant to—"

"I'm not." She winked up at him. "But we're going to be drenched before we make it back."

By the look of the sky, before they made it to the nearest House, even. He tugged on her arm, and Elera let him draw her to his side just as the first fat drop struck the tip of his nose. Both glanced warily up … and the sky tore open, pelting them with icy sheets of rain as they raced to an overhang in the nearest cliff.

She ducked under the ledge, laughing as she pulled him in after her just as hail followed the rain. The pebble-size pieces bounced off the ground, drumming over the roof of their makeshift shelter. Lightning quickly followed, spearing across the dark horizon in brilliant bluish streaks.

"Came in fast," Karl muttered, shaking the rain from his hair and eyes. His nostrils flared when he noticed Elera's figure beneath her sodden outfit.

She saw the look, and stepped close to run her hands up his bared chest. Her tongue darted out as she licked the raindrops rolling down his collarbone.

"Elera."

Sliding her hands beneath his hair and wrapping them around his neck, she pressed her body into his. "Mmm?"

He groaned … but recalled the challenge in her eyes from earlier. Just because he was seeing her world did not mean he should not begin seeing to his mate as well.

Perhaps it was time for Elera to grow accustomed to surrendering to his will. He loved her strength, loved the way she challenged him, but with enemies everywhere the time might come when he needed her to obey without argument in order for him to keep her safe.

He would start with something small ... and considering the woman, he would start in an area that would not seem so threatening to her warrior's pride.

The best battle won was the battle an opponent never knew he had lost ... *she had lost*, he corrected, grinning. Before she could whisper his name once again, he turned her abruptly against the cliff wall. His hands roamed over her stomach, cupping her breasts, warming her skin, staking a claim as he owned every curve. She gasped when he slipped his hand beneath the waist of her low-slung pants to brush his fingers through her damp curls.

"Are you wet from the rain"—he scraped his teeth over the curve of her shoulder—"or from me?"

He pressed one long finger inside her, and changed her answer to a moan.

"Please ..." he murmured, flicking her nub once with his thumb. He waited. "I want you to say it...."

"Karl ..."

"*Uben, ja'ik, abbari, toma ...*" he murmured the word he had demanded from her in the four other languages he spoke, desperate to hear her say it in hers.

From over her shoulder, he saw her lips curve. He growled and immediately stilled the movements of his thumb.

"*Naro*," she moaned, reaching down to cover his hand with hers, trying in vain to force him to touch her. "Please ..."

"More ..." he rasped, nipping her ear in encouragement. He flicked her slick nub once more, circling it until her soft cries filled the overhang with her scent.

Once more he stopped when she did not submit.

"*Dayana*," Elera cried, releasing his hands to reach back and twine her fingers in his hair. "*Dayana naro* …"

More, please …

He rumbled in approval, but he wasn't finished with his mate yet. He wanted to hear the words of his claiming on her lips. "I am yours.…"

"*Nea me lin* …"

Karl narrowed his eyes even as his body burned and throbbed behind her. She had given in too easily. The curve on her lips said she played him, as did the defiant light in her eyes when she peered over her shoulder to stare at him.

"Clever, mate …" His grin was fierce, and he repeated what he suspected she had said to him. "'You are mine.'"

She bit her lip, refusing to speak.

His chuckle was as dark as the passion and possession inflaming his blood … and he groaned when she arched her back and brushed against his shaft with the curve of her bottom.

Cursing the rain that made his pants stick to his skin, he backed away long enough to rip them off. He stood behind her then, his hot breath skimming the nape of her neck as Elera shoved the dark mass of her hair aside. He pressed his thighs against the back of hers, savoring her quick gasp.

The rim of his shaft slipped between her buttocks to tease her moist folds.

"You are mine.…" He snarled it, and the combination of fear and excitement in her gray eyes as she glanced back at him nearly sent him over the edge.

He would not lose this battle.…

He stroked his hands possessively up her stomach and plucked at her nipples. Elera screamed at once and a surge of heat dampened his sex as it slid along her folds. Again he plucked at her breasts; again he felt that heat rush from her.…

"Yours!" Elera screamed brokenly, her head falling to his

shoulder as sensation took her. "*Me ti'maen*, Karl…I am yours!"

She was still screaming it when he wedged her thighs apart…and drove as hard and deep inside her as he could go.

Her legs gave out. Karl wrapped an arm around her waist to hold her in place. She was scalding, and the contrast between that and the icy temperatures around them drew a long moan from his throat. Her own sounds of pleasure were shattered by every furious pump of his hips, every sharp pulse and lost breath as his arms tightened around her. Release came as a hot, clenched fist within them both that slowly eased to shivering waves.

He stayed deep inside her soft heat as the patter of rain mingled with the sound of hail hitting the ground. Eventually, the rolling sounds of thunder faded into the night.

"If you wanted to learn my language, you had only to ask," Elera whispered, panting in the aftermath of his sensual assault. "You shocked me…."

But he could hear the smile in her voice, and since his lesson would be for naught if he spoke of it, he did not respond.

Her breath hitched as he slid out of her. He knelt, untangled her pants from around her ankles, and pulled them back up her thighs. He lingered there, smoothing her buttocks with his rough palms. She purred when he stood and wrapped his arms around her stomach, burying his face in her hair to hold her close.

"I love the sounds you make," Karl murmured, turning her in his embrace and pressing his lips softly to hers. "We forgot to do that in all the rush."

"*You* forgot to do that in all the rush. I believe I was at your mercy." Elera's mouth curved under his, and there was humor mingling with the passion still glazing her eyes. "But I'm not complaining."

No, she never did, he thought. It was the reason he showered her with so many little courtesies. He loved to watch the way they flustered and pleased her all at once.

He ran the tip of his finger along her jaw, savoring her sigh before he straightened and peeked out of the overhang.

Clouds blotted out the moonlight. "I think it's just a lull in the storm. But if we hurry, we might make the nearest—"

Elera shook her head. "The nearest House is Ronin's."

"The nearest behind us is Ronin's," Karl corrected. They had passed it earlier in the day. "I mean to go forward." When she frowned, he tapped her chin. "I would see every House before we return home. Will none lend shelter to us for the night?"

"Most will," Elera said, pulling back from him. "But you could have let me in on your plan. I would have told Warwick not to expect us back, or at the very least packed a change of clothing. I would have—"

"I spoke to your grandfather, Elera. He knows." Stepping out from beneath the shelter, Karl grabbed her hand and pulled her on a fast trek through the cliffs. "And I like what you're wearing."

When she saw the evil glint in his eyes, she glanced down. The twisted material of her shirt had left one breast exposed, and the other scantily covered. In the midst of her colorful, albeit whispered opinions on the male sex, his grin never faltered.

Though the next House belonged to one of Ronin's staunchest supporters, they were offered shelter from the storm. While he would have preferred not to be spending the night in this particular manor, Karl still wanted to speak with its rider.

Elera had nodded off a few hours earlier in the room prepared for them. *The lavish room,* Karl corrected silently. This House was filled with all the riches so absent from hers. But he would not have left her alone if the bull hadn't come looking for his rider and settled on the ground under her window.

Looking into the hostile eyes of the warrior seated across from him, Karl decided that not even the presence of the bull was enough to set him at ease. He stayed alert to any sounds that might filter down the stairs, and tried to focus on the conversation at hand.

"I have no desire to rule your world." It was about as honest as Karl thought he could be. The old warrior looked considerably stunned by his admission.

They measured each other silently, before the warrior, Loren, finally responded, "I have no desire to be ruled by any outsider, much less a Mattaen slayer."

"Most of your people agree, I suspect," Karl said quietly, ignoring the implication that all Mattaen were slayers. "Though I have no wish to rule, I do have a fierce desire to keep my mate safe. If that means securing the world she loves, as well as safeguarding the bond between rider and dragon, I will do so with my life."

Loren took a long swallow of fire-brew, then rose from his seat to stand before the fire. The flames turned blue when he ran his hand across them. "It is as much as can be expected from a seeker. There is no understanding between you and a dragon, and there can be no bond other than the one you share with your mate. This my people might accept, if not for the tainted past that lingers like a bad smell behind every step you take."

"Your people might accept me, but not you," Karl said, letting the insult pass ... for now.

"Nor the one I am pledged to follow." Loren turned back. "Ronin will—"

"Ronin will die for any further attempts to harm my mate," Karl said coldly, quietly, filling his voice with as much menace as he could.

Loren inclined his head. "If the strength of the love you bear your mate weren't already the main topic of conversation between Verteva's bedsheets at night, I would know it. Some might consider that kind of devotion a weakness and seek to exploit it."

"Some might, and they would fail." He fought to keep from clenching his jaw.

Something close to approval shone from the other man's eyes for a moment, and then Loren's stare hardened once again. He took his seat and leaned urgently forward.

"I will tell you the truth, as you have been truthful with me. Elera's misfortune has always been that her mate must ascend to rule. Such a woman would be hard-pressed to find contentment in her mating, much less desire. I speak not of the physical," he added with a snort when Karl grinned. "She chose well for a mate, if not for a ruler."

He sat back, staring out the window at dragons flying between the streaks of lightning in the sky.

Karl also stared, entranced by the eerie beauty of the scene. "They like the challenge."

"The thrill, I always thought," Loren murmured, and glanced at Karl. "More than a few have come home with their scales scorched, but looking right pleased despite it. You'd understand if you went riding into the storms with one. Stirs the blood more than the best sex you'll ever have."

Thinking of the interlude beneath the cliff, Karl grinned. "Do you have no mate, then?"

"She never made the journey." It was all he would say on the subject.

Never chose to make it or never survived it, Karl wondered, but he sat in silence as the man studied him. Loren seemed torn between his oath to Ronin and his affection for Elera, and he hoped the rider would eventually trust him enough to give his oath to the rightful sovereign of this world. Until that happened, Karl would remain on guard.

Taking a sip of his drink, Loren turned back to the sky and

searched for his dragon.... His face relaxed when he found her. "I've offered you the safety of my home this night, and I will honor my word in this as in all things."

His subsequent pause was just long enough to let Karl know that it was his oath to Ronin to which he referred. Loren leaned forward once more. "Be warned. Ronin is single-minded in his pursuit for sovereignty. Any man with the discipline to deny himself the pleasures of a woman for nearly forty years will not be so easily swayed from his..." Karl's bland stare had the rider blushing and stumbling over his words. "Aye, you've that discipline too. The difference..."

"Karl," he insisted, when Loren hesitated to use his name.

"The difference ... Karl ... is that you did sway." His eyes crinkled at the edges. "If you had not, you might well be hunting those you are now sworn to protect."

"I find it ironic that I would have been condemned for either choice."

"Did you get a choice?" Loren's eyes grew sad. "I do not recall giving she who would have been mine a chance to resist." He blinked rapidly, startled by his confession.

It was the most strategic time to leave, so Karl rose and inclined his head. "I am grateful for this night's shelter, and the conversation."

He made it halfway up the stairs, where Elera had clearly been eavesdropping. He saw her shadow retreating when Loren called his name. Obviously uncertain about speaking further, the rider ran a hand through his gray-streaked mane.

"If I did not know it would destroy my world to lose the bull, I would tell you to take her and run. As it is, I will tell you to be on your way before I rise in the morn."

Karl tilted his head. "You care for her."

The old warrior paused again, which seemed to be his way. "I was there when she first rode the bull. A slip of a girl, beautiful and bruised, riding with her head thrown back and her arms spread wide. Her laughter rode the wind." He sighed. "It was not a sight to forget."

Karl stood in place until the sound of Loren's footsteps faded. The creaky stairs testified to Elera's continued attempts to creep away. She squealed when he rounded the stairwell and spun her around to stand face-to-face with him before she could slip back into their room.

"I—"

"Caught in the act," Karl whispered, tilting her head to inhale the scent of her neck. "But since you are awake …"

They were gone from the manor before the sun peeked over the ridges of Verteva's highest cliffs, and spent the day in relatively the same manner as the one before. Karl made a strong impression on the people of every manor they visited, though it was not always in his favor.

The seeker turned sovereign was making it known that he meant to stay.

As the day progressed, word of their journey spread, and the Houses of Verteva expected their arrival. Some welcomed them with warmth and hospitality, others with stiff-necked courtesy that did little to hide the anger lurking beneath the facade.

They visited four Houses that day, having walked hard and fast to get around the cliffs. There had been one river that he had insisted Elera cross on the bull. The strong current had nearly cost him his own footing, although seeing her poised to leap from the bull to assist him had carried him to the opposite edge quickly enough. He'd snarled at her when she'd stayed in the sky to avoid what would have been a long lecture.

She was exhausted by the time they approached the last

House of the day. Karl quickly forgot his lecture, which he'd been saving for when he got her on the ground, and simply caught her as she dropped. Swerving to avoid the bull's lashing tail—the reaction was becoming habit—he held her hand the rest of their walk.

"This House has been in Tem's family for generations."

"But Tem—"

"Was chosen by his beauty long before his father died and left his own dragon to search for another rider. Tem's aunt Andia holds this House in trust until the dragon's current rider comes of age." Elera nodded toward a matronly woman stepping out of the manor. She raised her hand in tentative greeting and smiled. "I spent most of my summers with Tem and his family. There's no danger here, unless it comes in the form of a switch to my poor youthful and innocent bottom."

"Between you and Tem, I doubt there was an innocent bone in either of your poor, youthful bodies," Karl muttered, though he patted the curve of her behind.

She swatted his hand away, turning pink as Tem's aunt marched toward them. Karl watched in fascination. She rarely blushed. Unless it was after …

He coughed, lest the color rise in his own face. The elderly woman was now close enough that he could see every stern line etched into what seemed an even sterner face. Before he could marvel over the gall of any child willing to misbehave in this woman's presence, she jabbed an elegant finger toward Elera's chest.

"Shame. Shame on you and your grandfather for doing this thing…." Andia's eyes narrowed as she studied Elera. She smirked, leaning in to whisper, "Without letting me get in on the action first. At the very least, you wicked, wicked girl, I should have been present to see the look on Ronin's face when …"

She straightened then, and lifted her chin, giving Karl the impression that she was staring down at him ... when in truth he stood a good foot and a half over her head.

"Never did have a redhead in the family," she said finally, and the sudden warmth in her smile transformed the severity of her features. "Ought to make a pretty baby."

Karl blinked and nervously swallowed. The two women exchanged amused glances over such a typical male reaction.

His gaze lingered on Elera as she walked arm in arm with Tem's aunt. Did she want children? He glanced at the sky ... unsure whether he should feel pride or terror at the possibility of giving her a babe of riding blood. He was still trying to handle the riding woman.

But he had a sudden and desperate longing to see his mate growing large with their child ... so intense he could actually feel his hand caressing her rounded belly.

"I do not recall the rider of your House, madam," Karl said, forming a fist to stem the sensation before scanning the sky as he climbed the stairs behind them.

"My great-nephew, Tornak," she explained, waving her hand to a thick cloud where a dragon of near-translucent coloring had just burst free. A gleeful whoop drifted down from the sky. "Nine years old and a rival for Tem and this one"— she jerked her chin toward Elera—"with his wild ways. Thinks he's a warrior too. Ronin's, unfortunately, since he is the strongest rider in Verteva, and such is the meat of young boys' dreams."

"No wrong in that," Karl reassured her, seeing the hint of fear in her eyes. "I would like to meet him, with your permission."

She shrugged. "If you can get him down, he's yours. You're family now; I'll trust you to see to his safety."

Karl grabbed her hand before she entered the manor, attempting to snag the attention of the boy pretending not to watch the stranger in his territory. "There's no blood between

Tem and Elera, which left you with no obligation to show her any concern. I'm grateful for the mothering you gave her."

"Well," Andia said, slightly flustered. "Well."

Elera rolled her eyes, and received a smart cuff on the back of her head.

"Never mind the insolence of this one." Gathering her composure, the woman beamed up at Karl. "Someone had to help that dried-up husk raise a decent girl rather than a hellion. He's coming in fast, by the way."

He was indeed, Karl thought, ducking low as the sharp tip of a wing missed him by a hair. A moment later, when a bundle of mad stormed up the stairs, the women hastily retreated indoors.

Indecision clouded the boy's fury when he noticed the red hair. "You're that outsider who wants to be king?"

Keeping his eyes on the dragon hissing in the background, Karl shook his head. "I'm the outsider who *is* king."

The bull swooped down from the sky just then. Abandoning her annoyance on her rider's behalf, the female flew off to welcome him.

Tornak cursed, then fearfully searched for his aunt. When no cuff to the back of his head came, his slight shoulders slumped in relief.

He lowered his eyes to Karl's stomach. "I heard Ronin chopped you in two."

"Very nearly." Karl grinned. "Want to see?"

They spent the night at Andia's insistence. Despite her taunts from earlier in the day, Elera succumbed to sleep the moment her head touched the pillow of her childhood bed. Slipping beneath the sheets with a sigh, Karl gathered her close ... and slept with his feet dangling off the bottom.

TWENTY-ONE

The morning chill succumbed to the dry midday heat much too quickly for Elera's liking. They were walking through the endless wheat fields on Andia's lands. But while most stalks stood a few feet higher than his head, they still did nothing to provide shelter from the glaring sun above.

Elera grumbled under her breath. It was the same low growl she'd been making since they'd started out not two hours earlier. When sporadic glares began to accompany the sound, he braced his shoulders ... and waited.

"I hate wheat," she muttered suddenly.

So she would start out slow. Keeping his grin to himself, he said, "At least you got new clothes."

Ceremonial clothes, she'd grumbled when Andia had pulled them out, and nearly identical to the crimson gown she'd been wearing on the night of Karl's arrival. Ignoring his pathetic attempt to cheer her, Elera swiped at the wheat stalks.

"It's dry and itchy and ..." She hissed as she sliced her finger, then glared at him as she brought it grumpily to her mouth. "Why are we walking to every blasted House in Verteva? It'll take a week, even at this pace. You could have asked Tem to let you ride with him, and then I could have ridden—"

She shrieked when Karl leaned down and scooped her up into his arms.

"Don't argue," he said. Transferring her weight to one arm so he could bring her injured finger to his lips, he sighed. "I never thought the bull would leave you to walk all this way. I thought he'd carry you for most of it, even if he was just walking nearby instead of flying. Since he has not …"

"You will?" Elera narrowed her eyes when he shrugged. "You can't carry me all the way to the next House, Karl. I was only grumbling … I'm perfectly capable of—"

"Just for a while then," he said, tightening his arm around her middle to stop her squirming. After tossing an annoyed glance toward the empty skies, he leaned down and pressed a soft kiss to her lips. "I have no problem exhausting you, Elera, but I can think of many more enjoyable ways to do so."

Relenting enough to rest her cheek against his shoulder, she murmured, "Karl?"

"Elera …" he drawled, enjoying the way her lips moved against his throat.

"I do love you."

His slow grin wavered, then fell away completely.

"Don't tell me I can't," she continued hurriedly, holding on to him when he stumbled and nearly sent them sprawling. "I know my mind and I know my heart. I brought you here to be our king … and I never expected to have more from my mating than affection and safety—"

"I know that, Elera … that's why I can wait."

She covered his lips with her fingers. "But I watched you fall in love with my dragons and my world, and then there was the way you claimed me that night in the ancestral ruins, and, Karl … how could I not have loved you from that moment …?"

Karl shifted her quickly in his arms, swinging her upright so she straddled his waist. At the flash of annoyance in her eyes, his lips curved. "I ought to get you angry more often."

"You seem to have a talent for it," Elera whispered. She studied his face, as if searching for something. When she found it, she closed her eyes and whispered, "You believe me."

"I remember the look in your eyes that night." His voice shook with reverence as he brushed his lips over her brow.

Elera sighed and savored the feel of his touch for a long moment ... and then her eyes popped playfully back open as she tilted her head. "Shall we go swimming?"

Karl lifted a brow and turned full circle. He didn't even see a puddle.

Elera explained with a grin, "There's an underground stream near the borders of Andia's land. Bit of a challenge to access, but ..."

When she gnawed at her lip and looked away, he prompted her. "Bit of a challenge?"

"It's hot, Karl," she complained. "If you're dragging me across the land, I think we should stop so you can get to know it, as well as its people. Isn't knowledge your ultimate pursuit?"

"It was once." His eyes sparked with amusement as he leaned forward to brush her lips. "You've made a good argument, though, and so I suppose I should indulge you."

He couldn't deny her anything at the moment, not with her confession still ringing in his ears.

"Can you lead the way?" he asked.

"On hot nights, Tem and I used to sneak through this wheat to get to the water. I still—"

Shifting her in his arms, Karl boosted her onto his shoulder before she could finish her sentence. He winced when she yanked two handfuls of his hair.

"Swing your leg around the other side of my head," he offered helpfully.

Elera did as he'd asked, raising the material of her skirt to her thighs and letting it hang to one side.

"The bull would know my preferences by the way I shift my seat, but I suppose for you ..." Using the hands entangled in his hair, Elera pulled to the left.

Karl turned his head and nipped at her thigh. She giggled, and he started off in the direction she'd indicated.

Sometime later he stood at the edge of a waterfall that flowed out of one cavern before plunging directly into another.

He glared. *Bit* of a challenge, indeed.

"I did it as a child," she countered, and nearly succeeded in concealing her astonishment that neither she nor Tem had been crushed on the rocks lining the tunnel down. "It wasn't so long ago, Karl, and it looks exactly the same. I guess I just didn't recall …"

He swung her down, rolling the stiffness from his shoulders while glancing dubiously at the path of rushing water.

"*Baya*," Elera muttered. "It didn't frighten me as a child."

"How do you get out?" Karl asked.

She nodded into the distance. "The river widens into a pool, then flows through a few other tunnels that we were never brave enough to explore. Too dark." She shrugged. "But there's a chain of rising vents just off the main cavern. We always climbed out there."

"I'll go first."

Elera blinked, already resigned to the fact that he would refuse. "We're going in?"

It wasn't as dangerous as it looked. Karl had already measured the distance between the gaps and the cliff, and also studied the velocity of the water. He shrugged, saying only, "I'm hot too."

"And how am I supposed to know if you make it through?"

"I'll make it," he said, and teased, "Don't be afraid, Elera; I'll be there to catch you when you come through."

"I never said I was frightened." He stared at her until she ducked her head. "Okay, I did. You really want to jump?"

Karl cupped her cheek, kissed her hard ... and leaped while she was still catching her breath....

When he plunged into the pool below, the current sucked him into a dark underground tunnel. Karl decided that he was going to kill her ... if he survived to do so. She hadn't warned him about this, though surely she had known. The flow of water through the tunnel was shallow, but it was quick enough to keep him sliding over the smooth rock at breakneck speeds.

Suddenly the rock fell away and he *was* free-falling into a seemingly bottomless pool below, where he slammed belly-first into the water with stunning impact. He broke the surface near the bottom of the falls with a curse and Elera's name on his lips. Perhaps they were one and the same.

The chasm was not immersed in total darkness, as he'd feared during his fall. There were deposits in the walls, some kind of precious stone that glimmered in the brief patches of light filtering in from the vents far above. He hoped these weren't the vents they would be climbing out of.

This was even more fun than she'd remembered, Elera thought. She squealed as she hurtled out of the tunnel above Karl's head. When she hit the surface of the pool, he dove and wrapped his arm around her waist as he pulled them both to the surface.

"If I were Andia, you and Tem would have gotten more than a bruised bottom for daring such stunts." He tried to look stern, but his lips twitched. She laughed and wrapped her limbs around him like tentacles.

"Admit it, Karl: You loved the thrill," she teased. His eyes sparked in the light zipping around the cavern. She hadn't re-alized he could let go of his control this way and just enjoy the moments as they came.

He smirked and ran his hands beneath her dress to cup her bottom. Just as she arched into the caress, he lifted her out of the water and tossed her a fair distance away. She came up sputtering, surprised and loving this playful side to him ... but just as eager for revenge.

She grabbed his shoulders and pushed him under ... then laughed triumphantly until he caught her ankle and dragged her down, kissing her until her chest heaved for air.

"All right," he murmured, drawing her close. "I did enjoy it, though a warning—"

"A warning would have ruined the thrill and you know it. Besides, we are cooler."

Karl winked at her before scanning the narrow banks beside the pool. "Do we swim to these vents that lead out?"

"Too far," she said, stroking lazily into the soft current. "But the banks are wider a bit farther down. It's pretty. I had forgotten."

They watched the light from the luminescent stones sparkling along the ceiling and the walls, teasing the darkness.

When Karl reached for her hand and twined their fingers, she decided a lazy float down a soft current was just as good as the fast ride that had gotten them there to begin with.

Enjoying the serenity of the moment, they drifted for a while. They abandoned the water to walk along the embankment after her teeth began to chatter. Eventually, they rounded a bend that led them to the open cavern ahead. Here, a series of thin falls flowed from fissures in the walls, making their jutting ledges slick with water and algae. A few of those falls were wide enough to conceal the tunnels behind them. Light streamed through the open vents.

"We use the ledges to climb up."

Karl frowned. "The ledges overflowing with water?"

She shrugged, nonchalant, but lifted her chin. "Race you to the top?"

"No." His arm shot out, snagging her waist before she could dart past him. "No, Elera."

"We're only going to fall back into the pool," she argued, raising a brow when he stared deadpan at the distance between the pool and the vents. "I fell from the top once, bloodied my nose and lip. My skin was chafed for days—"

"Good incentive."

She grinned. "I didn't die or break anything but my pride, and I was only twelve."

She was aching for the challenge. Her body was practically vibrating while she waited for his answer. When she saw the resignation on his face, she knew he'd relent.

And then he shoved her back into the pool.

To his credit, he waited in the stream on the lowest ledge until she emerged.

"I'll give you a three-ledge lead," he whispered, pulling her up and chuckling when she slapped his wandering hand from her bottom. He took a deep breath and dove backward into the water.

She moved fast, her hands and feet quicker to remember the path than her mind. But she had no more than a three-ledge lead when Karl lifted himself from the water and started bounding after her. She glanced back once, and shrieked to find him within inches of her feet. Long, lean muscles rippled through the fabric of his shirt as he leaped ahead to cut her off.

With a recklessness that would give Karl nightmares, Elera jumped to a ledge nearly six feet away and ducked quickly behind the falls. He was still eyeing the distance between his position and her falls when she climbed out on the opposite side.

Cliff, water, ledge … jump and hold. "You're cutting yourself off," Elera shouted, grinning maliciously when Karl cursed. He'd been too busy watching her, making sure she chose a safe path. Now he would have to backtrack to reach a vent.

She ducked behind a thin waterfall. From there, with the echo of the water ringing in her ears, she stopped to stare appreciatively at her mate.

Of course, he'd catch her for sure if she couldn't keep her mind on their race and off his splendid body. Shaking her head with a rueful grin, Elera began to turn... then gasped when something cool and sharp pressed against her throat. She whimpered as an arm pressed hard against her stomach. Rancid breath seared her ear.

"Another sound and I'll slit your throat," Ronin rasped, pressing her painfully against the wall of his chest as he led her back into the dark tunnel. "Your lover can watch your lifeless body fall to the pool below."

He leaned down and touched his lips to her neck. Elera swallowed her cry and focused on Karl's approaching form.

"Did you enjoy your swim down in the water?" He squeezed her hard enough that she could feel the erratic beat of his heart against her back. "Did you think I wouldn't get to you, that I couldn't with your lover at your side?"

"Ronin—"

His blade bit, leaving a trickle of blood to slide down her neck.

"He'll never touch you again," he whispered, moving his hand from her stomach to her breast. Cruel fingers dug into the soft flesh and her stomach roiled. "Do you still think he'll save you?" Gripping her chin hard enough to bruise, Ronin forced her to her knees so she could crane her neck and see beyond the lip of the tunnel. Shadows moved outside the vents on the ceiling above the cavern.

Dragons and riders, she realized in horror, glancing back at Karl. He'd already hesitated on the wall, one foot hovering over a ledge as his gaze shifted up to those same shadows. Then slowly he swung his head toward the falling stream Elera had slipped behind.

He *seemed* to see her, though she knew that was impossible. Ronin had dragged her too deeply into shadow. But Karl leaped suddenly, three quick lunges that brought him to her ledge, fingers scraping as he tried to pull his body through the gentle rush of water.

His face twisted in fury when he saw the man at her back. "Let her go."

In answer, Ronin splayed his fingers across her stomach and rocked against her from behind. She could feel his arousal pressing against her buttocks.

Karl rushed forward until Ronin pushed the blade even higher under her jaw. Elera struggled to stay absolutely still.

"I'm sorry," she whispered, twin tears slipping down her cheeks.

Karl didn't look at her. He stared straight at Ronin. "You cut her."

"I'll do worse if you don't take a full step back, and now." When Karl hesitated, Ronin dragged the edge of his blade across her throat not hard enough to cut her skin, but enough to make them both think for a moment that he had.

Enough to warn them both that he could.

Karl stepped back at once. She could see his hands shaking. "Don't. Don't cut her again."

"Then jump."

The ceiling above them splintered. Slabs of stone and earth crumbled, splashing into the pool below. Another crack resounded through the cavern as Karl spoke. "I know what you've done."

"Jump," Ronin repeated, this time with an edge to his voice. "Unless you want her blood to flow like the water at your back."

"Elera." Karl's eyes glittered with fear, but his voice was steady. "Don't be afraid. I'll come for you; I swear it."

Ronin moved to twist the blade....

Karl jumped.

Terror consumed her when he disappeared. Dark images flashed through her mind … Karl's vibrant green eyes turned dull and empty, his body crushed; Ronin's hot breath on her face as he raped her repeatedly; dragons slain in heaps of blood as their world plunged into a maelstrom of hate and war …

She hadn't realized she was screaming until the sound was swallowed up by the exploding vents as they splintered under the pressure of the four dragons diving through them. A huge shower of earth and stone plunged after Karl and buried him beneath the pool below.

"Still think he's coming for you?" Ronin screeched over the din. He grabbed her hair with one hand. The rock wall rushed forward to meet her, and everything went black.

Karl woke just as his body began purging itself of the water and muck sloshing in his lungs. It felt like fire coming out, just as his first breath felt like fire coming back in. It took every bit of his strength to climb onto his hands and knees in the muddy embankment.

He couldn't see a thing. Not the light from the sky somewhere above. Not even his own fingers moving before his face. He growled as he took stock of his injuries.

Ribs, was his first thought. A couple cracked, maybe even broken. Warmth trickled down his thigh. Blood, he figured, fingering a gash with a wince. More dripped down the side of his face from a generous lump on his head. Fighting back vertigo, Karl crawled along the embankment, cursing aloud when a mound of stone and earth blocked his path.

But the image of Elera with a blade at her throat returned to fill his vision. The remembered scent of her fear played upon the fringes of his senses, renewing his fury at having been forced to watch another man hurt her, draw tears from her eyes.

He couldn't find his calm through focused breathing, or even by concentrating on exterior sounds. Instead of suppressing emotion, as he had been taught, he embraced his rage until its dark burn honed his mind into sharp focus. Forgetting his pains, Karl took a deep breath and slipped back into the water lapping at his feet.

He knew the cavern was completely caved in. He'd seen the rocks entering the pool from beneath the underwater ledge where he had taken shelter against the debris. But some of the larger slabs from the ceiling had landed angled against the walls, forming spaces under the wreckage through which he could crawl.

He hoped only that the slabs would brace the weight of the wreckage above him long enough to allow him to find a way out. He would begin his search by following the current that had carried him and Elera along the earlier tunnels. It might lead to an easier way out than digging up through the cave-in itself.

Diving under the water and groping blindly along the embankment, Karl felt no pain from the sharp rocks slicing into his fingers. He cared nothing for the cold that numbed his aches and filled him with lethargy.

Though he could hold his breath a considerably long time, he still had to resurface three times. The last time he came up for air, he rapped his already bruised skull on a rocky protrusion.

He hung his head, letting the blood drip from his nose to coat his lips. He'd found the place where the current exited the pool of water. Not even a child could have fit through that long, tapered fissure.

TWENTY-TWO

The realm, Tem thought with a sneer. Overindulged and indifferent to the suffering of the surrounding lands ... the realm was the one place that brought him as close to hate as a man of his temperament was capable. That included its fine, upstanding ladies with their fancy jewelry.

He was happy to lift the pretty little trinkets from their persons with quick and clever fingers in order to provide the silver his people needed. But he never slept with the women here. Not once ... and not ever, he vowed. Even if his people didn't consider them to be weak and frivolous, they fell under the jurisdiction of the Mattaen.

The women in the barrens were a different matter. Unlike the ladies of the realm, who seemed to care only about the power of luring a dark stranger into their bed, the village women were honest in their passion. He'd made love once with a girl bathing in a stream, and again with a young widow doing laundry ... also in a stream, now that he thought about it. Walking along the perimeter of the Mattaen monastery, Tem grinned wickedly as he recalled that particular memory.

He'd found pleasure in the barrens, but still not a woman who might possess the strength needed to be his mate. Nor had any of them caught more than just the interest of his loins.

This hardly seemed the place to be indulging in fantasy, sexual or otherwise. He'd left his beauty deep within the barrens to keep her from being spotted by the realm, then proceeded to sneak across the great wall directly beneath the notice of its vagrant guard. He moved quickly to reach the center of the realm and the temple.

Tem chuckled as he stood outside the smaller wall of the monastery, waiting for the fourteenth hour and the spot the sun would strike.

The time drew close. Tem watched with tense muscles.... Patience was always a battle for him, and when the sun finally flashed over the stone wall, he grinned. A large tree sheltered the location from prying eyes. Perfect.

Moving within the shadows, Tem leaped up and sought cover within the tree. A fruit-bearing tree, he discovered quickly, sampling one fuzzy treat as he climbed further into the needle-sharp leaves.

Karl hadn't mentioned how long it would take this *monk* to make his way to the spot. For the remainder of the day, Tem wavered between keeping his oath and the desire to stretch his cramped legs.

The night air was cool and comfortable, but if he had to eat one more *bayan* piece of fruit from this *bayan* tree, he thought he might hack it to shreds on principle alone. Someone might have pointed out the folly of forgetting his sack of rations back in the barrens ... but she was in Verteva, probably in her bed with the arms of their new king keeping her warm.

Grumbling quietly over the scratches on his own bare arms, Tem tilted his head.

Someone was approaching the wall. A long black robe concealed the man from head to toe. Tem tossed a glance down at the grounds, but his eyes were too accustomed to the elevated lands of Verteva. Down in the barrens, the moonlight was too weak for him to make out the face behind the hood.

The man walked to the exact spot Karl had described, then leaped onto the wall and crouched there. Tem waited, a half smile on his face when the monk stilled, and very slowly turned his head to catch the gleam of strange eyes staring from a nearby bough.

His crooked smile faded the same moment the monk threw back his hood and tilted his head. "Did you think we did not know you were here?"

Tem growled in disgust as he noticed the many shadows emerging from the grounds.

"I would ask who you are, but I can see the color of your eyes." With a shrug that had probably lulled many opponents into complacency, Simon glanced toward the monks gathering below. "Say what you've come to say, rider. They'll be upon you in less time than it would take to jump from—"

Tem jumped from the tree to the wall, pleased to address the folly in that assumption, though he did nothing to bring the monk harm. Simon glanced curiously at him, then held up his hand. The monks coming toward them advanced more slowly.

"Deliver, then, what it is that you have come to deliver."

Tem reached into his vest and pulled out the blade with the black and red locks twined around it. Simon looked at it with a flash of recognition ... then struck Tem in the mouth with the heel of his hand. With the metallic taste of blood filling his mouth, Tem dropped the blade as he ducked to avoid a second monk lunging up the wall. He kicked a third off its edge, but more shadows than he could count were coming now.

Not that it mattered. The monk, Simon, tilted his head ... and swept Tem's feet out from under him. He went from teetering on the wall to flying head over heels until he hit the ground below. Landing on his back, the wind knocked from his lungs, Tem unfurled the blades on his wrists ... and just barely managed to get his arm between his neck and the noose thrown around it.

One of his blades fell, and the other was useless after a second noose encircled his wrist. Two more ropes snagged each of his legs, jerking him back to the ground after he had only just stumbled to his feet. He did manage to send a monk flying toward the wall by tugging hard on the ropes. But the monk simply flipped in the air, kicked off the wall, and dove back into the fray.

The monks who weren't holding the ropes taut surrounded him now. Tem couldn't even reach the blade on his thigh, since the hand he'd thrust between the noose and his neck was now imprisoned. Sweat beaded on his brow as he strained for freedom, but that mocking smile stayed on his lips, even after Simon leaped down from the wall.

Simon landed lightly, fingering the bare black blade in his hand.... The coil of hair was gone.

"Is that your dragon, then?" he asked, lifting his eyes to the dark speck moving in the distant clouds. "Coming in response to your dilemma, perhaps?"

With his cheek in the dirt, Tem turned his head, hissing as the rope rubbed his skin raw. The sight of his beauty stole whatever little humor remained in him, dark or otherwise. Closing his eyes in concentration, he rasped, "Go back."

A rumble sounded, slow and heavy. It carried on the wind and vibrated over the hairless bodies of every ordained monk surrounding her rider.

"Station the wall," ordered the monk nearest Simon. "Send slayers to ensure the beast doesn't come any closer than this. Send others to track and kill it if it does."

"The beast heeds his warning," someone spat, nodding to the dragon that had indeed retreated into the distance.

"It doesn't matter," another said softly. "They've broken truce trespassing here, especially after killing one of ours and then taunting us with the proof."

He nodded to the Initiate blade gripped tightly in Simon's hand.

"And the rider?" Simon asked, staring down at him without feeling.

"Take him below," the elder ordered quietly, accepting the blade Simon offered him. "Find out why he's here and how much he knows."

From the corner of his eye, Tem saw one monk nod to another. He saw the shadow of something swooping down. But despite the sharp pain that accompanied the blunt blow, his gray eyes were laughing just before they rolled back into his head.

His stomach growled, demanding food. Tem twisted wildly against the chains shackling him against a stone wall. His wrists were chafed and bloody, as were his ankles. He ignored the pain as he strained to study the confines of his prison.

He'd been conscious for hours. He couldn't see the stars, moon, or even the sun to tell the time. There was only the thin light slipping under the door in his dark, dank prison. Probably torchlight, judging from the way it flickered. But Tem was a rider, as in tune with the passage of time as the dragon he rode.

Thinking of her made him feel as if there were a ball of ice in his gut, and for a while he resumed his fierce struggles. He couldn't feel his beauty. He *thought* she'd heeded his command the night before, but he was sick with the thought that it might be her death, and not her distance, impeding the connection.

In very little time, Tem slumped as far as his restraints would allow him, too exhausted to even feel the rough rope still encircling his neck. He felt a sharp sliver of stone near his arm. He peeked down and saw the blood dribbling down his arm from where that shard had sliced his skin. Tem pushed his wrist further into the manacle. His skin tore in the process, but he reached far enough to bend and grasp the sharpened rock.

It sliced into his fingers as he worked the lock binding his hand. Twice he nearly lost it, and twice he clenched hard enough to drive the shard half an inch into calloused flesh.

But excitement gleamed from his eyes when the manacle finally clinked and his arm fell free. The promise of retribution steeled him against the pain in his shoulder and gave him enough energy to lift his arm back up and slice through the rope at his neck.

Tem quickly set to work on the other three manacles.

Once he was free, he conducted a more thorough examination of his surroundings.

And with a grin, he walked straight out the unlocked door.

Fools, to have counted on mere steel and rope to hold him.

Monitoring the rider from within a shadowed alcove, three pairs of eyes crinkled at the corners. Such arrogance, such misguided confidence!

They were both amused and thrilled.

Following him, the three crept quietly along the inner wall paths, intercepting four other monks also arriving to stand guard. They would learn how much this intruder knew by watching which path he took ... without ever using force to coax the information from his lips.

It was the Mattaen way. If it failed, they could then apply the various other techniques to extract the information.

Adaptation, also, was the Mattaen way.

Tem knew exactly where he was. Well, perhaps not exactly ... but he knew he was close to something. He could smell it in the damp air, feel its vibrations in the rocky walls. He could even hear it rushing through the tunnels under his feet.

He swung over the edge of a steep incline and started climbing down the narrow grooves cut into the rock wall. If his fingers hadn't been bloody and raw, he might even have been able to descend the entire distance, instead of falling once he was two-thirds of the way down.

Landing hard on his back, shaking his head until air filled his lungs once again, Tem rose slowly to his knees. Black water lapped against an embankment less than a wingspan away.

The hidden silver pools. There was no possible way to access them outside of the realm—unless one was inclined to tunnel underground through the barrens for many leagues.

However, he knew there were access points staggered through various corners of the realm itself. If he could find one of those by following the water, he could escape....

It was pure reflex that had him smashing his elbow into the first body that emerged from the shadows behind him. Knocked off his feet when the monk slammed into his knees, Tem rolled and rose.... He scanned the area and noticed half a dozen monks stalking him from alongside the cliff. He craned his neck and spotted three more descending along the wall.

"You have nowhere to go, rider," called a voice from the top, as Tem retreated into the pool. The cool water soothed the angry, torn skin around his ankles. As the group marched relentlessly forward, Tem froze.

Mistaking his hesitation for submission, one of the younger monks flashed his teeth. He'd done no more than lift his hand to beckon the prisoner back, when Tem leaped at him in a rush.

He wasn't concerned with attacking. He was still trying to flee. Leaping up the wall, climbing where the deeper grooves allowed, Tem moved like a man possessed. His eyes gleamed when he reached the top, and he laughed mockingly at the men left in his wake. But more monks were racing through the tunnel leading into the cavern now, all armed.

"You made it this far because we let you," warned a monk holding a long and spike-tipped spear. He made a point of raising it. "Do not let arrogance lead you to death."

A second monk closed in and lifted a torch from the wall. He tossed it over to Tem. "Scrolls say you can change the properties of this fire, rider."

So this was why he lived still. Tem's lips curved lazily as he retreated along the ridge of the wall, careful to keep close to the ledge.

"Change the fire and we'll keep you alive, as our ancestors did for the prisoners of centuries past."

Say nothing, Karl had commanded. Tem decided laughter did not fall into the category of speech. He flung the torch away and laughed, low chuckles that shook his shoulders, before blooming into full, braying mirth. His long golden hair fell across his chest as he doubled over, clutching his stomach.

"We cannot let you leave," the young monk shouted, hefting a short spear from the many lining the walls. Other monks were entering the cavern from below and also from above, racing through a maze of tunnels honeycombing through this vast underworld. "If you had not known of this place, we might have been content to ..."

The monk frowned, his words forgotten when a gulping ripple came from the waters below. For just that brief moment, all eyes fell away from the rider ... but by then it was too late.

The water exploded in a burst of black frothing spray, instantly blinding the men along the banks. Emerging from the very center of the pool were the smooth spreading wings of a dragon.

His beauty had come for him. She was alive! Teeth bared, she hissed with enough menace to instill dread into the hearts and minds of the surrounding slayers. One of them managed to find a foothold and plant his weight so he could launch his spear, but her tail slammed against the rock wall as she rose. Stone and earth crumbled, sending dozens of monks scrambling for purchase.

But not Tem. He dove from the ledge and landed on her back. Gripping tightly with his thighs, he sent her spinning with an agility that put the slayers to shame.

A spear whizzed by them, missing her wing by a hair.

Tem laughed as he guided her along the ceiling, angling their flight so every other spear flew short. He reined in his dragon's desire to dive back beneath the water by tightening his grip, and instead guided her between rock fissures no wider than the length of two men.

The limited space forced her to furl her wings and run along the rocks. Her claws bit into the stone as if it were mud. But the tight quarters would force the slayers to abandon their spears and arrows, which was what he had counted on.

"Be strong," Tem whispered, as much to himself as to his dragon. Solid stone blocked the passage ahead....

Holding fast to her neck, Tem ducked his head as she burst through the stone with a powerful leap. Rubble exploded in the air, nearly cloaking the staircase looming in front of them. His beauty didn't run so much as hop up those steps before clearing the top and finding sufficient room to spread her wings.

Tem threw his head back in exhilaration, and then nearly lost it when she bunched her powerful hind legs and jumped directly through the central floor of what appeared to be the Mattaen temple.

Shock, fear, disbelief... the monks' expressions were as varied as their attempts to flee what was, to them, a mythical beast.

Three levels, four, and still she forged on, using her head and shoulders to muscle through what men had taken centuries to build.

She breached the highest ceiling and regained the sky. The beacon tower cracked beneath a vengeful lash of her tail. Teetering in slow motion, it fell to the earth and nearly impaled the first monk who raced from the building.

It was Simon. Even as he stared at the dragon in awe, he pivoted, dislodged a long metal shard from the wreckage itself … and sent it whizzing after the escaping pair.

Tem saw it coming and knew it would be true. He flipped off his dragon's back and dove straight into the path of that lethal projectile. He caught it in midair, spun, and hurled it back into the ground.

It lodged three feet into the earth, dead center between Simon's feet. He hadn't moved an inch, and stared now as Tem reached and grabbed his dragon by one of its extended claws just before he would have crashed into the earth. They hovered in the air as a contingent of Mattaen stormed out of the temple.

Tem tipped his head and met the ice blue eyes of Karl's lost brother. "Knowledge without experience, slayers …" He laughed, then scrambled onto his dragon's back.

Simon watched them until they vanished behind the clouds. His brow furrowed in thought before he tilted his head and murmured, "Is weakness."

TWENTY-THREE

Her head pounded, her wrists burned, and nausea churned in the pit of her stomach. Biting back a moan, Elera opened her eyes ... and saw nothing at all. Wherever she was being kept, it was completely devoid of light. The only thing she knew for certain was that she was lying on a mattress with her arms bound and twisted above her head.

Her feet were tied too, she discovered, tugging against the ropes. A bellow shook the air, and her heart started racing. It was the bull, roaring beyond the walls.

She writhed on the bed, desperate to soothe the rage and panic in his deep-throated bellows. Light flooded the room as the doors opened. Pain stabbed her eyes as they struggled to adjust.

She blinked. The figure of a man approached. Ronin, judging by the roughness of his hands and the anger in his voice. After slicing through the bindings with his knife, he yanked her off the bed and pulled her to his chest. "Calm him, Elera."

She curled her lip, and then gasped when he slammed her against the wall. The lights already dancing before her eyes doubled. Ronin's face wavered out of focus as he yanked her even closer. Now they were nose-to-nose.

"Your lover is not the only man of yours whom I can end, my love. There is still Warwick." He touched her cheek as the bull's cries grew even more deafening. "Calm him, or see your grandfather torn to shreds by the warriors surrounding your home."

Dragging her through his manor, Ronin finally shoved her onto the terrace beyond his room.

Elera gasped as she glanced out from between the rails. Hundreds of warriors occupied the grounds, with nearly thirty riders taking point in the sky. Nearly all of them tried to distract the bull as he continued to dive and attack.

Elera clenched her fists when she saw his distress. It was one thing to allow a man to rape her, since the dragon didn't understand the concept ... but it was another thing entirely not to be able to get to her when he could sense that she was hurt.

She looked past him just then and noticed that a separate line of riders had formed just outside the borders of Ronin's land. It consisted of all those who had sworn allegiance to Karl, but they stood undecided, unsure of what course of action to take when their sovereign was silent and under suspicion.

Before Elera could do anything more than lift a hand to them, the bull spotted her.... Every warrior standing between him and the manor was sent flying with a single whip of his wing.

"Do it now," Ronin whispered in her ear before pushing her forward and racing back into his room.

Elera fell to her hands and knees, wincing just a little when the bull slammed into the manor above her head. He sheltered her with his wings and snarled viciously at anyone who might try to approach. Elera glanced back inside the manor, and trembled when she saw the glare Ronin sent her.

If she hadn't been in such turmoil, she might have sneered. He'd retreated deeper into his room before turning to face her. Instead, she twisted around and raised her hands to the underside of the bull's neck.

He flinched, but then his growl lowered, becoming almost

a purr as she stroked his scales. His eyes still burned red, but the tail that had been weaving back and forth in search of a target now slowed and lowered.

Ronin took a step toward the terrace, and that tail slammed straight through the wall. Its bladed tip missed the man by a hair, but the sharp rubble that sliced into his skin as he rolled seemed to spill enough of his blood to appease the bull's ire.

"No!" Elera yelled, before Ronin could call his men and speak the words that would sentence her grandfather to death. "I'll send him away."

Though the bull's growl returned as he sensed his rider's agitation, Elera kept her hands steady upon his snout, smoothing away his snarl and pressing her forehead to his jaw. She whispered nonsense designed to ease him by the rhythm and cadence of her voice. And so it did.

With the bull calm, her own heartbeat slowed, which meant Elera could finally search for the echo of Karl's pulse in her veins. If he was dead, she would feel nothing, and fear of that possibility made her tremble anew.

The bull tensed, and she restarted the calming process. It was easier this time, because she *had* found that resonance in her heart and blood. Rising to her toes, Elera leaned against the bull and whispered quietly enough that no one would overhear, "Karl. Find Karl."

The bull tossed his head, and she toppled to the floor. He wouldn't obey … she wasn't sure if he could without Karl's scent. But then he lowered his snout, nuzzled her briefly, and leaped from the manor. A plume of stone, dust, and dirt sprinkled the terrace in his wake.

Ronin's hand brushed the grit from her skin. "The first sign of betrayal, Elera, and I will have your grandfather—"

"Ripped to shreds," she interrupted, lifting her chin and staring defiantly into his face. "I heard you the first time."

"You think me a monster," Ronin said, hauling her upright and dragging her back to the room. "But I warned you this would come to pass if you did not submit. Anything could have been yours, Elera. *Everything.* Am I not the one who pulled this world together when we would have fallen apart?"

Her head bounced off the bed, so hard did he thrust her upon it. As the world grayed and doubled, Elera fought back her nausea and pushed to her knees.

"You may have pulled our world together, but you can't lead us from the destruction that lies in our path. If you had accepted this, you could have continued to lead Verteva's army. Karl would not have unseated you—"

"Karl," Ronin sneered, stalking her until she pressed against the headboard with her knees drawn up to her chest. He studied her, enjoying her wide eyes and trembling hands. He gripped her chin and forced her to look at him. "Tell me, Elera. Where is your good friend Tem during these last few days when you and your lover have trekked across the land?"

With a shake of her head, Elera jerked free of his fingers. The swift motion sent the room spinning again.

"Head bothering you, my love?" Tracing the angry bruise on her temple, Ronin ran his fingers over her blood-encrusted hair.

"You can't keep me here," Elera whispered weakly. "The people took Karl as king.... For you to do this ... it will bring war to our world."

He chuckled. "There will be no war. The people know their king intended to betray us to the slayers." When she shook her head, his voice turned harsh. "Your lover sent Tem to the Mattaen on the very evening of his rise to rule, and then set about distracting you and the great Houses with his journey of *knowledge.* How many secrets has he discovered on his path, how many of our weaknesses?"

There was a rebuke there, she knew. But it was so very hard to think with her vision swimming and her stomach roiling. "If he did so, there was good cause—"

"Then why keep it secret?" Ronin's fingers tightened in her hair, the pulse in his neck increased, and still he waited for the answer she would not give. "Because he always meant to betray you, and Tem, and this world. He is Mattaen, Elera."

Elera lifted her chin. "When Tem returns, he'll set things right. Whatever you've done to turn the people against Karl, it will be for naught."

Ronin stared in astonishment before shoving her back against the headboard to pace the room in fury. Finally, he stopped and turned to face her.

"If you are right, Elera, I will step down." Her lips parted in surprise. "I've already sent riders to help Tem if it isn't too late ... or to retrieve his dragon and body if it is."

Horrified by the image his words produced, Elera lifted her hands to her mouth and moaned. *Tem ...*

Ronin paused, then walked back to her and settled on the edge of the bed. Reaching out, he lifted a single tear from her cheek.

"Why do you fight me? I am no gentle man, I realize. But I am of this world, and I would give my life's blood to see it strong and pure. You went to another man, an *outsider*, and that is my failing for not having forced our union sooner. I had wanted so very much to be your choice. To rule with your breath and not only my strength."

The last statement rang with sincerity, but it crawled over her skin in the same manner as his eyes did.

"Your lover is dead. He betrayed you and our people." His voice grew harsh a second time, his fingers cruel on her chin. "Can you still have faith in your abilities to decide what this world needs?"

If he'd simply left then, she might have dwelled upon his words and given in to doubt. But he climbed onto the bed and pressed his body to hers until the pounding of his heart blocked out any other sensation. For a moment, she had a glimpse of what it would be like to have this man only, and feel naught from her mate. No! She would not give in.

She kicked out and sent the pair of them rolling off opposite sides of the bed. Standing her ground when he leaped across the mattress and towered over her, Elera whispered, "You're lying. Karl would not have betrayed us, and Tem is not dead, at least not by Karl's hand."

Neither was Karl dead, but she didn't want Ronin to read that in her eyes, so she ducked her head when he raised his fist, and let him believe that her trembling came from fear of him.

Only after his steps receded and the door slammed did Elera give in to her uncertainties and let her tears fall.

Loren was waiting outside the door when Ronin stormed out of his room. Nothing in his face revealed his sympathy for Elera's plight, even when he heard Ronin giving orders to the two warriors at his side.

"Find Tem. Kill him, and bring his body to my door."

Loren fought to keep from cringing. Had it come to this?

"And his dragon?" asked the youngest. "She will fight for him."

"Then kill her too!"

He watched their shocked expressions as Ronin continued down the stairs. These warriors were young. Their loyalty had been bought with strength, fear, and the heroic tales of tired old men. With no more than a glance, they nodded and left the manor.

He, however, was not young.

"Ronin," he called, racing down the stairs to catch the man

he had served with blind obedience for nearly two decades. "You must send me with them."

Stopping, Ronin turned with narrowed eyes. "You question me?"

Loren shook his head. "Never. But I am more than a jailer, and you waste my strength by leaving me in charge of one mere girl."

"One mere girl who has always held my fate, and the fate of this world, in her hands," Ronin spat.

"I understand your anger," Loren said quietly. "But if the blood of a dragon is to be spilled, you'll need more than strength of steel. You'll need strength of heart. Send me with them, Ronin. They will fail otherwise."

"You understand, then?" Ronin asked softly, deceptively.

Loren nodded and didn't have to feign sadness. "Better one dragon falls to a rider's hand, than many to the hands of the Mattaen. I understand your heart, Ronin. Know mine and be easy."

Making no sign to show that he noticed when Ronin's hand fell away from his ax, Loren lowered his eyes in a gesture of respect. Rain pooled and gathered beyond the windows, and still the younger man studied the older.

"You have always been loyal." Placing his hand upon the old warrior's shoulder, Ronin nodded. "Go then. Send one of the others to guard here in your place. See the deed done."

He concentrated, trying to find that faint echo of Elera and their bond, but he felt only the furious burn in his ribs and the sting in his hands as he dug into the dirt beneath a boulder. His breathing was shallow. The amount of oxygen in the cavern was decreasing ... and his body was failing fast.

He had been unable to escape the cave by following the current, and so had returned to the source of the cave-in and begun tunneling up through the collapse. He'd spent the entire night working. He had fallen twice from exhaustion and once from dizziness stemming from a knock on his head. But each tumble had him groping a path up the incline and relentlessly starting anew.

A sudden shift in the boulder he was trying to dislodge made him redouble his efforts. He clawed at it and then moved quickly aside as it toppled down the incline. Stretching his arms into the darkness, he squeezed into the empty space, using his forearms to feel his way to another boulder above.

He slipped then, as a sudden boom shattered the earth above his head. Dust filled his tiny pocket of air, leaving him gasping. Smaller chips of rock flew into his face, lodging within his hair.

Another thud had the rocks shifting yet again with no assistance from him. If stone and dirt hadn't been closing in around him, Karl might have roared in victory when he felt the fresh air filtering in from above. Instead, he took his first clean breath and started crawling upward through the maze of falling debris.

Something hard and heavy pummeled his chest before rolling past him. That was another cracked rib, if he wasn't mistaken. But at last he could see light slipping through a wedge in the rock. Reaching out, Karl grabbed hold of what seemed to be a sturdy ledge and pulled his body through a tight crevice that stripped the skin from his shoulder.

He rolled to his back, prone and exhausted, and felt the growling breaths of a much larger being gusting over his skin. Karl cracked a lid and stared into the red-eyed gaze of the beast himself.

"Yesterday would have been better," he rasped from his parched throat. Rolling to his knees, he saw that the entirety of the collapsed ceiling had created an uneven floor of debris that spread across the cavern itself. The bull's claws had left gouges in the stone. "But better today than never."

As he staggered to his feet, his vision swam, and he reached out for the nearest sturdy object. That the nearest sturdy object just happened to be made of scales, teeth, and a spiked tail didn't dawn on him until he heard the bull's low hiss.

"If you're going to do it, dragon," Karl whispered, removing his hand when those glowing eyes swiveled down and glared into his own, "I don't have the strength to stop you."

The bull held his tail poised, his muscles quivering with rage. But the sounds of a female in flight filled the air, and for just a moment the beast looked away. It was long enough for Karl to dive beneath his wing, slide under his belly, and duck into an alcove against the wall.

The tip of the beast's tail sliced a superficial line across Karl's shoulder blades, instead of his neck. Roaring his defeat, the bull leaped the entire length of the collapse and vanished into the storm clouds above.

Karl sank to his knees, too busy trying to slow his rapid pulse to see the arrow flying toward him until it pierced into the rock right beside his ear. He ducked instinctively, then tore out of the alcove with his pulse leaping anew. He stared across the wreckage at the boy with the bow.

"Tornak." The child drew his bow back again, when he saw Karl stalking across the uneven rubble of the fallen ceiling. The second arrow whizzed harmlessly past his ear, and the third he caught in midflight. Snapping it over his knee, Karl sprinted the remaining distance and ripped the bow away.

"I'll kill you," the child screamed, swinging wildly, laughing through his tears when his small fist split Karl's lip.

Enough, he decided, cursing quietly and restraining his temper just enough to pin the boy's arms without hurting him. For the first time, the thought of throttling a child did not seem completely abhorrent. In fact, when a tiny knee landed square in the center of his groin, the idea of placing his hands around that slim neck became thoroughly appealing.

"Enough!" Karl roared, tossing the boy to the ground, holding him down with a foot to the chest. Tornak squirmed and spat. He reached into his belt, and before Karl even realized what was happening, the boy had unsheathed his small dagger and stabbed it into the leg holding him down.

Karl's curses rang in the air as he hauled Tornak into the air by his shirtfront. Holding the boy an arm's length away from his aching body, he snatched the dagger out of his grasp ... and let the brat flail.

"Go ahead," screeched Tornak. "Kill me like you killed him."

Sensing the boy's pale eyes on the dagger still in his hand, Karl tossed it to the ground. "I haven't killed anyone, though I'm damned tempted at the moment."

"Bastard, *bayan* liar ..."

His struggles resumed until Karl shook him hard. The boy's racking sobs were loud enough to give him pause, and he eased his grip. "I said I haven't—"

"You sent my uncle to your people," Tornak cried. "You lied to him, and you sent him to die. I hate you. I *will* kill you...."

When he shuddered, Karl lowered him gently to the ground. Sitting at his side, his injuries throbbing, he waited. When the sobs turned to sniffles, Karl held the boy by his chin and stared into those mutinous eyes.

"Who told you I sent Tem to the Mattaen?"

"Everyone knows," Tornak whispered. "Ronin said ..."

"Ronin said?" Karl pressed, unintentionally tightening his fingers when the boy faltered.

"Ronin said you tricked Elera, and that you were a Mattaen spy come to export our weaknesses—"

"Exploit," Karl corrected absently.

"And pulverize the secrets of our steel," Tornak finished, proudly lifting his chin for having remembered it all.

Karl hid his smile. "Pilfer, Tornak. Pilfer the secrets of your steel. It means steal."

"Yes, the steel." Rolling his eyes, Tornak mumbled, "That's what I said."

"No, not . . ." Karl ran a weary hand over his face. "Never mind. You overheard these things from Ronin personally?"

"Some men came to our home. There was a lot of yelling, and Aunt Andia was crying. . . ." His gaze turned hard, filled with a rage much too large to belong to someone so young. "It's all your fault."

Karl nodded, bearing the weight of the blame. "These men brought Tem's body?"

Swiping at his tears with the back of his hand, Tornak shook his head. "They just said. I listened at the top of the stairs."

Karl brushed off the dirt and rocks, and then lifted the boy to his feet. "I'm going to tell you once, Tornak, and never again after this. I am no one's spy. I didn't lie to your uncle, or to Elera, or to you. And I have never killed anyone. But I am going to."

Karl knelt, lowering himself until he was eye level with the frightened child. "Ronin took Elera against her will. He hurt her, and is probably hurting her even more right now."

He had to stop there to control his panic. But the boy was her family, at least in spirit, and if he was old enough to ride and attempt to kill, he was old enough to know the truth of the man he worshiped.

Tornak wiped his nose on his sleeve. "Like raping her?"

"Listen a lot, don't you?" Karl asked softly, but nodded. "Maybe. Is that the kind of man you want to be?"

The boy lifted a shoulder in a halfhearted shrug. But his lips were trembling and his little body quivered. "You didn't send Tem to the Mattaen?"

"Yes, I did," Karl said after a pause, and raised a brow when the boy's hands fisted. "I sent him with a message to a man I once called brother."

"To warn him about us?"

Karl shook his head. "To warn him that if war comes, and we meet, not to trust me to be that brother still."

"Wouldn't that make him mad?"

"I'm sure." With a thin smile, Karl retrieved the boy's fallen bow and handed it back to him. "But when he gets through being mad, if he is my brother, he'll fight as hard as I will to keep that war from happening."

They cleared the ruins of the cave-in, and then walked in silence for a while, though it took most of the night to draw near to the fields around Tornak's home. The clouds belched, drenching the boy and the man in sheets of rain as they walked through the fields of prickly wheat.

Tucking the child against his side, Karl eyed the sky. "Where's your dragon, Tornak?"

The boy shrugged.

"You sent her away thinking I would kill her?"

Tornak nodded, looking slightly guilty. "And because we aren't allowed to leave the house. Ronin's warriors said so, because we were loyal to Elera, and Elera was loyal to you. No one was going to think I was gone if my dragon wasn't." He sniffed. "Are you going to go get Elera back now?"

"I am," Karl said, ruffling the boy's hair. They were approaching the boundaries of his House, where three of Ronin's warriors prowled. He grabbed Tornak before he could race ahead and knelt at his side once more. "Are they looking for me?"

"They think you're dead."

Karl nodded, then tilted his head curiously. "Why didn't you?"

"I...I hoped..." His eyes lowered, fixing on his feet. "I hoped you weren't, so I could..."

So he could do the killing himself, Karl realized, lifting his brow. "And how did you know where to find me?"

"I hoped if I followed the bull that I would find you." He hesitated, swallowing his tears before asking, "If Ronin was lying about you, do you think...do you think maybe my uncle is still alive?"

"I don't know." When the boy shuffled his feet, Karl put a hand on his shoulder. "But when I have Elera, if your uncle hasn't yet returned, I'll go find him. I swear it."

He hid in the wheat as the boy sneaked toward the manor. Tornak scrambled over the rocks lining the grounds, careful to remain in shadow, and finally shimmied up the side of the manor to his terrace at the top. He tripped over a chair on the terrace when he turned back to wave. Only after the young rider ducked quickly behind the curtains did Karl turn his attention to the two warriors coming to investigate the disturbance.

The contented rumbling of the female overhead was all it took to set them at ease. With little effort, Karl sneaked up behind the two men, cracked their heads together... and *pilfered* what remained of their rations and water.

He wouldn't set foot in Andia's House, for that would put the family in even more danger. Instead, after consuming a handful of rations from the stolen pack, Karl raced through the rain. He continued to run, leaping over crevices, diving across streams... until a wall of scales slammed into the ground before him. Karl slipped in the mud when he tried to stop his momentum, fell to his back and slid to a halt directly underneath a set of slavering black lips.

"Still nursing a grudge, I see," he said softly, as the breath of the beast enveloped him. But with his blood rushing in his ears, Karl met that red-eyed fury with an arrogant toss of his head. "Good."

The time had come to ride this damnable beast.

TWENTY-FOUR

Tem lifted his hand to welcome the trio of riders swooping down from the sky. Flames crackled from behind him. It was the first fire he'd lit since racing the winds with greater speed than any rider ever before … or so he would boast at the next feasting celebration.

If he made it to the next celebration. Tem narrowed his eyes as he recognized Ronin's men, and glanced briefly toward his beauty cooling off in a nearby pond. He slowly reached for the harness at his back and the blade concealed there.

Loren guided his dragon to the ground with no more than a whisper of sound. He inclined his head. "Greetings, Tem of Pryor."

"And to you," Tem said cautiously, widening his stance after the older man glanced at his beauty as if noting the distance between them. "What brings you to the barrens?"

"What brings *you* here?" asked Thayer, the youngest rider, taking his place as all three formed a triangle of restless dragons around Tem.

There seemed no point in attempting to conceal his blade. Tem pulled it from its clasp and held it loosely at his side. His fist clenched around its hilt, sending muscles rippling up his forearm as he waited for one of them to make a move.

"You should not have betrayed him," rebuked the third and final warrior as he slid from his dragon's back. Newly bonded to his dragon, but not as new to Ronin's army, Brenn drew his weapon. The blades at either end of his long spear glistened in the moonlight. "Nor given your loyalties to the wrong side of a rebellion that will be vanquished in the blood of dragons."

"Have a care whom you name a rebel, lest you become one yourself." Tem lifted his blade a fraction higher. "My oath is given to the rightful sovereign of Verteva."

Loren threw his head back and roared with laughter. "Brave words, rider, but slightly out of character for one who flouts custom and rule with every breath he takes."

Tem inclined his head. "We have not had a king in power during my lifetime, old man."

"Power belongs to the one who can keep it," spoke Thayer.

It was Tem's turn to laugh. "Do I debate with monks of the Mattaen this day?" His smile faltered when the men started closing in. "Or do I fight warriors, come to slay a rider of the blood?"

He parried the first blow, sent Thayer sprawling with a hard kick to his chest, and just barely managed to avoid the spear swiping the air above his head. It was impossible to keep his beauty unaware of this battle. She lifted her head from the water at the first thud and lunged forward with a snarl on her lips.

The other three dragons swiveled as the female approached, hissing as they sensed her intent to defend her rider by attacking theirs.

"Dragon cannot spill dragon blood," Tem shouted, struggling to calm the fire in his veins as he battled the spear wielder.

"You're right," Brenn drawled, slipping through Tem's defense to slice his shoulder. Over his own shoulder, he roared, "Kill her now!"

Tem lost his footing after seeing Thayer lift a longbow from a pack slung over his dragon. Taking advantage of his distraction, his opponent spun his spear, grazing the edge of Tem's neck as he rolled along the ground to avoid the blow.

Now he was too far away to stop the arrow from being released from its bow. Tem's mind railed against the coming slaughter, and he screamed for the beauty who wouldn't think to evade a strike from another rider. In the whole of their history, there had never once been a rider who sought to spill the blood of any dragon.

Tem's throat burned with his anguished roar, but the arrow never flew. The young rider slumped to the ground instead. Not dead, but not moving either. Loren stood over him, a small line of blood staining the flat of his ax. The dragons were facing the greater threat of the approaching female, and none but Loren, Tem, and Brenn were witness to the act.

Before Brenn could recover from his confusion and feel the alarm that might bring his dragon back, Tem planted a fist beneath his jaw and sent him slumping to the ground.

By the time the trio of dragons turned back—no longer threatened by his beauty, who had calmed the second she ceased to sense a threat to her rider—both he and Loren were standing well away from the pair of unconscious riders. Their confused beasts nosed them, but their scaled bodies no longer rippled with menace.

Tem's beauty landed before him, nudging him in affection. From beneath her snout, he met Loren's eyes. "Why would you help me?"

"Because you are *not* standing here debating with Mattaen slayers." With a sigh, Loren caressed the scales of his own beast. "Our oaths should be first and foremost to the dragon, and not the rider. I once pledged myself to the lesser of the two. I will rectify that mistake now."

"I think you already have."

Loren shook his head, wilting where he stood. "Your sovereign is dead, and mine ordered the killing of a dragon. And he has Elera."

Tem immediately stamped out the fire, retrieved his blade, and swung onto his dragon. "Then we race the wind—"

"You race the wind, rider," Loren interrupted, pointing his ax toward himself. "There are none to stop him now, and I will not live to see a world that sets dragon against dragon...."

"No!" he shouted, but too late. Loren had impaled himself on the blade of his own weapon. His dragon stood with her head tilted curiously until the scent of his blood reached her snout. Only then did her screech bruise the very winds on which Tem already raced.

He was insane. And that was the sanest thought in his head, Karl decided, as he rolled under the bull's tail and leaped into the air when its tip swung back around for a second lash. Clearing it by a hair, he landed on his heels, and sighed when he felt blood trickling over his left eye.

"Sure could have wished to be in better condition for this," he grumbled, leaping onto the wing that came swiping toward him. He ran along its membranous edge and nearly seated himself behind the bull's crest before the blunt side of that damnable tail caught him in the ribs.

This time Karl landed on his back, engulfed by the fire spreading across his battered torso. He had no opportunity to catch his breath, however, for the beast pounced with claws extended. They scraped rock instead of flesh, and sent sparks flying after his fleeing form.

There was no restraint in the bull's speed or attack, for he was truly furious at having been touched by man, and twice in the same day. Every time Karl dodged one blow, a wing, spike, or claw came around to swipe at him where he landed.

He lost his footing in the mud and nearly fell, yet even as the beast's tail plunged to skewer him, Karl ducked with his arm raised and grabbed hold of one of the spikes on its tip. Torn from the ground as the tail whipped around, he hooked his feet around its girth for balance, took one deep breath ... and leaped.

He landed on the dragon's back, swerving as the ridge of its spine extended. He nearly slipped off the beast's sleek scales before his fingers gripped the cracks between them. The bull's massive wings tried to beat down upon him, but were hindered by their range of movement, which gave Karl just enough space to scramble up the bull's neck and grab his crest.

The bull bared his teeth as Karl planted his feet atop his powerful shoulder. "Let's ride," he whispered.

The beast wasn't exactly willing. He carried Karl through vines that whipped at his skin, flew between jutting cliffs that would have scraped him loose if not for the wide crest that limited exactly how near the ragged stone the bull could skim.

The speed was phenomenal, stealing his breath and making his eyes water. The strength of the wind threatened to tear him from his precarious perch. Compared to this wild and frantic battle of wills, the ride with Tem had been as tame as a walk through waist-deep water.

It was the spine that actually saved him, for with it extended the dragon could not engage in the sharp swerves that might have thrown him off. Nor could he lower it without the risk of granting Karl a firmer seat ... although the bull could have sliced the man in two the moment he settled atop the lowered spine. Animal instinct apparently did not include the intelligence to lay such a trap.

They flew to the very boundaries of the sky, far above the people turning too slowly to catch more than a glimpse of fleeting shadow. Straight to the edges of Verteva, where the bull dove toward the ocean. Karl's stomach leaped into his throat, and he suddenly regretted eating the rations he'd stolen.

Once his heart started beating again as the dive leveled out,

Karl dared to open his eyes. They were gliding *through* the very honeycombed matrix he had risked life and limb to climb. The beast's flight brought them close enough to the rock and earth and clay that Karl could actually smell the different properties in each until finally they whizzed through to the opposite side.

"This cannot continue, my friend," he shouted, pressing flat against the beast when he bulldozed through the frail mesh of an earthen wall. It wasn't that Karl was growing weary. Riding was exhilarating. But Elera . . .

Spreading his legs, Karl started weaving with the bull, learning the movements of his muscles, anticipating when to dig in with a heel or press with the balls of his feet . . . swaying in whatever direction the bull took. Though it seemed like only moments had passed, it must have been hours later when the bull started responding.

Only then did Karl begin initiating the changes in direction, instead of simply weaving with them. Until finally, from his position on the beast's shoulder, he was guiding their flight.

It was a seduction so thorough, so efficient and sly, that as they flew over the borders of Verteva, the bull didn't seem to notice his own surrender.

Elera paced the confines of her windowless room. Sometime during the night, she'd woken to find Ronin sitting on the bed. His breathing had been shallow, and in the little light that seeped under the door, she'd watched his shoulders trembling. He'd done nothing more than stare at her, but she'd feigned sleep even as her skin had dripped with cold sweat.

He would not be content, she knew, to merely watch for much longer.

With that thought foremost in mind, Elera worked on the

rope binding her wrists until tears burned in her eyes. If Ronin had tied her hands in front instead of at her back, she might have freed them sooner. But finally, with her blood slicking the bindings, she managed to slip free. Quickly, she moved behind the door.

Getting out of the room was simply a matter of waiting for the guard to enter with her evening meal. He would be expecting to see her huddled on the edge of the bed...as she had been on each previous occasion.

As anticipated, the man marched swiftly through the door with little regard for his surroundings, and Elera was able to hug the wall and slip out behind his back.

She was halfway down the corridor by the time he shouted, and she slipped into a room that connected the east and west wings of Ronin's manor. A group of warriors raced past the door a moment later. She held her breath until their steps faded, then exited the room and edged along the alcoves in the hallway.

More warriors neared her hiding place, but these men were slowly and deliberately searching each room, shadow, and corner.

Elera hissed. She'd counted on gaining a bit more distance from the manor before having to deal with an organized hunt. Her eyes darted to an open terrace two levels down from the central stairs. She remembered, from former functions that had required her presence here, that the terrace overlooked the eastern grounds. The sun was setting, and that area should already be cloaked in shadow.

Dashing out of the corner, Elera leaped over the banister and landed hard on the stairs two levels below. She grabbed the railing before she stumbled and fell, then squeezed through the bars. She cried out when something caught her hair. Tears burned in her eyes as she left a dark lock in someone's clenched fist, but she shot back to her feet, racing down the corridor with a second pursuer on her tail. Three more approached from the opposite direction, cutting her off.

Elera scrambled into the terrace room and kicked the door shut in their faces. Searching her surroundings quickly, she barred the door with a nearby chair. It creaked as the men began slamming against it.

Elera climbed over the lip of the terrace and started climbing down the latticework. If she could reach the cliffs, she could call the bull and get clear of—

Without any warning at all, a pair of large hands grabbed her by the waist, tightening cruelly before pitching her to the grass.

Breathless, Elera looked up and rasped, "Ronin..."

She cried out when he wrapped his hand around her throat, hauling her up and knocking her back into the manor. "I have done everything to give you time. I've been lenient, and still you seek to betray me!" Forcing his thigh between hers, catching her wrists with the hand not around her throat, he sandwiched her against the wall. "I have waited and waited...."

He hissed when Elera started struggling, then caught the knee she raised to his groin, shoved it against the wall, and settled fully between her legs.

He was going to take her here, she realized in panic, watching his eyes go black. She felt his shudders, heard the animalistic sounds tearing from his throat as he fumbled with the fastenings on his pants. He would take her here, against the wall, with her hands held over her head and a scream on her lips.

It was the scream that saved her as he tore at her clothes. Ronin's hand left her wrists to cover her mouth. And that quickly, Elera grabbed the blade clasped to his thigh and pressed it against the erratic pulse in his throat. For a moment, she was afraid he was too caught up, that he would take her without even noticing. But his eyes cleared, his body froze, and he very slowly pulled his hands away from her flesh.

"Stay," she ordered shakily, when he moved to step back. She had the upper hand only as long as she held his blade against his throat.

"Elera ..."

The steel bit into his skin. She meant it as a warning, but Ronin wisely shut his mouth.

"Walk with me," she said, willing her legs to remain steady. Slowly, inch by painful inch, Elera pushed him out of the shadows, rounding the manor as the hunger in his eyes caused the blade to tremble in her hand. A thin stream of his blood trickled down the edge of the knife, but still they walked together ... a single misstep away from death.

Even after she heard the approaching rush of many feet, Elera continued to push Ronin toward the front of his home. She heard him growl a warning to the warriors forming a circle around them, and listened as their steps immediately stilled.

His charcoal eyes never once left hers. "How far do you expect to take this?"

"To the riders on the fringe," she whispered. She saw motion out of the corner of her eye. "Make them stay!"

Ronin raised his palm to stop the silent rush of his swiftest guards. "An adequate plan, Elera. If ..."

Her eyes narrowed, and he grinned.

"If my riders didn't outnumber yours two to one, with more than a hundred warriors to back them up on the ground." Shifting his eyes back to the guard before Elera could anticipate his motives, Ronin ordered, "Kill every rider that supports her."

By now, the riders on the fringe had spotted Elera. They saw her bloodied and bruised face and tensed.

"Release her!" shouted a rider closest to the border.

Ronin smirked when one of his own men shouted back that it was Elera who held the blade. Not that it mattered. The grounds already resonated with the sounds of weapons being unsheathed by hands restless to draw blood.

When she heard one dragon snarling at another, Elera knew her advantage was worthless. She could not allow dragon to fight dragon. "Call your men back, Ronin, and I won't—"

"Why would I bargain?" Leaning into the blade, he breathed, "How many arrows do you think are aimed at your throat even as you stand with a blade to mine? I'll wager the mettle of my men against the speed of your wrist, Elera."

Shifting her eyes without moving the dagger, Elera realized that he held his warriors back ... not for his sake, but for hers. Silent tears of defeat slid down her cheeks. "Why are you waiting, then? I can't stop you. There's no one to stop you."

"For those words," Ronin whispered, tilting his head as if in regret, before lifting his finger to signal the kill.

Elera closed her eyes and wondered if there would be any pain, or just the cold and empty feeling of death. She wished, she truly did, that she had the strength to end Ronin as she'd threatened instead of simply standing here shaking in the shadow of ...

Wasn't this taking just a bit too long?

Elera opened her eyes and stared into Ronin's stricken face. With a frown, she turned her gaze to the nearest warriors and found them frozen, their weapons hanging limply at their sides. Even on the fringe, the battle had stilled before the first clash of weapons.

Every man was staring at the dark mass descending from the sky.

It wasn't death, or at least not hers. It was the bull, and riding him, with that mane of fire tangling wildly in the wind, was the sovereign king of Verteva.

The blade fell from Elera's fingers to lodge harmlessly in the soil between her feet. Ronin could have snapped her neck or slit her throat. Instead he watched in disbelief with the rest of his men, frozen as the bull slammed into the earth with enough force to send vibrations skittering from her toes to her spine.

The bull trumpeted as Karl jumped to the ground and strode furiously toward them. He studied her face, and she could see his mouth tighten when he noticed her bruises and bloody lip. He murmured her name ... then smashed his elbow over her head and into Ronin's face.

TWENTY-FIVE

It wasn't the entrance he had meant to make, but Karl decided it would do. The sole reason he wasn't pounding Ronin into the ground was crushed tightly against his chest. Karl buried his face in Elera's hair as he fought to control his fury . . . until he caught sight of the unfastened pants on their would-be warlord.

Karl's vision turned black with rage.

Maintaining enough sense to give Elera a gentle shove toward the bull, he reached down and hauled Ronin upright by the throat. Two fast strikes sent the rider back to the ground.

Karl hesitated just once, when Ronin's dragon dropped from the roof of the manor with her teeth bared and her tail poised to strike, until a single hiss from the bull sent her cowering in submission.

Ronin's eyes wavered uncertainly between the two beasts. When Karl pulled him to his feet a second time, he offered no resistance. Nor after being stuck down a third time, or even a fourth.

Before he could fall again, Karl dragged him up until they were nose-to-nose. He roared, "Fight back!"

The warrior merely stared weakly at his feet . . . and Karl dropped him in disgust.

Elera.

Not another glance did he spare for Ronin as he sprinted to where Elera stood in the shadow of the bull's outstretched wing. He stopped a few feet away, after he noticed the stricken look on her face. "Elera?"

She shook her head, backing away.

"He hurt you," Karl said quietly, aching for her bruises, her torn clothing, her blood. Forcing his hands to unclench at his sides, he held one out. Anguish contorted his features when still she moved closer to the bull. "Do you think I would hurt you, that I could?"

She shook her head again.

Relief flooded through him, but she was silent still. Karl tilted his head as another thought occurred to him. "Did you think I had betrayed you, Elera?"

This time she hesitated, tears filling her eyes as her lips trembled. "For a moment."

Ignoring the warriors closing in around them, Karl stepped closer, speaking softly. "It's all right."

"No. It isn't." Her eyes flashed fire then, as annoyance replaced her wariness. "And what else could you expect, sending Tem off without saying a word to me? Do you even—"

"I don't make much of a figurehead," Karl murmured. "You brought me here to save your people, and that is what I'm trying to do." He closed the distance between them and wrapped her in his arms. "Don't be afraid of me, mate; I couldn't stomach it."

"It's not that," she whispered, melting into him as he pressed soft kisses over her brow, her cheeks, her jaw.

His fingers shook as they fingered the torn band of her skirt.

"He didn't," Elera whispered, and again when his fingers tightened and his body shuddered: "He didn't. I ... He tried, but he didn't. I—"

Karl clutched her tightly, strangling her words as he thought of all he might have lost. He had forgotten the battle they'd interrupted. The bull snarled as riders from both sides began to form a semicircle around them.

Forcing his mind to focus on the crisis at hand, he nudged Elera behind his back, then stood and faced the horde.

Their faces wore expressions of awe and distrust as the ones who stood closest took a few steps back. His spine stiffened. Though his lips parted to speak, it was Elera's choked whisper that carried on the wind: "Tem."

Karl turned and followed her gaze to a shadow approaching from the clouds. While he watched, the rider's name was whispered throughout the crowd, as more than a few fingers pointed skyward.

Slumped against his manor, Ronin watched the sky with dark and weary eyes. His riders must have failed.... How could they not, when his own defeat lay bitter upon him. He glanced at Elera, at her hand tucked firmly within her mate's, at the bull standing protectively over the pair. And finally, he glanced at the army he'd formed out of chaos. They hadn't spared him a glance since the usurper had arrived riding the bull.

Last, Ronin stared in despair at the magnificent creature that had carried him in flight for three decades. "I'm sorry," he whispered to her. No one noticed him rise to his feet, or reach for his ax lying on the ground a few paces away.

Gathering what remained of his strength, Ronin pivoted on his heel, swung his ax behind his shoulder ... and with a roar that had all eyes spinning toward him, he launched it at the bull.

It was his own dragon that leaped into the path of the blade. Horror twisted Ronin's face as his hoarse shout of denial rang out. He never saw the wing of the bull knock the female out of danger, or the leap of the new sovereign as he grabbed the ax by its spinning hilt and hurled it to the ground.

Ronin never saw any of these things. The bull's tail had slashed through the air and severed his torso with its bladed tip.

Tem leaped from his dragon before she had even touched the ground. He had seen Elera's blood. He had also seen Karl, who evidently was not dead after all, shift his weight to shield her from the remains of the man who had once been her future. With no thought except to reach her, Tem rushed forward.

A snarl from the bull halted him midstride. Karl tugged Elera back before she rushed out from the protective shelter of the bull's wing.

Slowing his advance to assume a less threatening manner, Tem ducked under that same wing and moved to the couple's side. "I take my eyes off the two of you for a few days ... and look what happens."

His immediate concern had been for Elera, and then the keening dragon guarding Ronin's corpse, but he finally noticed the motionless army surrounding them.

With a frown, he leaned into her. "Ah ... what did happen?"

"Karl ..."

Her whisper caught in her throat, overcome by the fierce sound of a hundred steel blades being unsheathed. Axes, swords, maces, spears ... all raised to shimmer in the light of the full moon.

Surprisingly, one of Ronin's men was the first to kneel. Perhaps he staggered a bit, but there was nothing hesitant in the way he shouted his name and the name of his House before plunging his sword deep within the earth.

Tem watched a wave ripple through the crowd as riders leaped from their dragons, offering their steel along with the riderless standing among them. Individual names were lost in the din, but the meaning of their pledge rang as clear as their blue-flamed heritage.

Cursing her tears, Elera reached back and grabbed his hand. Her voice was steady with pride as she told him, "Karl rode the bull."

She seemed to suddenly realize that this might have been

an extreme source of distress for her dragon, and left both men to rush forward and smooth the snarl from his lips.

"Right." Tem snorted in disbelief. He took another look around the grounds, his gray eyes lingering over the kneeling horde. He glanced warily back at the bull and cocked his head slowly to the side. "Truly?"

"If you go speechless on me, I'll knock you on your ass," Karl growled, frowning when the dragon flinched away from Elera's touch.

"But you rode the …" Tem breathed, grinning as his taunting earned him another glare. "I believe you sent me away just to miss all the fun."

"Looks like you had your share," Karl said, nodding to the gashes and bruises littering his arms and face.

"Some," he said quietly. "From your friends in the realm, and from the riders Ronin sent to see me dead."

He gave Karl the details, watching as something close to compassion flashed across the other man's face when he heard how Loren had died.

"You knew Ronin had Elera?" Karl asked.

Tem nodded. Without further delay, he withdrew both his blades as he knelt and plunged them into the earth.

"You don't need to …"

Karl fell silent and both of them looked at the bull, who was still shifting restlessly away from Elera's touch. It took Tem only a moment to understand what was happening, and he lost his breath as emotion swamped him.

"Elera?" Karl called.

"He won't let me touch him," she said softly, appearing lost and vulnerable as she stepped back.

Karl looked stricken. "Because I rode him? Elera, sweet stars, I never meant to—"

Though every other warrior remained bowed and watching, Tem rose and clasped his hand over Karl's shoulder, bringing a quick halt to his forward rush. "That's not the problem."

With a stiff nod, Karl stayed back as the dragon shied farther away from her before leaping over the heads of the men in his path. He landed at the side of Ronin's keening female and nuzzled her softly. With a harder nudge, he sent her soaring clumsily to the sky, where she flew in the shadow of his wing.

Elera watched them go, then turned to face her mate. Her dazed look quickly faded to scorn. "There's such a thing as taking arrogance too far, you know." She tossed her head. "I am hardly in danger of being usurped as the bull's rider by any male, no matter what you did to get him to tolerate you. In truth, you're lucky your head is still atop your ..."

Elera shuddered, and Tem watched carefully as she purposely avoided Ronin's remains when she walked back to where he stood with Karl.

"Grant your mate a little mercy, Elera," Tem rebuked her softly, "and tell him."

"Tell me what?" Karl asked, taking her hand and pulling her to his chest. "What keeps the bull from you?"

With a small smile unlike any Tem had ever seen on her lips, Elera dragged Karl's hands to the gentle slope of her stomach. "Your son," she whispered. "He senses your son."

Karl said nothing. Not a word. His fingers tightened on hers before splaying wide across her abdomen.

"Don't think he's quite that size—"

Her mate kissed her gently before whispering, "Of course he is."

His eyes changed then, blazing with intent. In front of more than a hundred warriors, he fell to his knees with his arms wrapped around her waist and pressed his lips to the place where their child rested.

A multitude of voices rang out in cheers as each warrior withdrew his blade and thrust it skyward. Karl looked up in surprise, cheeks bronzing when he realized he'd just made the news public. He stood slowly to face the men, and Tem heard him whisper, "A man might have wished for a more private moment to learn of such a thing."

Elera's eyes narrowed, but before she could argue, Karl whipped her off her feet and swung her atop his shoulder.

"To the future of Verteva!" Tem shouted, overcome by pride and love as he moved to face the couple. The warriors echoed him as Karl slid Elera slowly down his torso.

"To the future of our son," Karl added quietly, raising her fingers to his lips. Her eyes misted, and then flared in alarm. Karl placed his fingers over her mouth. "Tem."

Distracted by the depth of emotion he could see in Elera, Tem did not answer. His oldest friend had found love in her bond. It was the greatest joy that could come of seeking, but it did not always happen. Even though he had wanted nothing less for Elera, it was disconcerting to realize he was the outsider now.

Sighing when Karl continued to stare at him with his brow lifted, he murmured, "Yes?"

"Did you see to Warwick on your way in?"

"Of course. I—Elera," he rebuked, belatedly recognizing that this was the cause for the returning alarm in her eyes. Mate or no, she should know he would see to the concerns of her heart as well as her safety. Caring nothing for the watching army, he stepped forward and brushed his lips over her brow.

"Your grandfather is hale and hearty, with a couple of new footstools bound and tossed onto his front step."

He stepped back before his touch could be deemed inappropriate before the eyes of their people ... another first that left him feeling unsettled.

He winked to help keep things light.

"Have a little faith in those who love you," Karl whispered with a nod of gratitude to Tem. He steadied Elera when she swayed on her feet. "You need to be home."

She shook her head. "I don't want to leave you, and you have to be with the men, making sure—"

"I rode the bull for the men," Karl said roughly, then arched his brow as his eyes glazed. What a wild ride it must have been, Tem thought with a low chuckle.

Karl grinned ruefully at him. "It was a side benefit, at the least. But I think it's enough to satisfy them for a night or two … or …" He growled, because Elera was shaking her head … and Tem knew he must have realized the truth.

The king could not leave.

Karl dragged his fingers through his hair … and Tem nodded before he could ask his question. "I'll get her home … and see her safe," he assured the king, when Karl seemed reluctant to release Elera's arms.

"Dane," Karl ordered. "Take Dane and two others who have your trust. We'll speak later."

He didn't touch Elera again, but Tem saw his struggle in the working of his jaw. But with a final nod, Karl headed off … stopping just on the brink of the dispersing crowd to call over his shoulder, "The names of the riders sent to kill you?"

Tem gave them, and Karl vanished behind the waiting men.

It was nearly morning when Karl brushed his fingers over Elera's cheek, softly enough that he wouldn't wake her. The shadows under her eyes had yet to fade, although Tem had reported that she'd fallen asleep halfway back to the manor … stirring just long enough to check on Warwick and have her injuries tended. Karl's own wounds still ached, though he had been immersed in the sunken tub for the last hour, washing and bandaging each laceration.

But he did not touch her again...yet. He had something he needed to find...and that was the echo of Elera's pulse. The immediate danger might have passed...but he refused to ever again be uncertain when it came to his mate's well-being.

Dropping to his knees on the floor beside their bed, Karl stared at the pulse in her throat. When he thought he had the rhythm committed to memory, he closed his eyes...and waited.

He felt nothing at first...only the strong beat of his own pulse tapping against his wrist. But he would not be denied. Letting the love he felt for Elera flow into him, through him, around him...he listened until the sound of her breath moved as a caress within his ears, until her scent consumed his senses.

Something...Afraid to lose the tiny sense of a second pulse, Karl held his breath...and he thought perhaps...

He had found it! His blood thrummed loud enough to fill his mind in his excitement...but behind each heavy pulse skipped that softer echo she had described...almost too faint for him to feel, but moving steadily through his veins while she slept.

Karl opened his eyes and gazed with love at the beautiful woman who had given him such a heart-wrenching gift. Slipping over the edge of the bed, he leaned close and curled his body around hers.

Elera's lashes fluttered. "Karl?"

"Who else holds you thus?" he whispered, and felt her lips curve against his neck. "You're awfully warm and cozy."

Snuggling deeper into his arms with a yawn, Elera whispered, "And sleepy."

His hands quickly ceased their roaming. "You will be for the first few months. And nauseous. Are you? I could..."

With a chuckle, Elera pushed him back into the mattress, leaning over him so her hair tickled his shoulders. "So the scholar tells me what my body will feel?"

Color rose in his cheeks as his hand cupped her nape and he pulled her down to his lips. One brow lifted arrogantly. "Has it ever been different?"

For a while, they lost themselves in the taste and warmth of each other. His lips and hands moved slowly, gently. He was conscious of the soft shivers that might have been due to fear or discomfort.

"Is there trouble?" she asked, confused when he pulled back.

"In a world where each citizen is as bullheaded as the next?" Karl asked dryly. "Never say so."

His tone coaxed a smile from her lips, and set her enough at ease that she rested her head in the hollow of his shoulder. "Did you speak to Warwick?"

"I did," he whispered, absently stroking his thumb along her hip. "He was frightened for you, and angrier than any elder I've ever known."

"With you?" Elera asked sharply, sitting up. "Why?"

"For letting things get this far." He hushed her with a finger to her lips. "He has a right to be, Elera. I gave Ronin the chance to hurt us when I didn't slay him the night of my acceptance. It was a mistake that nearly cost me …"

He traced her cheek, running his fingers along her breast, her ribs … and finally rested his hand atop her stomach.

"Those who were absent last night have three days to pledge fealty or they'll be banished below." Her eyes widened, and he frowned. "It is the way of things, is it not? I spoke at length with Tem."

"With the few warriors who cannot work the flame, yes," Elera said. "But for the others, there can be no banishment.

The Mattaen could capture them and force them to manipulate fire. There is only—"

Execution.

Karl claimed her lips before the word could be spoken aloud. Tem had been adamant on that point also, and although Karl had agreed, he hadn't wanted to burden her with thoughts of further bloodshed.

Elera's eyes narrowed. Evidently, he was not as good at hiding his intentions as he had believed. "Do you wish me to kneel before you, Karl?"

His nostrils flared and his hands tightened on her arms, and then he slumped as he realized she had not meant …

"No. At least, not in the manner you imply." He brushed his thumb over her lips. "You know this."

"Then you wish for me to stand at your side?"

"I said so, did I not?" His fingers traced the bruise on her jaw, roaming across her neck, moving lower. "But that doesn't mean—"

"In all things or in nothing," she whispered, closing her eyes when he cupped her breast. "I'm not weak in mind or heart, Karl. I can bear up under any burden that falls to you."

"I know this. But that doesn't change my right to keep you from harm," he murmured, rolling her under him, watching for the first sign of fear. He gently parted her thighs, painfully conscious of her bruises as he stroked deeply into her.

She was wet already, and so hot that he groaned into the sweet curve of her neck. His rocking remained soft and slow, completely at odds with the rapid pounding of his heart.

"Elera," he whispered, holding to his unhurried rhythm when her legs wrapped around his waist and urged him to rush. His breathing grew ragged, his control shredded with the sound of her moans, and her hands …

Locking them in his, he continued to increase the heat

and friction and torture...until she threw back her head and cried her release into the red dawn. Only then did his touch roughen, his fingers tightening on her skin as he whispered her name through the long, sharp tremors racking his body.

His home, Karl thought later that day, looking out over the crumbling walls of the manor at the overgrown grounds. For the first time since sneaking into a world that should never have existed, he felt at peace.

The bull lifted his head from the nearby hill, glancing over and holding the gaze of the man standing on his rider's terrace.

Karl's spine tingled with the ... *consciousness* ... of that stare. He wondered, not for the first time, over this seemingly instinctive bond between rider and dragon.

"He'll keep them with him for years," Elera whispered, coming to stand at his back. She nodded to the two riderless females tucked beneath his massive wings. "Until they find new riders. And until he can accept my touch again."

The last was spoken with humor, but also with pride in the arrogant beast.

"I can accept your touch," Karl whispered, tucking her beneath his arm in much the same manner as the bull had his females.

Thunder erupted overhead, releasing a downpour of rain amidst streaks of hot, white lightning. He sighed, knowing she was still waiting to see if he would be honest, rather than overbearing in his desire to protect her.

"The Mattaen will come now."

Closing her eyes in relief, Elera sank into the arm that tightened around her. "Because you sent Tem to them?"

He nodded. "They might have been content to let this

world continue until it fell of its own means. With the destruction of the silver pools, the dragons die, and an entire war is averted with next to no blood spilled." Feeling the shiver that skipped over her skin, he pulled her beneath the shelter of the overhang. "Now they know that their secret has been discovered. That sooner or later we'll come for the silver pools under the realm. So they'll train, and plot … and this war will begin in truth."

"We can't win, can we?"

"No one wins in war." Cupping her cheek, Karl leaned down for a soft taste of her lips. "But I haven't failed you or your people yet, Elera."

"Because you still believe in your friend?"

"Not a friend, but a brother. And it doesn't matter what I believe." Straightening, Karl stared out at the bull, the cliffs, and the borders of the lost world he had joined. "So long as Simon remembers that he does believe in me."

He chuckled then, as he twined their fingers together.

"He's going to have a difficult time keeping the realm in ignorance of the dragons' existence, now that they've seen one bursting out of the temple itself."

When the citizens of the realm turned on the Mattaen for answers, perhaps even retribution, Simon's hands would be every bit as busy as Karl's. Smiling at the twists of fate, he lifted Elera into his arms and walked back into the rain.

"I would have come here after I found the scrolls," he murmured, tightening his hold when she burrowed against him with a laugh. "I wouldn't have been able to resist knowing. But I wouldn't have had you."

"Or our son," she whispered, sipping the rain from his neck, fingering the lock of red and black in his hair.

His lips curved wickedly as he ran a finger along the waist of her pants. "I suppose I owe you. Care to collect?"

"Of course." Elera shifted in his arms, wrapping her legs around his waist and moving enticingly against him. "But I warn you, it's a large debt."

"Thank the stars," Karl murmured, and swallowed her laughter with the rain.

Marjorie Liu

Long ago, shape-shifters were plentiful, soaring through the sky as crows, racing across African veldts as cheetahs, raging furious as dragons atop the Himalayas. Like gods, they reigned supreme. But even gods have laws, and those laws, when broken, destroy.

Zoufalství. Epätoivo. Asa. Three words in three very different languages, and yet Soria understands. Like all members of Dirk & Steele, she has a gift, and hers is communication: That was why she was chosen to address the stranger. Strong as a lion, quick as a serpent, Karr is his name, and in his day he was king. But he is a son of strife, a creature of tragedy. As fire consumed all he loved, so an icy sleep has been his atonement. Now, against his will, he has awoken. *Zoufalství. Epätoivo. Asa.* In English, the word is despair. But Soria knows the words for love.

THE Fire King

A DIRK & STEELE NOVEL

ISBN 13: 978-0-8439-5940-6

To order a book or to request a catalog call:
1-800-481-9191
Our books are also available at your local bookstore, or you can check out our Web site **www.dorchesterpub.com** where you can look up your favorite authors, read excerpts, glance at our discussion forum, and check out our digital content. Many of our books are now available as e-books!

MELANIE JACKSON

Author of *Night Visitor* and *The Selkie*

A ghostly hound stalks Noltland Castle. For years, such appearances have signaled doom for the clan Balfour, and there is little reason to believe this time will be any different. Wasn't their laird cut down while defending the Scottish king, leaving a boy to take a man's place?

Frances Balfour has done all she can, using guts and guile to keep her cousin safe in his new lairdship, but enemies encroach from all sides, and now the secluded isle of Orkney is beset from within. A stranger has arrived, and his green gaze promises to strip every secret bare. The newcomer is a swordsman, a seducer and a sometimes spy for the English king, but for all that, he seems a friend. And Colin Mortlock can see into the Night Side, that spectral world between life and death. He shall be the destruction of all Frances loves—or her salvation.

The Night Side

ISBN 13: 978-0-505-52804-9

To order a book or to request a catalog call:
1-800-481-9191
Our books are also available at your local bookstore, or you can check out our Web site **www.dorchesterpub.com** where you can look up your favorite authors, read excerpts, glance at our discussion forum, and check out our digital content. Many of our books are now available as e-books!

C. L. WILSON

LORD OF THE FADING LANDS

Once he had loved with such passion, his name was legend....Tarien Soul. Now a thousand years later, a new threat calls him from the Fading Lands, back into the world that had cost him so dearly. Now an ancient, familiar evil is regaining its strength, and a new voice beckons him—more compelling, more seductive, more maddening than any before. As the power of his most bitter enemy grows and ancient alliances crumble, the wildness in his blood will not be denied. The tairen must claim his truemate and embrace the destiny woven for him in the mists of time.

ISBN 10: 0-8439-5977-0
ISBN 13: 978-0-8439-5977-2

To order a book or to request a catalog call:
1-800-481-9191
This book is also available at your local bookstore, or you can check out our Web site **www.dorchesterpub.com** where you can look up your favorite authors, read excerpts, or glance at our discussion forum to see what people have to say about your favorite books.

C. L. WILSON

LADY of LIGHT And SHADOWS

He had stepped from the sky to claim her like an enchanted prince from the pages of a fairy tale, but behind the mesmerizing beauty of his violet eyes she saw the driving hunger of the beast and an endless sorrow only she could heal. Only for him would she embrace her frightening magic and find the courage to confront the shadows that haunted her soul. Only with him could she hope to defeat the terrifying evil that had pursued her all her life. No barrier could stand between truemates, not of the body, mind or soul. For an epic battle was fast approaching and only united could they hope to turn back the armies of darkness.

ISBN 10: 0-8439-5978-9
ISBN 13: 978-0-8439-5978-9

To order a book or to request a catalog call:
1-800-481-9191
This book is also available at your local bookstore, or you can check out our Web site **www.dorchesterpub.com** where you can look up your favorite authors, read excerpts, or glance at our discussion forum to see what people have to say about your favorite books.

USA Today Bestselling Author of *Dragonborn*

Jade Lee

Horrific are a dragon's claws, its fiery breath and buffeting wings. Potent is its body, fraught with magic down to the very last glistening scale. But most fearsome of all is a dragon's cunning—and the soul that allows it to bond with humans.

"Exotic and unique!"
—*Romantic Times BOOKreviews* on *Dragonborn*

DRAGONBOUND

Sabina was the one girl of her generation chosen as Dragonmaid, friend and caregiver to the copper dragon of her nation's tyrant king. There she witnessed the greed, lust and rage such a beast could incite—and acquired her own very dark secret.

Handsome of face and mighty of sword, Dag Racho ruled Ragona with an iron fist and the help of his wyrm. But the line between man and beast has blurred, and a woman has come for them. Revenge, salvation and three kingdoms hang in the balance—and the fate of two hearts.

ISBN 13: 978-0-8439-6047-1

To order a book or to request a catalog call:
1-800-481-9191
Our books are also available at your local bookstore, or you can check out our Web site **www.dorchesterpub.com** where you can look up your favorite authors, read excerpts, or glance at our discussion forum to see what people have to say about your favorite books.

✂

☐ **YES!**

Sign me up for the Love Spell Book Club and send my
FREE BOOKS! If I choose to stay in the club, I will pay
only $8.50* each month, a savings of $6.48!

NAME: _____

ADDRESS: _____

TELEPHONE: _____

EMAIL: _____

☐ I want to pay by credit card.

☐ **VISA**   ☐ **MasterCard...**   ☐ **DISCOVER**

ACCOUNT #: _____

EXPIRATION DATE: _____

SIGNATURE: _____

Mail this page along with $2.00 shipping and handling to:
Love Spell Book Club
PO Box 6640
Wayne, PA 19087
Or fax (must include credit card information) to:
610-995-9274
You can also sign up online at **www.dorchesterpub.com**.
*Plus $2.00 for shipping. Offer open to residents of the U.S. and Canada only.
Canadian residents please call 1-800-481-9191 for pricing information.
If under 18, a parent or guardian must sign. Terms, prices and conditions subject to
change. Subscription subject to acceptance. Dorchester Publishing reserves the right
to reject any order or cancel any subscription.

GET FREE BOOKS!

You can have the best romance delivered to your door for less than what you'd pay in a bookstore or online. Sign up for one of our book clubs today, and we'll send you *FREE* BOOKS* just for trying it out... **with no obligation to buy, ever!**

Bring a little magic into your life with the romances of Love Spell—fun contemporaries, paranormals, time-travels, futuristics, and more. Your shipments will include authors such as **MARJORIE LIU, JADE LEE, NINA BANGS, GEMMA HALLIDAY,** and many more.

As a book club member you also receive the following special benefits:
- **30% off all orders!**
- **Exclusive access to special discounts!**
- **Convenient home delivery and 10 days to return any books you don't want to keep.**

Visit www.dorchesterpub.com
or call 1-800-481-9191

There is no minimum number of books to buy, and you may cancel membership at any time. *Please include $2.00 for shipping and handling.